Dear Reader,

He's the man who makes you swoon, makes you forget everything but his face, his eyes, his voice. He's the man you can't get out of your mind. The man who's too hot to handle. But you just can't keep your hands to yourself.

Three of those men are heating up the love stories in this collection, written by three of your favorite authors, Mary Lynn Baxter, Ann Major and Laura Parker.

So whether you're reading *Summer Sizzlers: Too Hot To Handle* under the sun, or curled up in a comfy chair, or even on a bus or train, prepare to need something to cool you down....

Wishing you a wonderful summer,

The Editors
Silhouette Books

SILHOUETTE

Summer Sizzlers

"Too Hot To Handle"

Mary Lynn Baxter
Ann Major
Laura Parker

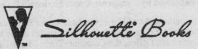

Silhouette Books

Published by Silhouette Books
America's Publisher of Contemporary Romance

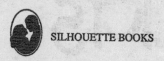

SILHOUETTE BOOKS

ISBN 0-373-48287-6

TOO HOT TO HANDLE

BOOT SCOOTIN'
Copyright © 1995 by Mary Lynn Baxter

FANCY'S MAN
Copyright © 1995 by Ann Major

CHARISMA
Copyright © 1995 by Laura Castoro

Printed in U.S.A.

CONTENTS

BOOT SCOOTIN'

Mary Lynn Baxter

Chapter One

Kelly Warren stared at the paper in front of her and frowned. On impulse she crushed it into a tight ball, arched her right hand and aimed it at the wastebasket.

"Two points," she said with a sarcastic grin as the wad hit the target.

She stood then and stretched her back, the grin having disappeared from her face. Today had not started off to be a good one. She had already torn up several sketches, and it was only nine o'clock.

Maybe she shouldn't work today, after all, she thought, especially as it was her twenty-seventh birthday. Maybe she should just lock up the shop, go get her grandmother and spend the day doing something wonderfully outrageous.

A frown rearranged Kelly's smooth, porcelain skin at the same time that she axed that idea. She *was* doing something wonderfully outrageous; she was doing what she wanted to do and not what her father wanted.

Kelly had recently opened her own business, a small stationery and gift shop called Exclusively Kelly. While the shop itself was a dream come true, her long-range goal was to design cards with a Western theme and sell them to a reputable card company. She wasn't choosey about the company, either, just as long as she proved successful in her venture.

Before she'd left Houston and moved in with her grandmother in the sleepy East Texas town of Lufkin, she had been at her father's beck and call since she'd graduated from the University of Texas five years earlier.

Finally Kelly had grown tired of acting as hostess for Simon Warren, a grocery store magnate who entertained with a vengeance. She often wondered how, or even if, her life would have been different had her mother lived instead of dying from a blood clot shortly after Kelly was born. She suspected it would have been vastly different; Simon would not have relied on her so much.

In addition to the hostess gig, the endless rounds of parties and bridge games in which her "friends" involved her had bored her. Kelly's only interest had been her charity work—enjoyable, but not fulfilling enough in itself.

After a close friend's death and her beloved grandmother's heart attack, Kelly had realized how precious life was and that she was recklessly throwing hers away. So when Simon had mentioned putting her grandmother in a nursing home, Kelly had suggested instead that she leave Houston, move to Lufkin and take care of Claire.

Only after she'd been in Lufkin six months did she decide to open the shop, having inherited a flair for art from her mother. Of course, her grandmother's encouragement had gone a long way toward forcing her to stake her claim for independence.

"Have you lost your mind?" Simon had scoffed when she'd told him her plans.

"No, Dad," she'd said calmly. "Quite the contrary, in fact. For once I'm doing something I want to do, rather than what *you* want me to."

Simon's sharp blue eyes, which Kelly had been blessed with, as well, had heated up. "Well, I can tell you right now, it won't work."

"And just why not?" Kelly had retorted.

"Because you don't have the self-discipline it takes to stick to it, that's why. Ever since you finished school, you've flitted from one thing to another."

An answering heat had flared in Kelly's eyes. "And just whose fault is that?"

"Go on with your crazy scheme, then. Get it out of your system." Simon had batted a hand in the air. "But when you fail and run back home, don't say I didn't tell you so."

That pompously spoken statement had been all the incentive Kelly needed. If there was any "I told you so," it would come from her lips. Even if she had to bribe every friend she'd ever known to drive to Lufkin and buy something from her shop, she would prove her father wrong.

She hadn't had to resort to such a drastic measure. At least, not so far, she reminded herself with a satisfied pat on the back. Her shop had been open for two weeks, and customer interest had been gratifying.

Not that she'd made that much money, because she hadn't. But she'd had interested "lookers" who'd said they would return. She prayed they would, though not for the reason most people went into business, which was to make money. While that was important and was the barometer by which success was measured, Kelly didn't need the money.

Her grandmother had set up a trust fund for her shortly after she was born. When Kelly had turned twenty-five, the money had become hers. No, this change in her life was not about money. It was about independence and self-satisfaction.

Kelly paused in her thoughts and peered at her watch. In thirty minutes, at nine-thirty, it would be opening time. She'd been here since seven, though, working on her sketches.

Giving in to the urge for a cup of coffee, Kelly made her way from the loft to the kitchen downstairs, where she heated the water for a cup of French Vanilla Café. Once the mug of steaming liquid was in her hand, she made her way into the shop proper.

She stopped and stared at her masterpiece, trying to see it through her customers' eyes. She knew it was different from any other shop in town; she'd made sure of that.

The house, a cottage-type brick that she'd leased with the intent to purchase, was close to the downtown area and provided the ideal location and charm that Kelly wanted to project.

Besides the kitchen, the downstairs was comprised of a bedroom and large living room that housed the inventory. Along with displays of greeting cards and stationery, the majority of which Kelly had designed and had printed herself, was a hodgepodge of "pretties."

Various baskets were filled with heart-shaped sachet pillows; shelves were littered with unusual picture frames, while an assortment of candles and potpourri occupied the small bedroom.

The upstairs, which Kelly had converted into a loft, was her studio, where she actually designed her cards. A huge skylight that she'd had installed added the proper atmosphere she deemed necessary to do her best work.

Now, as Kelly made her way to the checkout counter, she walked with pride. She hadn't made her mark yet, but she would, or die trying. The main thing she'd inherited from both her father and her grandmother was hardheaded stubbornness.

With that in mind, she set her coffee down, grabbed the petty cash bag and opened the cash drawer. Moments later she heard a rap on the glass door. She looked up into the face of a smiling customer.

Darting from behind the counter, she muttered a victorious, "Yes!"

Kelly massaged the back of her neck. Jeez, but she was tired. But it was a good tiredness, she told herself, staring at the clock and watching as the hands registered five o'clock. In thirty minutes she would close the shop, drive home and celebrate the remainder of her birthday with her grandmother.

Suddenly the door chimed. She turned just as a man strolled through the door. Her mouth gaped open.

He chuckled at her obvious surprise. "Close your mouth before you catch something contagious."

"What on earth are you doing here?" Kelly demanded, continuing to stare at her attorney friend, Charles Lipton, a man she'd dated several times before leaving Houston.

"I figured that would be obvious." He hitched the pants of his expensive suit and sat at the end of the

counter on the stool that she kept for customers who
had the urge to stay and chat.

"Oh, how's that?"

Charles quirked an eyebrow. "Hey, it's your birthday. I thought you might like to celebrate, maybe go
out on the town."

Kelly had mixed emotions about Charles's presence—mostly unpleasant, though she tried to temper
those feelings by forcing a smile. He had her father's
vote, of course. He was exactly the kind of man Simon wanted for a son-in-law—solid, with a good head
for business. To Kelly, both qualities spelled boring,
despite the fact that there was nothing boring about
Charles's looks.

He was movie star handsome, though he was only
about five foot seven. He had been blessed with a thick
head of light brown hair and green eyes, but his smile
was his main attraction. He seemed to always know
when to flash it, too, exposing a set of perfect white
teeth.

Like Kelly, Charles came from a moneyed background. His family owned a chain of hotels in Houston. It was their influence that had zoomed him to a
partnership in a prestigious law firm at the young age
of thirty.

However, none of these pluses overcame the notion
in Kelly's mind that he was a know-it-all who was
more of an aggravation than an asset.

"So, are you interested?" he pressed, forcing her
back to the moment at hand.

"Well, since you drove two and a half hours to see
me, how can I turn you down?"

Charles stood and, as if on cue, flashed his grin. "You can't."

It wasn't until a few minutes later, after they were in her grandmother's driveway and about to get out of the car, that Kelly realized he'd made no comment about her shop—good, bad or indifferent.

On the heels of that realization came another one— she didn't give a damn.

"You two have a wonderful evening."

Kelly smiled at her paternal grandmother, then leaned over and kissed her on one parchment-thin cheek. "Will do. Only I hate leaving you alone."

"That's silly," Claire Warren said. "This is your birthday, and I sure can't raise any hell."

Charles smiled, and Kelly laughed out loud. "Maybe not tonight, Grandmom, but hopefully soon."

The smile faded from Claire's face at the same time that she touched her perfectly styled white hair. "That's only wishful thinking on your part, my dear. This old gray mare is truly not what she used to be, only you won't accept that."

"You're right, I won't," Kelly countered, determined that her grandmother, at eighty, was going to get over her latest heart attack and be able to do the thing she loved most—putter in her garden. "You've already made great strides toward a miraculous recovery. I refuse to let you give in now."

Claire sighed. "Oh, you don't have to worry about that. As much as I love having you here with me, I'd like nothing better than to be completely on my own again."

Kelly smiled down at the beloved lady who had been more like a mother than a grandmother, and fought back the stinging tears. "You will be, though you can forget about kicking me out. I'm here to stay."

Claire showed some of her old spunk. "We'll see about that, only later. You two go on now, and get out of my hair. My favorite TV show's about to start."

A few minutes later Kelly and Charles walked out into the July sunlight, which was still strong, even though it was approaching eight o'clock. Charles opened the door to his Lincoln, and Kelly got inside.

Only after he was behind the wheel and the engine was purring did he turn to her and ask, "Where to?"

"Boot Scootin'."

He blinked. "Excuse me?"

"Boot Scootin'," she repeated.

"If that's what I think it is, forget it. I want to take you to a first-class place for dinner."

"You can forget *that*. It's my birthday, remember?"

Charles gripped the steering wheel and cursed. "Okay, so what is this place?"

"A country-western dance club."

"Where I assume they issue you a gun at the door— if you don't already have one, that is."

"Funny."

"Believe me, I'm trying to be."

"Look, if you don't want to take me, just say so. I'll go alone."

"Like hell you will."

"I wouldn't push it if I were you," Kelly warned in a controlled tone, wishing she'd told him that she'd already had plans for the evening.

"Okay, okay. You've made your point. We'll grab a quick bite somewhere, then Boot Scootin' it is."

"Besides the fact that I love to dance, I have another motive for wanting to go there."

He cut her a frustrated look. "You're serious, aren't you?"

"I'm in the process of designing some cards with a Western theme. Right now, country is the hottest thing going. As far as I know, no one else has capitalized on that."

Charles yanked the car into drive. "Whatever you say."

A short time later they were seated at a table in the club, the sound of the latest "hot act's" voice surrounding them. While they waited for their drinks, Kelly looked around, her excitement building.

She tapped her booted foot in time to the music, aching to dance. But first things first, she reminded herself, her eyes perusing the club, which was the hottest and most talked about one in town.

It lived up to the talk, especially with its large, oval-shaped dance floor located in the center of the room and surrounded by tables and chairs on an elevated platform. But it was the rustic decor that held her attention and that she was busy committing to memory.

"So what do you think?" Charles asked as a waitress served their drinks.

"It's exactly what I hoped it would be and more."

Charles took a healthy swig of his scotch on the rocks. "I'm glad you're pleased."

His veiled sarcasm wasn't lost on Kelly. She swallowed a retort and fought down the urge to throttle him. Instead she sipped her soda and continued her perusal.

"There's a guy standing over by the bar who's giving you the once-over."

Kelly didn't bother to look in that direction. "So what? That's what usually happens in these places."

"That's why I didn't want to come," Charles muttered.

Kelly raised her eyebrows. "My, my, but our mood seems to be souring by the minute." She patted his hand. "Give it a rest, okay? I want to dance."

"What if I don't?" Charles said, a petulant twist to his lips.

"Then you'd best take a hike," Kelly said in a sugary tone that was anything but sweet.

Charles seemed to sense he was treading on thin ice; he smiled, then stood abruptly. "Okay, you win." He reached for her hand. "Let's go."

Moments later, Kelly's hips were swaying provocatively on the dance floor.

Chapter Two

Tucker Garrett leaned against the corner of the bar nearest the dance floor as if he hadn't a care in the world. But those with even the slightest acquaintance of him knew better. Underneath that lazy, good-old-boy persona was a man wound as tight as a coiled spring.

As Tucker watched the blonde on the dance floor, that tightness inside him reached a level he hadn't experienced in a long time, if ever. Damn, but she was beautiful, with her delicate features and short, stylishly cut blond hair. Although he couldn't see her eyes, he would bet they were as striking as the rest of her face.

But it was her body, with the slim hips and seemingly never-ending legs moving in perfect time to "Boot Scootin' Boogie," that kicked his blood pressure up several notches. He cursed, then took a deep breath, trying to calm himself. No luck. If anything, his blood pressure increased, along with the pace of the music, which in turn, upped the sway of her hips.

He was thirty-five years old, and he'd never seen any woman's rear fill a pair of jeans to such perfection. And he couldn't neglect her breasts, not by a long shot. They were round and jutted against her tangerine silk blouse with every quick step. Sweat broke out on Tucker's upper lip, and he cursed again. Hell, he was behaving like an animal in heat. And all it took

was just watching her. How would he react if he were
to touch her?

He turned as James Arnold, known as "Crusty"
because of his gruff demeanor, ambled up beside him.
For a moment Tucker considered hugging Crusty for
interrupting his insane thoughts, then smiled. Despite
the inhibition of a wooden leg, Crusty could and
would have decked him on the spot.

"What's so funny?"

"Nothing."

Crusty shrugged, then said, "Place is filling up real
good, don't you think?"

"Yeah, the best yet," Tucker mumbled, his eyes
back on the woman on the dance floor.

Crusty followed his gaze. "Mmm, I see what you
mean."

Tucker jerked his head around, narrowing his eyes
into slits. "Why, you dirty old man."

"Takes one to know one," Crusty quipped.

"Go to hell."

Crusty laughed, showing teeth that maybe at one
time had been white. Now they were brown and
stained with nicotine from years of smoking and
chewing.

"Okay, so I'm a dirty old man, too," Tucker said.

"Not a damn thing wrong with that, son."

Tucker didn't say anything for a moment, thinking
instead of how lucky he was to have Crusty as a friend
and employee. He couldn't have run the club without
him. Crusty acted as part-time bartender, assistant and
general handyman. Tucker had met Crusty through
the uncle who had raised him, and for that he was
thankful.

"As long as you don't go thinkin' you can touch that pretty little tush, that is," Crusty was saying.

Tucker stared hard at Crusty. "What did you say?"

"You heard me. But I'll repeat it just in case it didn't soak in."

Tucker snorted. "Did anyone ever tell you that you're too damn nosy for your own good?" He paused. "I ought to fire you, you know."

"Yeah, you oughta, but you won't. Who'd keep this place in shape?"

Tucker snorted again, but he didn't respond, because he knew the old geezer spoke the truth. "Speaking of shape, have you ever seen her here before?"

Crusty didn't pretend to misunderstand. "Nope, don't reckon I have."

"Have you ever seen anyone who can move like she can?"

Crusty scratched his bald head. "Nope, can't say that I have. She ain't like most who come in here. That's why I said what I did."

"You mean, she's a cut above the average and completely off limits for the likes of me."

"I couldn't have said it better myself, son, and not because you ain't good enough, either. It's just that women like her are trouble. They'll break your heart. Hell, you oughta know that."

"You're damn right I know it. But that still doesn't stop me from wanting to—" Tucker broke off. "Oh, the hell with it. She's probably married to that fellow she's with, anyway."

"I hope to hell not. It'd sure be a waste. He doesn't seem man enough to handle her."

Tucker cut him another sharp glance. "Well, either way, it's none of our business, especially since we've got more urgent things to attend to."

Crusty looked around. "By golly, you're right. The club's filling up. I'd best make sure everyone's happy."

"I'm right behind you," Tucker said to Crusty's retreating back.

Still, he didn't move. He did, however, look around and watch the patrons pour in. Relief brought a smile to his face. Nothing like success, he thought, his smile growing.

That smile disappeared when he found his gaze returning to the couple on the dance floor. The disc jockey had switched on the TV screen and psychedelic lights, which made them stand out that much more.

The urge to strike out across the floor, shove the jerk she was with aside and take his place, was burgeoning out of control. What astonished Tucker even more was that he didn't give in to that urge, that he actually hesitated and weighed the consequences of such a move.

But then, he was no longer a roughneck on an oil rig where lack of manners made little or no difference. Instead he was in a legitimate business, where manners made all the difference in the world. Besides, he knew it wasn't wise to mix business with pleasure.

It was hard, though, to contain himself, he'd always been a man of action and still was. Having been raised by an old uncle who was now dead, for the most part Tucker had had to fend for himself and answer to no one—except Crusty, on certain occasions.

Old habits died hard. When Tucker wanted something, he simply bulldozed his way toward it and usually got it, only to find out that he'd oftentimes gotten far more than he'd bargained for.

His marriage was a prime example. He'd gone after Sheryl Hemple with a vengeance, only to regret it shortly after the vows were exchanged. His marriage had ended about the same time he'd gotten fed up with life on the oil rig. When the opportunity had presented itself to buy the club, he'd grabbed it.

At first Tucker had feared he'd made a mistake. The building was dilapidated, both inside and out. But his dreams of owning a country-western club overcame his trepidation, and he'd begun the manual labor to transform the place from something ugly into something functional.

Once he earned the money to pay off the bank note, Tucker hoped to fulfill another life-long dream, which was to invest in a small herd of cattle and run them on the tract of land his uncle had left him.

For the moment, though, his future plans were the furthest thing from his mind. His immediate attention was again on the blonde on the dance floor.

"Want something to drink, boss?" Alf, the bartender, asked.

"Nah, not right now. Thanks anyway."

"Something pretty special must be happening on that floor. I've never seen you stand still for so long."

"Mind your own business, Alf. You sound like Crusty."

Alf grinned. "She's sure a looker, ain't she?"

"Ah, to hell with it," Tucker muttered again, then turned in the opposite direction, only to swing back around and stalk toward the dance floor, cursing all the way as he listened to Alf's loud chuckle.

The beat of "Pretty Woman" by Roy Orbison had just begun playing when he tapped the blonde's partner on the shoulder. "Mind, buddy?"

The couple seemed to freeze for a moment, and Tucker realized that if the man told him to go take a hike, he would be within his rights.

But the pretty-faced man merely looked him up and down, then said, "Be my guest."

"Charles!" The woman seemed appalled by the unexpected turn of events. "Come back here!"

Charles paused just long enough to say, "Hell, I told you I'm tired. I need a drink."

"Charles!" she seethed under her breath. Yet she remained on the floor and watched as he threaded his way through the other couples, then stalked back toward their table.

Tucker peered into her confused, upturned face and forced a smile past the turmoil stirring inside him. "Sorry," he said.

"No, you're not," she snapped, glaring at him.

Ah, the lady had spunk as well as beauty, Tucker thought. Up close, she was even lovelier than he'd ever imagined. Her eyes were sea blue and so big they seemed to take up the majority of her face.

"You're right, I'm not," Tucker countered, his grin spreading from his lips to his entire face. He was smitten, pure and simple, which made him feel more like an idiot than ever.

When she didn't respond, he went on. "Look, I promise I'm harmless." His attempt at humor seemed to have fallen on deaf ears. But he had to say something. She was staring at him as if she would like nothing better than to tell him to go to hell—or worse.

But all she said was, "Who are you, anyway?"

"Tucker Garrett."

"So does that make you special?"

"Considering I'm the owner of the club, I guess it does."

She almost smiled, to Tucker's delight, feeling he was definitely making headway. "One dance, all right?"

"Why not? Despite your rudeness, I'd hate to see this song go to waste."

"Yeah, that would be a shame, now, wouldn't it?" Tucker said, and began to move with her in unison to the music.

Jerk! But then, this Tucker Garrett dude wasn't any bigger of a jerk than Charles. She didn't know which one she wanted to clobber the most—Charles, for leaving her at the mercy of this roughneck who was looking at her through bottomless black eyes as if she were a dessert that he would eat at any moment, or the man himself for *looking* at her like that.

Yet Kelly couldn't have left even if she'd wanted to. Roughneck or not, the stranger's body was perfection in motion as he moved to the beat of the music. Too bad his face didn't live up to his agile body, she thought, taking in uneven features that were much too craggy to be labeled handsome.

Still, all was not lost. His distinct nearly black eyes and the thick, dark brown hair, slightly mussed, that touched the collar of his blue sports shirt, made him intriguing. Or was *sexy* a better word? It didn't matter, because she wasn't interested.

She'd had encounters with men like Tucker Garrett. And they'd been just that—encounters. She had him pegged as both charming and dangerous, an explosive combination that was to be avoided.

So why didn't she simply tell him to go straight to hell, and walk away?

"You're a great dancer," he said at last.

She didn't quite meet his probing gaze. "So are you."

They fell into another silence, and when the song ended, they broke apart. "Thanks," she said, then turned toward the table.

"Wait."

She didn't know why she hesitated. Maybe it was the authoritative tone of his voice. Or maybe she wasn't as eager to leave as she'd thought. But the reason didn't matter. She paused and faced him again.

He held out his hand.

"You said only one dance."

The throbbing sounds of a soulful country ballad suddenly filled the air.

"So I lied."

Kelly opened her mouth, but that was as far as she got before his hand circled her neck and pulled her against him.

"No," she whispered, feeling his arousal, instant and strong.

He knew she felt it, too, for they both stiffened at the same time, as if struck by an electric current.

Chapter Three

Tucker's guttural curse didn't even register with Kelly, nor did anything else going on around them—the spinning lights, the large-screen TV, the other couples—nothing. She was only aware of the man who held her as if he would never let her go.

For a split second neither of them seemed capable of moving; even the air between them vibrated with electricity.

Flee, Kelly! she told herself. Get the hell out of Dodge! She couldn't. She could have sworn her feet were stuck to the floor. Then it was too late. Without warning, Tucker's eyes took on a smoldering intensity and he began to move in perfect time with the music, drawing her into his spell.

"Relax," he whispered into her ear. "I don't bite."

She realized his second attempt at humor was twofold—to force himself to relax as well as her. She heard the sandpaper edge to his voice and knew he was just as uncomfortable and mystified as she was by the internal combustion their touch had created.

"I'm not so sure about that," she responded, feeling herself relax now that she was no longer plastered against him. One contact had been enough.

Her face stung with unwanted color. She wasn't a prude, not by any stretch of the imagination. Still, she wasn't in the habit of sampling the feel of a stranger's arousal, for heaven's sake!

"Did anyone ever tell you that you move like an angel?"

This time his words, along with his rough voice, sent a chill through Kelly. He seemed to sense it, because he chuckled, then drew her closer. She immediately stiffened. He sighed.

"No, not...not in those exact words," she finally said, desperate to break the hold this stranger had on her. Something had—something *was*—happening to her, and she seemed powerless to combat it.

Tucker chuckled again, his minty breath caressing her ear. She forced herself not to react visibly; she simply refused to give in to this insanity any longer. Damn, was the song ever going to end?

Seconds later Kelly got her wish. Immediately, and with as much dignity as she could muster, she backed out of his arms. For another moment they stared at each other; then she forced a smile. "Er...thanks for the dance."

Tucker's lips quirked at the same time he cocked his head. "My pleasure."

Feeling as if he was making fun of her for behaving like a teenage virgin, she bowed her shoulders, turned and made her way toward the table and Charles. She knew Tucker hadn't budged; she could feel his eyes boring into her back. Damn him! And damn her for letting him rile her.

"Well, well, did you finally get enough of that low-rent cowboy?" Charles said, slurring his words.

"You're drunk," Kelly said, not bothering to hide her disgust. She'd smelled liquor on his breath earlier and should have been forewarned. What a way to spend her birthday. First she'd encountered a stranger whose mere touch set her on fire, and now her date was drunk and belligerent.

"Whadda you care?" Charles laughed before taking another pull on his scotch. "It's obvious you're more interested in stepping in cow dung than in being with me."

"And just whose fault is that?" Kelly fired back, jerking out her chair and sitting down across from him.

"Well, it damn sure isn't mine."

"Need I remind you that *you* let him cut in."

"Hell, I didn't have any choice."

"Baloney!"

Charles's lips turned down. "Well, let's just say I was tired of dancing."

"Now *that* I can believe." Her disgust had turned to contempt. "You never did like to dance, and that was your way of getting back at me."

Charles leaned toward her, his breath reeking of alcohol. She pulled back, repulsed.

As if he sensed that repulsion, his mouth twisted. "That's a lie. I just don't like that lowlife cowpoke mauling you in front of me."

Kelly rolled her eyes, though she felt the color return to her face. "Oh, pleeeze."

"I wanted this to be a special night," Charles whined in a slurred voice. "Our night."

Kelly sighed. "There's still time. If you'll stop drinking and order coffee, that is."

Charles's answer to that was to indulge in another healthy swig of his drink.

"So, what's it going to be?" Kelly demanded. "Me or the scotch?"

Charles looked at her strangely. "I wish you meant that."

"What?" Kelly asked in a strained voice, suddenly weary of Charles and his immaturity. All she wanted to do was dance again. She wondered if Tucker Garrett was back out on the floor, sweet-talking and arousing another woman. She wasn't about to give him or herself the satisfaction of looking.

"If I could have you, I'd gladly give up the scotch."

Kelly blinked, trying to force herself back to the conversation at hand. "Look, Charles...I—"

"I mean that, Kelly."

"At the moment," she said uneasily.

"Forever."

"How do you expect me to believe that when you're drunk?"

"Damn it, I'm not drunk."

She shrugged, deciding that she was wasting her time and energy arguing with him. "Okay, so you're not drunk."

When Charles didn't answer right off, Kelly took a sip of her soda and pressed her lips together. Insisting that their coming here had been a mistake. Still she didn't intend to let the evening become a total loss. Even now she was busy taking mental notes on her surroundings. As far as talking to the owner—well, that was out of the question. Kelly felt her face turn scarlet again. She wanted nothing more to do with Tucker Garrett.

"Will you marry me?"

"Pardon?" Kelly asked distractedly.

"Damn it, I said, will you marry me?"

Kelly's eyes widened, and her mouth gaped. When she could find her voice, she asked, "That's a joke, right?"

Charles's face turned white at the same time that his mouth stretched into a bitter line. "It's no joke, but judging from your reaction, it should be."

Kelly groped to come to grips with Charles's bombshell, even as he added, "I think we'd make a good team. We're both from the same background, have the same friends, like—"

"Wait, wait a minute." Kelly shook her head. "This is all happening so fast. But you really are serious, aren't you?"

"I've never been more serious in my life, and I'll prove it."

Charles reached into the pocket of his coat, pulled out a velvet-covered box and extended his hand. When Kelly hesitated, he said, "Go on, take it. It's yours— if you want it, that is."

Kelly stared at the box, then swallowed hard. What else unexpected was going to happen?

"Take it," Charles urged.

Kelly took the box and, with a sinking heart, slowly opened it. Her breath caught at the beauty of the huge, marquise-cut diamond. She snapped the box shut, along with her mouth.

"You don't like it," Charles said.

Kelly picked up on both the hurt and anger in his tone but was at a loss as to how to comfort him. "Actually, I love it. I think it's beautiful, but..."

"But you don't want it," Charles finished for her.

Kelly didn't so much as flinch. "That's right. I don't want it."

He reached out and jerked it out of her hand. "One of these days you'll get what's coming to you. I just hope to hell I'm around to see it happen."

"Look, Charles, you're a good friend and a good person," she lied. "But I just don't happen to love you, and I don't think you love me, either."

"You don't know how I feel," he snapped.

"Maybe I don't. But have you stopped to think that now I live in Lufkin and have a business here?"

"So what? You can move that business to Houston. You never should've left in the first place."

"What about Grandmom?"

"She's your father's problem, not yours."

Kelly gritted her teeth against the urge to slap his face. "That's where you're wrong," she said instead, her tone low and hard. "Grandmom's *my* problem because I want her to be. That's not going to change."

Charles shrugged. "So I assume the answer to my question is 'thanks, but no thanks.'"

"That's right," Kelly said, forcing a softness into her voice she was far from feeling. Why hadn't she seen how self-centered Charles was long before now? Well, it didn't matter; she could never love him, self-centered or not.

Falling in love and getting married were not on Kelly's agenda right now. She had just walked away from a man's dominance, started her own career and created her own identity. She'd left behind the stigma of being nothing but Simon Warren's spoiled socialite daughter who had more money than sense.

Now she was a person in her own right, one who got up, went to work and made her own money. It felt damn good, too, and she was happy with her life the way it was. She didn't need a man to feel fulfilled.

Besides, she didn't love Charles. He was too much like her father—all work and no play. And dull. When and if she ever married, she wanted a man who set her on fire, a man like— She axed that thought before it took a dangerous turn and watched as Charles toyed with his near-empty glass.

"So where does this leave us?" he asked, looking up at her.

"Friends, I hope."

"Friends, huh?"

"Yes."

Charles drained his glass, slammed it down on the table, then beckoned for the waitress. "What if I don't want to be your friend?"

Kelly didn't get the chance to respond as the waitress appeared at their table. "Give me another double," Charles said without looking at the young woman.

"Double coming up."

Once the waitress had gone, Kelly said, "Let's just leave, okay?"

"Hell, no!" Charles's voice rose. "This is how you wanted to celebrate your birthday, and I won't have you saying that I'm a party pooper. No, sirree."

"Charles, you're making a—" Kelly broke off in midsentence when someone tapped her on the shoulder. She swung around and looked into the face of another stranger. For a second she had thought it might be... Refusing to pursue that thought, she smiled as the man asked her to dance.

"Sure, why not?" she said, noticing that Charles's face was once again buried deep in a glass of scotch.

Kelly followed the young man onto the dance floor.

"What's with you, anyway?" Crusty demanded. "I can't remember ever seeing you get your shorts in such a wad over a woman, especially a woman you don't even know."

Tucker shot Crusty a look. "One of these days I'm gonna shove my boot in your big mouth."

Crusty shrugged off the threat with a grin. "So, let me in on the secret. What's that blonde got that the others don't?" Crusty massaged his leg. "Couldn't be her chest. From what I can see, she's not overly endowed."

"Shut up, will you?"

Crusty laughed again. "I'm serious, boy."

Tucker sighed as he ignored the old man and watched the woman, whose name he still didn't know, match her partner's steps to perfection. Dammit, he didn't like her dancing with anyone, most of all a strutting young dude who couldn't have been more than twenty, if he was a day.

Suddenly Tucker felt old, tired and foolish. He had about as much chance of getting this woman in his bed as he did of becoming the next president of the United States. He smirked. Hell, he figured the latter would be easier.

"Care to share the joke?" Crusty asked.

"Nope."

"Didn't figure you would."

"Look, just get off my case. One reason I'm keeping my eye on the blonde and her date is that I feel there's trouble brewing."

Crusty scratched his chin. "Think so, huh?"

"Lover boy's been sucking on straight scotch since they got here."

"Maybe he can handle it. Those 'suits' usually can."

"This 'suit' is an exception. If he's not already soused, he's well on his way, especially after she all but threw his ring back in his face."

Crusty did a double-take. "You mean . . ."

"Yep. I watched the whole thing."

"Damn, boy, you *are* smitten with this gal."

"Nah," Tucker lied. "Like I said, I smell trouble brewing, and I'm not about to let it happen."

"You want me to alert Max and have him on standby?"

Max was the off-duty policeman hired for security purposes. "Not yet."

Crusty gave him another knowing grin. "Wanna take care of it yourself, huh?"

"That's right, old man. You got a problem with that?"

"Nope, can't say that I have. But just so you'll know that I warned you, she ain't no good for you. She's silk, boy, through and through. If you're crazy enough to go after her, she'll chew you into little pieces. You watch."

"Hell, give me credit for having a little sense," Tucker said out the side of his mouth, watching as the blonde, escorted by the young man, made their way back to the table.

"Okay, have it your own way," Crusty said, turning and hobbling off.

It was in that moment that the commotion started. First Tucker heard the screech of a chair, followed by the woman's companion lurching to his feet, a finger pointed at the dumbfounded young man.

"Hell, no, she isn't going to dance with you again! Just get the hell away from here!"

"Charles, shut up and sit down! You're creating a scene."

So the fellow's name was Charles, Tucker noted. Fitted him perfectly, too. Tucker's eyes scanned the room, and he saw that the couples within hearing distance had stopped what they were doing and were watching the brewing ruckus with intense fascination.

Only there wasn't going to be a ruckus. Tucker shoved himself away from the bar and headed toward their table.

"Look, sir, I didn't mean any harm," the young man was saying as he backed away, his hands outstretched in a pleading gesture.

"Charles!"

The woman's hissed demand had no effect on Charles. He stood, lunged around the table and swung at the young man. One wild punch followed another.

"No!"

The woman's outraged cry met Tucker as he jumped between the two men. "Oh, no, you don't," he said, barely missing a punch in the nose.

"Get out of my way!" Charles hollered, now concentrating his aim on Tucker.

Instinct told Tucker that the only way he could stop this drunken idiot was to knock him out.

With that in mind, he raised his fist and aimed for Charles's chin just as the blonde moved, then cried, "No!"

Tucker tried to pull back, but his momentum was too strong. Even after his fist connected with her face, he didn't realize exactly what had happened, not until she crumpled into a heap at his feet.

Wild-eyed, Charles stared at Tucker. "Oh, my God, you've killed her!"

Without conscious thought, Tucker smashed his fist into Charles's face and watched as he, too, slumped to the floor.

"Damn," Tucker muttered, dropping to his knees beside the unconscious woman.

Chapter Four

The entire room fell as silent as a funeral parlor. No one moved. A pin could have fallen off a table onto the floor and everyone would have heard it.

Tucker let an expletive fly, then lifted Kelly in his arms and hurried toward his living quarters in the rear of the club. Once there, he placed her gently on his bed.

Crusty, who was right behind him, now hovered beside Tucker, but for once he didn't seem to know what to say. If the situation hadn't been so grim, Tucker would have laughed. Since he'd known Crusty, he'd never seen him at a loss for words.

Still, Crusty was the first to speak, all the while shaking his head. "Wha'cha thinkin'?"

"You don't want to know." Tucker's face was as pale as it was grim.

"You're probably right." Crusty was quiet for another moment, then added, "She's a looker, all right."

"Yeah," Tucker muttered absently, his mind not so much on how good she looked or how wonderful she smelled, though he was very much aware of both, but the trouble he could be in for the incident.

"Do you know who she is?"

"Nope."

"Great."

Tucker pulled his gaze off the woman and turned it on Crusty. "I'll take care of her. What I need you to do is help security make sure everything's okay in the club. You know, this could spell trouble in more ways than one." He paused, and his features turned grimmer. "And while you're at it, sober up the dirtbag she was with and kick his butt out the door."

"What if he wants to know about the woman?"

"Tell him to go to hell."

Crusty opened his mouth as if to say something else, only to snap it shut. "You're the boss."

Once Crusty had shuffled out the door and closed it behind him, the noise factor was cut instantly in half. But that was the way Tucker wanted it. If he had to live in the rear of his business, he wanted it to be as quiet as possible. He'd had the walls double insulated, which he'd never regretted, even though at the time the money had been needed elsewhere.

He rested his gaze on the woman, who continued to lie unmoving on the bedspread.

Tucker massaged the day's growth of beard on his chin and jaw, then stomped toward the bathroom, where he wet a cloth. Moments later, he placed it on her neck.

She moaned, and her eyelids fluttered, only to close again. Tucker pulled a chair close to the bed and eased into it, all the while keeping his eyes on her.

"You'll be lucky, Garrett, if you get outta this mess with your hide intact," he muttered.

She moaned again. He leaned closer to the bed. Maybe he should try to fully rouse her. No, he decided, predicting that she would come around in her own good time. Meanwhile, he was left with thinking about the possible ramifications of the incident and how the hell he would handle them.

"Everything's okay out front, boss."

Startled, Tucker swung around.

Crusty made a face. "Sorry, didn't mean to scare you."

"Yes you did, or you would've knocked."

Crusty grinned; then his face sobered. "The dirtbag's out the door, just like you said."

"Any trouble?"

"Nah, none that me and security couldn't take care of."

"Good."

Crusty craned his neck around Tucker. "So, how is she?"

"Still out, but she's moaned a couple times, which is a good sign."

Crusty gave Tucker a knowing look, then said, "Like I told you, boy, you'd best be careful. Them kind of women's poison."

"Get off that horse, will you? Hell, it's not the woman who has my belly tied in knots, it's the law."

"The law don't know nothin' about this."

"We're damn lucky they don't. If someone had called them, we'd be in big trouble."

"I can't argue with that."

"I've worked too damn hard on running a clean and decent business."

"Not to mention your pride."

"That's right," Tucker said. "And you know as well as I do that fights can tarnish a club's reputation quicker than anything."

Crusty shifted his weight off his wooden leg. "True, but so far, so good. So don't go gettin' your dander up. Right now, your job is to tend to the lady."

"Right," Tucker said, and watched as Crusty once again shut the door.

He turned his attention back to the woman, wishing like hell that he knew her name. Name or no name, she was sure to have a nasty black eye. In fact, the delicate skin around that eye was already swelling. A curse singed the air. He'd had his share of fights, but never had he belted a woman. The thought had never ever occurred to him, even though his old man had had a habit of hitting his mother before he'd died of a heart attack and she from kidney failure.

Even his uncle, who had been meaner than a junkyard dog, had never struck a woman. Leave it to him to pull a boner like that, Tucker thought, feeling the knot in his gut tighten. And not just because he'd struck her, either—although that in itself was unpardonable. But for the first time since he'd caught his wife in a compromising position with another man, feelings were stirring inside him that he'd thought long dead.

Tucker shifted in his chair, feeling himself grow hard, admitting that he'd like nothing better than to remove her clothing one piece at a time, then sample the delights of her curvy body. And not just once, either.

Feeling sweat pop out on his forehead, he got up and stalked to the window, where he took several deep breaths, struggling for control, control that he hadn't lost in a long time. Thoughts like those wasted time and energy.

"Where am I?"

Tucker stiffened, then turned and watched as she struggled into a sitting position.

"Hey, take it easy," he cautioned, hurrying to her side.

When he would have helped her, she cringed. "Stay away from me!"

Tucker jammed his hands into the pockets of his jeans and shrugged. "Whatever you say."

"So where am I?"

"At the club, in my living quarters."

She massaged her head and winced visibly.

"Do you remember what happened?"

She looked up. "Yes. You hit me."

"Not on purpose. You stepped between me and that a—" Tucker paused, cleared his throat, then started over. "That man you were with, who caused the brouhaha in the first place."

"While I'm certainly not excusing Charles, I'm not excusing you, either. You should've been able to control him without resorting to violence."

"Yeah, right."

His sarcasm wasn't lost on her, she flushed, then looked away. "What time is it?"

"Twelve o'clock."

"Where's Charles?"

"After sobering him up, we kicked him out."

She bit down on her lower lip and again shifted her gaze.

"Who are you?" Tucker massaged the back of his neck, trying to curb his mounting frustration. He didn't know whether to kiss her or shake her. Either way, he would lose. "I'm at a distinct disadvantage here. You know who I am, but I haven't been so honored."

She lifted her chin a notch. "Kelly Warren."

It wasn't so much what she said as the manner in which she said it that shot off a silent alarm inside Tucker's head. Women with that holier-than-thou demeanor set his teeth on edge about as quick as anything. Yet he kept his emotions under control. "Is that supposed to mean something to me?"

Her eyes widened, even her swollen one. "Warren Foods. My father owns the company."

Before he got a chance to respond, she stood, only to cry out when she got a glimpse of herself in the mirror.

"It'll get worse before it gets better. Sorry."

She moved closer and stared at her reflection. "Oh, no!"

"Under the circumstances, it couldn't be helped."

She faced him in outrage. "Couldn't be helped? How dare you say that? I'm ruined!"

"Your looks, for a few days, and maybe your pride, but that's all. You'll survive."

"But you may not!" she countered with heat. "After my father finds out about this, he'll—"

"Look, lady, I don't give a tinker's damn who your father is. You're the one at fault here. Shaking your tight fanny like you did got you into this trouble. So don't go blaming me!"

She glowered at him. "I want to go home."

Tucker's jaw tightened. "I thought you'd never ask."

Kelly gripped the phone until she thought her knuckles might crack. "You brought it on yourself, Charles."

"The hell I did!"

Kelly held the receiver away from her ear and felt the tension inside her lessen, especially when her grandmother lifted her eyes heavenward. Kelly almost giggled.

"If you hadn't gotten drunk, none of this would've happened," she said, turning away from her grandmother.

"Do you mean to tell me you're going to let that cowboy get away with giving us both black eyes?"

"What do you suggest we do?"

"Sue the bastard, that's what."

"You sue him if you want to, but leave me out of it."

Charles grunted. "Why, I do believe you've fallen for that hick."

"Look, you think what you like," Kelly said in a blistering tone. "And do what you like. I don't care. Right now, all I want is to be left alone." With that, she hung up the phone.

"My, my, but that sounded a bit tacky, don't you think?"

"Yes, but it's the truth, and he had it coming."

Claire simply looked at her.

Kelly sighed, then plopped down in a chair across from her grandmother and took a sip of coffee. They had both gotten up at the same time, an hour earlier, and stumbled into the kitchen simultaneously.

Kelly had dreaded Claire seeing her black eye, but since there was no way to avoid it, she'd faced the problem head-on.

"Oh, my dear, what on earth happened to your poor face?" Claire had whispered, her hand over her heart.

"Steady, Grandmom," Kelly had responded urgently. "I'm all right. Really I am. It's just a black eye, nothing more, nothing less."

"But how...I mean..." Claire had stammered as she'd eased into a chair. "Surely Charles didn't do that to you."

"Of course he didn't."

"Well, then, who did?"

Kelly hadn't heard that kind of spunk in her grandmother's voice since she'd had her last heart attack. That spunk had given her the courage to tell Claire the truth. "It's a long and not very pretty story."

"I've got all the time in the world." Claire had looked at the clock on the wall. "And so do you, young lady. It's only seven, and you don't have to open the shop until nine-thirty."

Kelly had laughed, then winced. The whole side of her face was sore. "All right, you asked for the sordid details, so here they are."

That unburdening had taken place an hour ago, and they were still sitting at the table, sipping coffee.

Claire spoke up again. "It's a toss-up, actually, as to who I'd like to strangle more, Charles or that...that cowpoke with—"

Kelly's laugh cut off her grandmother's next words. "Cowpoke, now that's a hoot. I'd bet he'd take issue with that word."

"So, what's his name?" Claire suddenly shook her head. "Never mind. His name's not important. *He's* not important. Any man who would hit a woman isn't worth a nickel."

"Hey, Grandmom, he didn't mean to do it." After last night, she couldn't believe she was defending

Tucker Garrett. But in retrospect, she knew he'd had no choice. If she had been thinking at all, she wouldn't have stepped between the two men. Remembering the look on Tucker's face made her shiver. He was definitely someone who didn't take any crap from anyone.

Claire gave her a strange look. "Surely you aren't..." She paused as if looking for the right words to convey what she wanted to say.

"No, I couldn't care less about him," Kelly said, reaching out and squeezing her grandmother's hand. "So get that frown off your face. Besides the fact that he's not my type, I'll never see him again. You can count on that."

"Well, I can't say I'm sorry."

"I can."

"Just exactly what does that mean?" Claire snapped.

"I'd like at least one more look at his club. You know I'm determined to design some cards with a Western theme."

"So visit another club."

Kelly turned and stared out the window. "I guess I'll have to, only Boot Scootin' had exactly the ambience I needed."

"Well, with your sharp mind, I'm sure you retained enough to sketch some great designs."

Kelly frowned. "I hope so. Anyway, I've got to get a move on and get to the shop."

"Why the hurry, and why are you working so hard, my dear? You don't have anything to prove."

Kelly kissed Claire on the cheek. "Oh yes, I do. To myself and to Dad, who thinks I'm doomed to failure."

"We both know better, don't we?"

"Of course," Kelly quipped with a smile, but that smile didn't reach her eyes.

Her back ached. She'd been sitting at her drafting table, sketching on tracing paper with the intention of transferring those sketches to the illustration board. But there was a catch. The majority of the sketches were terrible. Some, however, were salvageable.

Kelly peered closer at the drawings, made a face, then threw down her pencil and massaged her neck. She knew what her problem was, concentration—or rather, the lack of it. Plus, it was hard to see with one eye swelled shut.

Men! Why were they all such a pain in the backside? First her father, then Charles, now Tucker Garrett. But the latter didn't even bear thinking about. She'd meant it when she'd told him to go to hell, that she never wanted to see him again.

On the other hand, though, it was a shame. Not only was he intriguing and mysterious, he could dance like he had wings on his boots. Yet he was too rugged, rude and untamed. And even if she were looking for someone to go out with, she wouldn't pick Tucker Garrett.

Besides, her father would have a heart attack. Still, when she thought about the way he looked at her with those bottomless brown eyes and the way his buns filled those tight jeans . . .

The doorbell chimed. Kelly jumped, then collected her thoughts and breathed a sigh of relief. She suspected it would be her last customer from yesterday, back to pick up the gift she'd left to be wrapped.

"I'm coming, Mrs. Nelson."

She bounded down the stairs, only to stop midway and feel her jaw drop.

"Sorry to disappoint you," a husky voice said.

Tucker Garrett stood inside the door wearing a grin and holding a bouquet of flowers.

Kelly didn't know whether to laugh or cry.

Chapter Five

Kelly's first reaction was to tell Tucker Garrett to get the hell out of her shop, flowers or no flowers. Instead she found herself asking, "What are you doing here?"

He grinned sheepishly which made her heart pound a tad faster, even though she tried to ignore that fact.

"Surely you don't greet all your customers this way?" he drawled, two long strides placing him in the middle of the room.

"You're no customer," she snapped.

He raised his eyebrows. "How do you know?"

Enough was enough, Kelly told herself as she made her way down the stairs. He couldn't simply stroll into her domain and behave as if he were her prince in shining armor and not a wolf in sheep's clothing, which she knew him to be.

But dammit, why did he have to look so good? His still-damp hair told her that he'd probably just gotten out of the shower. She didn't know why that thought made her flush. Maybe it was the idea of him in the buff...

Yet nothing could discount the way he looked fully dressed, either. His yellow chambray shirt was tucked into jeans that hugged his muscular legs, down to his scuffed boots. The only things that seemed to be missing were a Stetson and spurs. She almost smiled. All in all, though, he was a fine specimen.

"It's threatening to be a scorcher," he said, dispelling the awkward silence while wiping the back of his hand across his forehead.

Kelly cleared her throat and forced a nonchalance she was far from feeling. "Again, *why* are you here? I know it's not to discuss the weather. Right?"

His response was to hand her the bouquet. "You'd better put these in water before they wilt."

Churlishly, Kelly grabbed the flowers and walked into the kitchen, where she located a vase. He followed her. Once the task was done, she leaned against the cabinet and faced him, her eyes challenging and hostile.

"Would you believe me if I said I was sorry?" he asked.

"No." Her terse comeback made it plain that she was unwilling to forget or forgive.

"Mmm. Didn't think so."

"Would you believe it if I said I wanted to see how your eye was?" He seemed to suddenly scrutinize her closer. "It's not nearly as swollen as I thought it would be."

"Look, Mr. Garrett—"

"I am sorry, you know." His drawl had turned low and husky. "I'm not in the habit of destroying beauty."

Tucker's words sent another hot flush through her. Kelly wanted to turn away, but she couldn't.

His gaze held her, and he went on. "I know we got off on the wrong foot—"

When she smiled, he broke off. "Well, maybe those aren't the right words, but you get my drift." He paused again. "And the name's Tucker."

"All right, Tucker, and I do get your drift. So you've apologized."

"So, is it accepted?"

"I guess."

"If that's the best you can do..."

"I wouldn't push my luck, if I were you."

He leaned against the counter. "So, what kind of business are you in?"

Why she answered him, Kelly didn't know. She should have told him to get out of her life and stay out. "Stationery and gifts, but it's the stationery that I'm concentrating on."

"Oh?"

"I hope to sell my ideas to a major card company."

"Any chance of that happening?"

"I've had a nibble here and there."

A silence fell between them, a tension-filled silence during which Kelly felt his gaze drop to her mouth, then lower. When his eyes darkened, heat filled her face.

"Tell me," he said at last, and she breathed a sigh of relief, "why is this so important to you? I mean, if your father is loaded, then why..."

Her relief was short-lived, and so was her coolness. The smirk on his face and in his tone was insulting. Red-hot fury raced through her. "Why would a rich girl like me play at making a living? Is that what you're asking?"

Tucker shifted his weight, but he didn't flinch at her harshly spoken words. "I guess so, even though I didn't mean—"

"Yes, you did," she interrupted coldly. "But I don't give a damn what you think. Now, if you'll excuse me, this dumb blonde has work to do."

"Kelly!"

"Goodbye, Mr. Garrett."

She knew he would have argued, but a customer chose that moment to open the door. He stared at her a bit longer, then saluted in a mocking fashion and walked out.

Kelly leaned against the counter for support, feeling as if her legs might give way under her.

"You all right, honey?" the woman asked.

Kelly forced herself upright. "I'm fine, thanks."

The woman winked. "Men. Can't live with 'em and can't live without 'em."

In spite of herself, Kelly smiled. "You got that right."

A while later the shop was empty, and for once she was glad. Thanks to Tucker Garrett, her insides were still in a turmoil. To offset that unwanted turmoil, she'd called and invited her grandmother to have lunch with her. Claire always seemed to be able to put things in perspective, and Kelly desperately needed perspective.

The buzzer sounded, and, thinking Claire had arrived, Kelly looked up with a bright smile, only to have that smile twist into a frown.

"You again!"

Standing just inside the door, Tucker lifted his shoulders in a seemingly innocent shrug. "I'm just like a bad penny. I keep showing up."

"You're not wanted."

"You're lying," he said softly, his eyes roaming her body.

"I—"

"Come to the club tonight?"

Kelly gasped. This man obviously had more personalities than a schizophrenic. "You're not serious?"

His face sobered again. "What do you think?"

"I think you're insane."

"Is that a yes?"

Kelly rolled her eyes.

"Good. I'll pick you up at nine."

"I don't think—"

He stared at her for a long, intense moment. "You won't be sorry."

"That remains to be seen."

He laughed and shut the door.

"There's a fellow here to see you," Crusty said, standing in the doorway of Tucker's apartment.

Tucker, who was sitting at his desk doing book work, looked up. "Did he give you his name?"

"Nope."

"Well, this isn't a good time, but send him in."

Seconds later a tall, rawboned man filled the doorway. Tucker winced visibly. "Hell, Wilder, you're the last person I wanna see."

Anson Wilder ambled to the nearest chair, plopped down into it, and grinned. "Now, is that any way to greet your ex-boss?"

Anson hadn't changed, Tucker thought. His loud voice still had that whiskey rasp to it, as though he'd been drinking all his life. Tucker knew better; he'd never seen the man take a drink, period.

"So, what brings you to this neck of the woods?"

Anson pulled on his beard. "I want you to come back."

"Not on your life."

"Not even for megabucks? We're drilling a new well, and it's a huge project with a huge budget."

"I told you I was through living out of a suitcase, and I meant it."

Anson looked around. "How much do you owe on this place?"

"That's none of your damned business," Tucker lashed out, his face red.

Anson snorted, then stood. "Well, think about it, 'cause you could pay this dump off with what you'd earn." He paused. "You're the best, and that's what I need. Think about it. I'll be in touch."

Tucker didn't bother to answer. Once his visitor had gone, he stared outside with brooding intensity. He was a fool not to take Anson up on his offer. And the main reason for it, was a sassy blonde with a cute butt who he could never have, despite the fact that he wanted her.

He pounded the desk with his fist.

"So, what do you think?"

"About what?"

Tucker grinned. "The club."

It was now past eleven, and for the two hours Kelly had been there, she'd sat at a corner table, sipped a soda, watched the dancers and sketched. She'd loved every minute of it, even though she found it difficult to digest that she'd actually come.

After she'd committed herself, she'd picked up the phone in the shop several times with the intention of telling him that she'd changed her mind, only to slam the receiver back down. When a customer had given her a strange look, she'd decided she was not only behaving foolishly, but overreacting, as well.

What harm could possibly come from her accompanying him to the club? After all, wasn't that what she wanted—to make sketches, something she hadn't gotten to do the time before? Of course it was. So what was she afraid of? It was a question she refused to answer.

So far the evening had been as Kelly had hoped—uneventful and productive. She hadn't expected Tucker to hover over her; he had his job to do, and he'd done it.

Yet she was always aware of his presence, which both irritated her and excited her. She likened her relationship with this man to a child playing with a packet of matches, dangerously striking each one.

Kelly sensed he felt the same about her. She had caught him staring at her several times with a brooding expression in his eyes. She'd pretended not to notice.

"Again, what's the verdict?" he pressed into the silence.

"I think it's neat."

"Is that all?"

Kelly hesitated. "Well, you could put a mechanical bull in that empty corner and it'd be even neater."

"What!"

"You heard me."

Tucker opened his mouth, snapped it shut, then laughed. When she didn't respond, his laugh disappeared. "You're serious, aren't you?"

"I wouldn't have said it otherwise."

"A bull, huh? Like in the movie?"

"And like other clubs have."

Tucker massaged his chin. "What makes you think I'd wanna play copycat?"

"I don't. And because of that, I think you're missing an opportunity to make good money."

Tucker continued to massage his chin. "Mmm, not a bad idea, actually. I'll give it some serious thought."

"Really?"

"Really."

Their eyes met, and for a second, they seemed alone in the room.

Tucker cleared his throat, which she noticed he had a habit of doing when he was uncomfortable. It served to break the tension, especially when he said, "Well, I could sure use a drawing card."

"Is that your way of saying the club's not doing well?" she asked, glad that things were back on a stable footing.

"It is and it isn't. Does that make sense?"

"Yes, since I'm in business myself."

"Well, when it isn't," Tucker continued, a bleak expression on his face, "I sorta get bent out of shape. The note on this place is pretty hefty." He paused, then changed the subject, as if he regretted his lapse into his personal business. "So, show me your sketches."

Kelly did, and several were of a cowboy riding a bull.

"These are damn good. *You're* damn good."

Again their eyes met, and again the tension thickened.

"Look, I should be going," Kelly said at last. "I have to get up early," she added inanely.

He stood abruptly. "Come on, I'll take you home."

A short time later Tucker maneuvered his pickup into the driveway of her grandmother's house. He killed the engine, then, staring straight ahead, asked, "So, when can I see you again?"

"Oh, I don't think—"

She never got any further. He turned, leaned over and placed his lips against hers.

At first Kelly was so taken aback, she couldn't respond. But when his tongue coaxed her teeth apart, she was lost.

Groaning, she answered his hot, hungry lips with a hunger of her own. Then, with the same abruptness the kiss had started with, it ended. He jerked back, leaving them both shaken and gasping for breath.

"Look, I didn't mean—" Tucker broke off and stared at her; agony darkened his eyes. "Oh, hell, I don't know what I meant. I—"

"Forget it! It...it doesn't matter."

Kelly opened the door, jumped out and never looked back, not even when she heard him holler, *"Kelly!"*

Chapter Six

Sweat oozed from every pore on his body. It wasn't because it was muggy and threatening to rain, either, though the sky looked as if it could explode at any moment. Tucker didn't care if it did. His mind wasn't on the wretched summer heat.

His thoughts vacillated from Kelly Warren to Anson Wilder. Dammit, both were the last people he wanted to think about. He leaned over, patted his horse, Duke, on the neck, then nudged him in the side. Duke took off toward the wide-open pasture behind the barn.

Tucker tried to clear his thoughts, tried to concentrate on the sounds and sights of the land he so loved. When nothing else could unscramble his thoughts, clear his perspective on things, this wooded acreage could. But today it seemed to fail him.

He knew he could make a go of the club, though at the moment he was barely managing to pay his bills. If only Anson hadn't shown up and dangled that lucrative carrot in front of his face. He didn't want to return to the oil rig. He wanted roots. He wanted a home. He wanted to own his own business. Well, two out of three wasn't so bad, he told himself, grimacing. One of these days he would have the club paid off, then he could build his dream house on top of the hill that Duke was heading toward.

Once horse and rider reached that hill, Tucker stopped Duke, shoved back his Stetson and simply stared at the woods around him. Twenty-five acres wasn't much, but it was his, left to him by his uncle. In fact, this land was the only thing his uncle had ever given him except whippings and tongue-lashings. He was the meanest old coot Tucker had ever known. Yet when he'd died, Tucker had been completely alone in this world.

"Ah, hell," he muttered into the wind, having just made up his mind. Anson could take that job and stick it where the sun didn't shine.

He wasn't going anywhere, not until he got a certain blue-eyed blonde out of his system. That kiss they had exchanged had nearly taken the top of his head off, not to mention another essential part of his anatomy. He'd been hard all night.

He knew she'd been affected, too. She'd responded, all right. Still, he'd sensed a reserve, and the thought of chipping away at that reserve was a challenge he couldn't pass up, even though he knew he was headed for trouble.

Someone of her caliber was off limits to the likes of him, which was okay. Hell, he knew the score, and since he'd already been burned once, he didn't intend to let it happen again. He wasn't about to fall in love—that word was no longer a part of his vocabulary. All he wanted was to have her in his bed, especially now that he'd tasted her sweetness. But he would have to use finesse. She wouldn't be a pushover, not by a long shot. But he wasn't about to give up.

Whistling, Tucker nudged Duke around and headed back toward the barn, a plan forming in his mind.

* * *

"Ms. Warren?"

"Yes, this is she," Kelly said into the receiver, not recognizing the woman's voice.

"I'm Martha Havard, Director of Marketing at Visions Card Company. I hope you don't mind me calling you so early."

Thank goodness the chair behind the counter was close by or Kelly's legs would have buckled beneath her. She licked her suddenly dry lips. "Of course I don't mind. I'm delighted to hear from you."

"Well, I'm delighted with the card samples you sent us."

Again Kelly was glad she was seated as waves of excitement rolled over her. Yet she forced a calmness into her voice that made her proud. "You are?"

The woman chuckled. "Are you surprised?"

"I guess I am."

"We'd like to see more of your designs, especially the ones with the Western settings."

"So, Visions is definitely interested?"

"Yes, we are. But I have to tell you that the acquiring process is sometimes quite lengthy."

"So I shouldn't get my hopes too high. Is that what you're saying?"

"Yes and no. We're very interested in your work, as I said before, but there are others we're considering, as well."

"I appreciate your honesty, and I'll certainly send you more designs. Even as we speak, I have several new sketches on my illustration board."

"Perfect. As soon as they're complete, send them to us."

"I will, and thanks so much for considering me."

"Our pleasure. Talk to you soon."

After replacing the receiver, Kelly sat unmoving, almost stupefied. Then, when it dawned on her *who* had just called her, she jumped up and let out a whoop.

Moments later she thought of her grandmother and was about to call and share the good news when the phone jangled again. Kelly gave a start. She took several deep breaths, then answered it.

"Exclusively Kelly's."

"Hi."

For the second time that morning shock waves rippled through her body, sending her back behind the counter to the chair. "Hi," she finally managed in return.

Tucker chuckled, which added fuel to her already racing heart. "Well, at least you didn't slam the phone down in my ear. Should I be encouraged?"

"You're incorrigible."

He chuckled again, then his voice turned serious And husky. "I'm not calling to apologize."

She didn't pretend to misunderstand. "I didn't think you were."

"Good. Now that we've gotten that out of the way. we can cut to the chase."

"And just what is that?"

"When I can see you again."

Kelly ached to slam the receiver down in his ear, but not before telling him to leave her alone. But she couldn't do that, because the unvarnished truth was that she didn't want him to leave her alone. The torrid kiss they had exchanged had left her shaken and confused. Yet his audacity and conceit attracted her, and she couldn't deny it, which was even more of a reason to call a halt to this madness before it went any further.

"Kelly?"

"I'm still here."

"Then answer me. Please."

"Look, I need to work, especially now."

"Why the sudden urgency?"

She told him about the woman from Visions calling, though with reluctance.

"All right!" Tucker exclaimed. "That's more reason why we should go out and celebrate."

Kelly chewed on her lower lip. "Do you really think that's a good idea?"

"No."

His honesty rattled her. "Then why..."

"Because I want to see you."

"And do you always get what you want?" The second she asked the loaded question, she wished she hadn't.

He hesitated. "Most of the time."

Again she was amazed at the man's high opinion of himself, and at herself for being a party to it. "What did you have in mind?"

"Dinner, then back to the club."

She would have liked to skip the dinner part, because it sounded too much like a date. But she didn't mind the club part. In light of the other phone call, she wanted to sketch couples on the dance floor, something she hadn't done.

"Okay," she finally said.

He chuckled. "Don't get too excited, now, you hear?"

She didn't respond.

"I'll pick you up at six."

With that, he hung up. She stared at the receiver a moment longer, then slammed it down. "Damn!"

They had been dancing for thirty minutes. First they tried the Texas two-step, followed by several line dances, including Achy, Breaky and the Cotton-Eyed Joe.

"You're damn good," Tucker said, while waiting for the song to change.

Kelly looked up at him. "So are you."

As planned, they had gone to dinner at the Tejas Café, one of Kelly's favorite places, and shared the chicken *fajita* dinner for two. She hadn't planned to enjoy herself, but she'd found herself doing just that. He'd entertained her with some of his exploits on the oil rig, the humorous as well as the dangerous ones.

When it came to anything personal about himself, though, he shied away. But then, she didn't press the issue. She figured the less she knew about this man, the better off she would be. After she finished her sketches, there would be no need to go to the club or see Tucker Garrett again.

Now, as another tune began, he stared down at her, but he made no move to take her in his arms. Suddenly uncomfortable, Kelly looked around. She noticed that they were the only couple on the dimly lighted floor, though there was another couple seated in a far-off corner, their hands entwined.

Kelly knew that soon the club would be bustling, as it had been on Friday night. But the minute she and Tucker had walked in, he had hustled her onto the dance floor, where they had been ever since.

"Tell me something," he said, reaching for her and beginning to move in perfect time to the music. "Are you in love with Charley-boy?"

Kelly shouldn't have been surprised by his question. By now, *nothing* he said or did should have surprised her. But it did. He seemed to have the uncanny ability to blindside her.

"That's none of your business," she snapped.

"Well, are you?"

She stopped dancing and backed out of his arms. "Why do you want to know?"

"Curious, I guess. He just doesn't seem your type."

"Are you saying that you are?"

He continued to stare at her through smoldering eyes. "Maybe."

Her heart lurched, and because this conversation was headed in a direction she didn't like, she turned to walk off. His words stopped her. "I'll behave, I promise."

"Somehow I don't believe that for a minute."

He chuckled and pulled her back into his arms.

After a moment she stared up at him and said, "You ought to give dance lessons here."

This time it was Tucker who seemed stunned.

"What's the matter? Did I say something wrong?"

"Nope. Just goes to show you that great minds think alike."

"Yeah, right," she said drolly.

He lifted one eyebrow. "I'm serious. That's one of the reasons I asked you here tonight."

"Oh, really?"

"Yep, to discuss that very thing."

"Well, I don't think you can go wrong."

"So, how 'bout it?"

"How about what?"

"Teaching."

"Me?"

He grinned innocently. "Yes, you."

"Oh, I don't think I—"

"Great! I knew you'd say yes."

Kelly gave him an incredulous look. That was when he kissed her, long, hard and hot. Finally he lifted his head and whispered, "This could become a habit, you know?"

Kelly gulped. "I know."

"But it's one I don't want to break. How 'bout you?"

"I—"

He didn't give her a chance to answer. His lips adhered to hers once again, this time longer, harder and hotter.

Shaken and limp, Kelly dug her fingers into his neck and reveled in their tangling tongues. Without removing his lips, Tucker pushed her slightly away so that his hand could find and circle a breast and already-protruding nipple.

"Sweet, oh, so sweet," he whispered.

Kelly moaned into his mouth and wasn't even aware that the music had ended until someone tapped her on the shoulder. She jerked out of Tucker's arms as if she'd been shot.

"What the hell, Crusty?" Tucker demanded in the dim light.

The old man's eyes were on Kelly. "Sorry, miss, but the hospital's on the phone."

Chapter Seven

Kelly disliked hospitals. She couldn't say why. She'd never been seriously ill herself, with the exception of an appendicitis attack when she was twelve years old. Perhaps it was the stark setting and the clinical smell that repulsed her. Or maybe it was the fear that this time her beloved grandmother would die here.

She must have whimpered aloud because when she turned away from the window and to Tucker, beside her, he was peering down at her, a concerned expression in his eyes.

"I'm sure she's going to be all right," he said.

"Me...too." Only Kelly wasn't sure at all, and that was what brought the sting of tears to her eyes.

"Dammit, Kelly, I can't stand to see you cry," Tucker muttered gruffly, looking miserable himself.

"And I hate to cry."

"Then don't. Please."

Kelly gritted her teeth. "Why doesn't the doctor come out and tell us something?"

"He will." Tucker glanced at his watch. "It's only been two hours since they wheeled her into surgery."

"That's an eternity."

"Yeah, I guess it is."

When they had arrived, a cardiologist had met them in the emergency room where he'd shown Kelly X rays of her grandmother's heart, explaining that bypass surgery was critical to saving her life. Kelly had signed the required papers, then called Simon.

"I'd like to hold you, you know." Tucker's eyes were dark and spoke more powerfully than his words.

Kelly licked her lips and looked around. Several couples were in the combined surgery and intensive care waiting room on the sixth floor of Memorial Hospital, so privacy was nonexistent.

"I'd like that, too, only—" She broke off and turned away, no longer able to endure his intense gaze.

Tucker gave a harsh sigh at the same time that he ran his hand through his hair. Then he took one of her cold hands in his. That gesture brought her eyes back to his.

"You're going to have to admit it, you know," he said softly and for her ears alone.

"What?"

"That it's okay to need someone . . . to need *me*."

Kelly tried to remove her hand; his grip tightened. "I want to hold you as much as you want me to."

Fear of another kind squeezed her heart. Kelly jerked her hand out of his. "This is not the time to talk about us."

His mouth tightened. "You're right, it isn't. And I'm sorry. But soon you're going to have to face something you obviously don't want to."

Ignoring the veiled but husky warning in his voice, Kelly gazed at the window once again, that squeeze on her heart tightening to unbearable proportions.

She felt bad that her thoughts were on something— and some*one*—other than her grandmother. But then, any time she was around Tucker, he seemed to consume her, which terrified her.

She didn't want to want a man in that way, not just Tucker, but any man. Yet, at the same time, she wanted to lean on him, draw from his strength, wanted to feel his hot, needy lips on hers. Again and again.

But why? What was there about him that was so intriguing, so all-consuming? She didn't trust him; her intuition told her that he didn't believe in the ties that bind. But she trusted herself even less. He'd kissed her twice, and those kisses had created a yearning inside her that went beyond wanting only more kisses.

Was it just sex she wanted? Was that it? If they made love, what then? Would it end there? But again, she didn't want to want anyone. She rebelled against that constant, heated ache inside her. She only wanted to be left alone, to do her job and prove her independence.

So why couldn't she tell him to take a hike?

"You want some coffee?"

Kelly turned to her right, only to realize that Tucker was still close. Too close. She stared up at him, her eyes brimming with unshed tears.

He muttered a curse, slung his arm around her and pulled her against his side. She tensed, but only for a moment; then she gave in and let him hold her.

"She'll be fine," he whispered into her hair. "I just know she will."

"Kelly?"

On hearing her father's voice, Kelly stiffened then jerked out of Tucker's arms. She turned and stared at Simon Warren, who appeared as unruffled and composed as ever. Not one hair on his iron gray head was out of place, nor was there one wrinkle in his suit.

"Hello, Daddy." Kelly's voice quivered in spite of her effort to keep it steady. Simon disliked any show of emotion, and she could imagine his reaction when he'd seen Tucker's arms around her.

Without saying anything, and with only a quick, disdainful look in Tucker's direction, he leaned over and pecked her on the cheek. "Any word yet?"

"Not yet. How did you get here so fast?"

"I had Walter fly me."

"Right," Kelly said, catching Tucker's movement out of the corner of her eye. "Uh, sorry." Her gaze jockeyed between the two men. "Tucker Garrett, my dad, Simon Warren."

"Sir," Tucker acknowledged, and extended his hand. Though his tone was outwardly respectful, Kelly heard the undercurrent of contempt in Tucker's voice.

Simon obviously picked up on it, as well, because his face reddened and his eyes hardened. "And just who are you?" he asked bluntly.

"A friend."

Simon rubbed his chin. "I see."

No you don't, Kelly thought. But it didn't matter. Not now, anyway. All that mattered now was hearing news of her grandmother's condition.

As if someone had read her mind, the volunteer worker walked up to them and said that the doctor had called and would meet the family upstairs on the seventh floor. Kelly hadn't even heard the phone ring.

"Let's go," Simon said, completely ignoring Tucker.

Kelly paused, however, feeling the pull between two strong men, one she loved and one she wanted.

Tucker smiled, though it never reached his eyes. "It's all right. Go on, I'll call you."

Then, without so much as a glance in her father's direction, Tucker turned and walked out of the room.

"Who the hell is *that?*" Simon demanded, grasping her arm and ushering her forward. "I'm sure I smelled manure on his boots, for God's sake."

"I'll tell you later," Kelly countered in a heated tone.

"That you will, young lady. And you'll also tell me where you got that bruised eye."

"Forget about me, okay? Right now, I only care about Grandmom."

Simon didn't respond, but Kelly noticed that his face looked as if it had been carved out of cement. She stifled a sigh.

Tucker hadn't called, and it had been three days since he'd walked out of the hospital. Her grandmother had come through her heart surgery successfully, though the doctor had warned both her and Simon that Claire was by no means out of danger and wouldn't be for a long time.

Still, Kelly was encouraged, and every evening, the second she locked the door on her shop at five-thirty, she went to the hospital and sat with Claire in intensive care for the allotted amount of time. In fact, she was hopeful that her grandmother would soon be moved to a private room, maybe even today.

Kelly paused in her thoughts, then massaged the back of her neck as she sat at the breakfast room table and watched two bluebirds splash in the birdbath in the perfectly manicured backyard. She sighed inwardly, thinking what a great day it would be to go on a picnic or spend at the beach with someone, that someone being Tucker.

She clenched her fists in frustration. Why hadn't he called? Why hadn't he come by the store? She suspected she knew the answer—Simon Warren. Her father hadn't bothered to hide his contempt at having found Tucker with her.

Thank heavens, though, she'd been spared the grueling question-and-answer session that he'd promised. Shortly after they had visited her grandmother, Simon had gotten a call on his cellular phone that an ex-employee had entered one of the grocery stores with a gun in tow and was threatening to shoot several customers if he wasn't rehired.

Simon had left immediately, but with the promise to return as soon as possible. So far, she'd been spared.

She had just taken a sip of her French Vanilla Café when she heard a brief tap on the kitchen door, followed by a key turning in the lock. So much for her respite, she thought, watching as her father thrust open the door.

"Good morning," he said, striding to the table and giving her a dutiful peck on the cheek.

"Hi, Dad."

"How's Mother?"

"Better. I just spoke to the hospital, and I'm hopeful she'll be moved to a private room today."

"Great," he said, easing into a chair across the table from her.

"Would you like a cup of coffee?"

"No, I've just finished several."

"So, how long can you stay?" Kelly asked.

"Since it's Sunday, hopefully all day."

Kelly drained the last of her coffee, then stood. "I'll get dressed, and we can head for the hospital."

"Don't be in such a rush. I think we should talk."

"About what?" Kelly asked, pretending ignorance, but knowing her ploy wouldn't work. It didn't.

"For starters, your grandmother."

Surprised that he hadn't launched into a tirade about Tucker, Kelly actually sat back down. "What about Grandmom?"

"I'm going to put her into a nursing home."

"No, Daddy, please don't."

"I've made up my mind. She needs more care than you can give her."

"But a nursing home?" Kelly wailed.

"Actually, it's a retirement home that the Methodist church has just completed. I've made all the arrangements."

Kelly had heard about the home and how lovely it was. Maybe it wasn't a bad idea, after all. "All right, Daddy. We'll try it for a while and see how it works."

"I knew you'd see it my way."

Kelly didn't say anything, preparing herself for the hatchet to fall. But again she was surprised.

"Charles told me how you got that shiner. He also told me that he's terribly upset about what happened between you two."

"Don't tell me you've become his mouthpiece, too?"

Simon's face paled. "Don't you get smart with me, young lady."

"Look, let's not argue, okay? I'm not interested in Charles. That's not going to change."

"And all because of that cowboy, the one you were mooning over at the hospital."

"Honestly, Dad, that expression is not only archaic but ridiculous."

Simon turned even paler. "Call it whatever you want, but I won't have you involved with someone of his caliber."

"You can't tell me what to do. I'll see whoever I want."

An incredulous expression appeared on Simon's face. "Surely you aren't interested in *him*."

"What's wrong with Tucker?"

"What's right with Tucker, don't you mean?"

"Look, just because he doesn't wear a suit and work in an office doesn't mean he's subhuman."

"I never said he was. All I'm saying is that he's not for you."

Kelly laughed without humor. "That's my call, not yours."

"So, you really are involved with him?"

"Come on, Dad, join the real world. I love to country-western dance, you know that. He owns a club, and I've seen him a few times. That's all!"

Simon leaned forward. "That isn't all. I saw the way you two looked at each other. I think you've fallen for that hick cowboy."

"You're mistaken."

"He's just after your money. You must know that."

Kelly was so angry she couldn't speak.

Simon had no such problem. "I had the bastard investigated."

"You did *what?*"

"You heard me. So simmer down and listen."

"That's unforgivable, and I don't want to hear it."

"Yes, you do," Simon countered in a controlled, unruffled voice. "He doesn't have a pot to pee in or a window to throw it out of."

"Since when did you become so crude?"

"Since I'm worried about my only child not only making a fool out of herself, but making the biggest mistake of her life, to boot."

"Oh, for crying out loud, Daddy. You're making a mountain out of a molehill."

"He's a loser, Kelly, a user of women."

Kelly glared at him. "I don't care what he is. How I feel about him and what I do about it is still my call."

With that, she turned and made her way toward the door.

"Bet he didn't tell you he's been married and has a child."

Kelly froze in her tracks.

Chapter Eight

Her skin was as soft as he'd imagined. And her breasts...well, they were even softer and fuller and sweeter than he'd imagined. And when his tongue licked over that sweetness, he felt he would explode before...

"Kelly!" he cried as he thrust inside her.

It must have been the sound of his own voice that awakened Tucker. Like someone who'd been shot, he sat straight up in bed, drenched in sweat. For a moment he looked around the room, not sure where he was.

"Damn," he said out loud, just as things refocused and he realized that he was in his own bedroom, dreaming about making love to Kelly.

Pitching back the sheet, he got up and stumbled naked into the bathroom, where he stepped into the shower, wincing when the water came out colder than ice.

Overindulgence was his problem, he admitted, thinking about the number of beers he'd consumed last evening and the evening before and the evening before that. He'd blamed Kelly, which, of course, was absurd. *He* was to blame for getting involved with her in the first place.

If only he'd never sauntered out on that dance floor like some kind of stud, then he wouldn't be having erotic dreams about a woman who was off-limits to him, and who had a jerk for a father, to boot.

Still, as he reveled in the feel of the water pelting his skin, Tucker's thoughts remained locked on Kelly. He would have liked nothing better than to have her in the shower with him while he soaped every inch of her delicious body.

Dammit, Garrett, give it a rest! he told himself, because that wasn't going to happen. If nothing else, her arrogant bastard of a father would see to that. In the few minutes he'd been around Simon Warren, Tucker had ached to knock him off the pedestal he'd put himself on. And the hold he had over Kelly was another story, one he couldn't do a damn thing about. Tucker knew that her old man would do everything in his power to keep her away from him. Simon's idea of a perfect match for his daughter was someone like Charles Lipton—God forbid!

Kelly was too much woman for that wimp. She would use him as a doormat. Kelly needed someone strong, someone who could match her temper and her intelligence, someone like himself. Yeah right, Garrett, only not in this lifetime.

Still, he knew he would have to see her again, father or no father, stupid or not. He wanted her as he'd never wanted another woman. At the same time, he was confident that once he made love to her, he could get her out of his system and get his libido *and* his life back on track.

He'd been burned once, and he didn't intend to play with that kind of fire again. No, Kelly Warren was out of his league, someone he knew he shouldn't want and could never have.

But knowing that only made him want her more.

"You're full of it, Garrett," he muttered as he climbed out of the shower, wrapped a towel around his waist and padded back into the bedroom.

"Who you talkin' to?"

A scowl rearranged Tucker's features as he stared at his uninvited guest. "Hell, Crusty, don't you ever knock?"

"Yep, only you didn't hear me." The older man grinned. "Too busy talkin' to yourself, huh?"

Tucker's mouth thinned.

Crusty laughed. "Well, I'm glad to see you're in your same old sour mood. What the hell's wrong with you, anyway?" Before Tucker had time to answer, he went on. "It's that Warren woman, isn't it? She ain't lettin' you inside her pants, is that it?"

"I'd be careful, if I were you," Tucker responded in a cold voice. "You're mighty close to letting your mouth get your butt in trouble, my friend."

As if Crusty realized he'd pushed Tucker too far, his demeanor changed. "Sorry, boss, I guess I did step outta line. But, hell, these last few days, you've been worse than an old bear with a sore paw."

Tucker wiped a trickle of water off his forehead and smiled ruefully. "You're right, I have. But I have a lot of things on my mind. And you're right, Kelly Warren is one of them."

"Does she feel the same about you?"

"How do I know? Hell, I don't even know how I feel about her."

"Mmm," Crusty said, rubbing his bad leg.

"You can 'mmm' all you want to, you old coot, but that's all you're getting out of me. So, did you want to see me about something?'' Tucker added pointedly. "If not, then I need to get dressed."

"Yeah, as a matter of fact, I did. But you ain't gonna like this, either."

"Tell me anyhow."

"There's been some rumors," Crusty began, only to stop suddenly, as if unsure about how to continue.

"Go on, spit it out."

"Okay. There's talk about another club going in on the loop."

Tucker cursed.

"Yeah, my words exactly. I didn't want to tell you, but I figured you'd hear it sooner or later."

"Do you think it's just talk?" Tucker heard the desperate edge in his own voice and hated it.

"Maybe, maybe not."

"Thanks, Crusty, that's a real help."

Crusty's lips twitched. "Hell, Tuck, you ask a stupid question, you get a stupid answer. Talk's talk, that's all I know. But if one does open, so what?"

"It'll sink us, that's what."

"That's garbage, and you know it. You've got a lot of loyal customers, plus you run a clean club."

"True, but you know the old saying—the grass is always greener on the other side."

"For a few weekends, maybe. But after that, they'll come back here, you'll see."

"Well, if the rumor's true, I hope you're right about our clientele. Otherwise—" Tucker broke off, unable to go on, mainly because he couldn't bear to think about that scenario.

The reason for his negativism, he knew, was Kelly Warren. He hadn't seen her in three days, and that was eating away at his insides and his good judgment. A little dose of her would cure what ailed him as nothing else could. He smiled.

Crusty gave him an odd look, then asked, "Something rattlin' around in your head I oughta know about?"

"Nope. Just keep your ear to the ground and let me know if you hear anything else. I'll be gone for a while. I have something pressing to take care of.

"Yeah, and I bet she's blond and blue-eyed."

Tucker unlatched his towel and tossed it at Crusty. "Get outta here, you dirty old man."

"Huh," Crusty mumbled as he turned and opened the door. "Seems to me that's what *you* are."

Tucker laughed, then began to whistle.

"Grandmom, is there anything I can do for you?"

Claire Warren smiled at her granddaughter, who was sitting in a chair close to the bed. "No, my dear. Just having you here is all I need."

"Rest assured that wild horses couldn't drive me away."

As Kelly had hoped, Claire had been transferred to a private suite shortly after Simon had left for Houston. Since it was Monday and the shop was closed, Kelly hadn't left her grandmother's side, though she would admit she was pulled in two directions. She longed to be working on her designs, yet she didn't want to leave Claire.

Now, after a long nap, Claire was much improved and wanted to talk. Still, she was a long way from leaving the hospital, and that concerned Kelly. One of these times, she feared her grandmother wouldn't rally. She wasn't going to think about that, though, not now when Claire was holding her hand and smiling at her.

"So, tell me more about Visions."

Kelly scooted closer to the bed, her eyes bright with excitement. "Oh, Grandmom, it's a dream come true. When that lady told me who she was and what she wanted, I nearly keeled over."

"Have you sent her any more sketches?"

"Not yet, but I'm close. Hopefully, these will be my best ones."

"I'm so proud of you, sweetheart, yet—" Claire broke off and stared at Kelly through suddenly clouded eyes.

"Yet what, Grandmom?" Kelly pressed, tightening her hold on Claire's hand.

"Something's bothering you, isn't it?"

"What makes you say that?" Kelly hedged.

"Don't try to fool me. I know you better than you know yourself. Sure, you're ecstatic about selling your designs, but that aside, something's troubling you. Is it Charles?"

Laughter erupted from Kelly. "Heavens, no."

"Good, because despite what my son thinks, he's not for you."

"You'd think Daddy could see that, too."

"Don't be too hard on him, my dear. You're his greatest treasure. He only wants you to be happy. And apparently he thinks Charles can bring you that happiness."

"That's why I'm no longer living at home. Dad just doesn't understand that he can't live my life for me, that he can't choose who I see and who I don't."

"So, who is he?"

Kelly blinked. "Excuse me?"

"You can forget about being coy with me, young lady." Claire paused and smiled. "I know the symptoms when I see them."

Kelly laughed. "You're a piece of work, Grandmom."

"Well?"

Kelly's features sobered. "I met him at that club, Boot Scootin'. In fact, he owns it."

"Ah, a cowboy."

"You sound like Daddy."

"Only I'm not saying it in a derogatory tone the way my son would."

Kelly pressed her lips together. "You should've seen the way Daddy looked at Tucker when he met him."

"Ah, so Tucker's his name."

Kelly smiled. "Yes, Tucker Garrett. He brought me here to the hospital the night you had your heart attack, and he was really concerned about both of us."

"Well, maybe I misjudged him, then. Suppose you tell me more about this young man."

"There's not much to tell, really," Kelly said at the same time that someone knocked on the door. She looked at her grandmother with raised eyebrows, then stood and said, "Come in."

When Tucker walked through the door, holding a bouquet of flowers, Kelly gasped.

"Hello, ladies," he said, though Kelly felt his eyes linger on her.

An intense longing rushed through her. It seemed like an eternity since she'd seen him. Dressed in jeans and a yellow shirt that enhanced his dark eyes and tan, he looked better than ever. Or did that deduction stem from the fact that when he was anywhere near her, her world seemed to tilt?

"Well, don't just stand there, young man. Come closer so I can get a better look at you."

"Grandmom!"

Tucker grinned and did as he was told.

"You're Tucker Garrett, right?"

"That's right, ma'am," he said, winking at Kelly, who blushed. "Hope you're not allergic to flowers," he added, taking Claire's frail, outstretched hand in his and holding it for a moment.

He had such a compassionate look on his face that tears pricked Kelly's eyes. She turned away and blinked them back.

"They're lovely. Thank you," Claire said. "Give them to Kelly."

Kelly avoided his gaze as she took the bouquet, then found a vase. When she turned back, Tucker and Claire were laughing.

"Care to share?" she asked, feeling suddenly awkward and hating it.

"It's our little secret," Claire said.

Tucker got to his feet. "You take care, now, you hear? I don't want to tire you, so I'll be going. But I'll be back."

"I'll count on that," Claire responded. "And thanks again for the flowers."

Tucker smiled, then drawled, "Anytime, ma'am."

Kelly followed him out the door, closed it, then leaned against it. For what seemed the longest time, they simply looked at each other.

"I've missed you, you know."

Kelly swallowed. "And I've missed you, only I wish you'd told me."

He frowned. "Told you what?"

"That you've been married and have a child."

Kelly knew she'd struck a raw nerve. He flinched; then his entire body went rigid. But she'd had to say it. The bombshell her father had dropped had gnawed at her until she could no longer stand it.

Tucker drew a sharp breath, then slowly let it out, but he didn't take his eyes off her. "You never asked."

"I shouldn't have had to."

"Look, now's not the place to go into all that. But just so you and your *father* will have the facts right— yeah, I was married, but the kid wasn't mine. She was part of the package when we married. And did I care about her? You're damn right I did. Only when my wife walked, she took Nancy with her, which was the way it should've been." He paused. "Will that do for now?"

Thinking about how much she would have liked to kiss him, Kelly nodded.

"I want to see you," he said urgently, as if he had read her thoughts. "Tonight."

She flicked her tongue across her bottom lip.

He groaned. "Don't."

"Don't what?"

"Don't tease me like that," he said in a low, gruff voice. "Unless you're willing to pay the price."

"And just what might that be?" *Her* voice was barely audible.

He leaned over and gave her his typical kiss—long, hot and wet. While she fought for breath, he whispered against her lips, "You on top, instead of me. *That's* the price."

Chapter Nine

Cocky devil! That description fit Tucker better than anything else she could conjure up in her mind, at least on this hot morning, two days after his brash statement.

You on top, instead of me! Imagine! No man had ever come close to speaking to her like that. But then, Tucker wasn't just any man. Nevertheless, those words had rendered her nearly senseless as the blood thundered through her veins. Before she could find her voice, he'd sauntered off, swaggering as if he truly owned the world.

Damn him! She should have nailed him on the spot for that brashness. How, though? By denying that she wouldn't let him make love to her, or that she didn't want him to? Kelly made an unladylike sound. She knew better than that, and so did he.

Fate had saved her from making any decision, however. Later in the day her grandmother had had an allergic reaction to one of her medications. That setback had kept Kelly at Claire's side that evening and the two following it. She'd spoken to Tucker only by phone, which had unnerved her.

Had she fallen in love? Or had she merely fallen in lust? Was that why anything she did had to be re-done, especially her work?

Now that Claire was much better, she was to meet Tucker at the club. So, would tonight be the night?

Would she know what his lips felt like on her body? Would she ... ?

"Stop it!" Kelly snapped aloud, hoping the sound of her voice would squelch the fantasies dancing in her head like sugarplums.

Tomorrow evening she was to begin teaching line dances at the club. Tucker had advertised in the paper, and the response had been tremendous. He'd thanked her over and over for that idea.

But she didn't want his gratitude, she wanted *him*. He drew her like a magnet, and touching and kissing were no longer enough. Once they made love, what then? Would he open up, lower that shield that he'd erected between them? So far, he hadn't exposed the real Tucker Garrett.

She suspected, however, that underneath that tough facade was a vulnerable man who longed to be loved. She wished he would confide in her, especially about his failed marriage.

Was it their differing backgrounds that created the wedge? She'd had the best money could buy, while he'd had no money at all. She knew he was uncomfortable with that and looked on her career as play rather than work. Yet she had seen admiration in his eyes when he watched her sketch.

Kelly sighed and tried to refocus her mind on those very sketches, but all she could think of was Tucker. She was unhappy when she wasn't with him and confused when she was. Maybe that crazy feeling *was* love, after all.

She shook her head vehemently, as if she could shake thoughts of him from her mind. Maybe manual labor was the key to driving away her discontent, she thought, brightening. In the storeroom were several boxes of "pretties" that needed to be unpacked, checked-in, then placed on the shelves.

But first things first—her cards. The storeroom would have to wait. She had purposely left the house early so she could check on Claire and still get to the shop long before opening time. But she had already wasted thirty minutes of that time. Clamping her jaw, Kelly grabbed her ink pen and put the finishing touches on three sketches before she added the watercolor wash. The drawings were of a saddle, a bucking mechanical bull and several couples performing a line dance. She considered them to be her best work yet and couldn't wait to send them to Visions.

Once she was satisfied with her work, she cleaned her brush, then made her way to the storeroom, where she attacked the unopened boxes with a vengeance.

By the end of the day, Kelly's body was as tired as her mind. Not only had she taken care of the freight, but she'd had a lot of customers, as well. It was a good tiredness, though, nothing that a hot bath and seeing Tucker wouldn't cure.

She smiled as she opened the cash register, looking forward to counting the money from the day's sales. She had the checks in hand when the phone rang.

"Exclusively Kelly's."

"How are you, baby?"

"Oh, hi, Dad."

"Well, that's lukewarm at best."

"Sorry, I guess I'm just tired," she said, feeling guilty because she would much rather have heard Tucker's sexy drawl.

"So quit."

"Don't start on that again. Besides, I love being tired, especially when I have something to show for it."

"Well, I didn't call to argue."

"If it's about Grandmom, she's recuperating right on schedule, or so the doctor said."

"I know. I just spoke to both of them." Simon paused. "I need a favor from you."

Why wasn't she surprised? He couldn't just call to say hello and that he loved her. "What is it?"

"Before I actually get to that, you should know that I'm looking into buying another chain of stores." When Kelly didn't respond, he went on. "What I need is for you to come home for a week and plan the party I want to give, then play hostess for it."

"Dad, you know I can't do that."

"And why not?"

"You know why!" Kelly lashed back. "I have a business to run, not to mention Grandmom."

"Your grandmother is well taken care of, so that's no excuse. And that shop—hell, just put a sign on the door and close the damn thing for a week."

"What if I told you to close your stores and help me out?"

Simon made an ugly sound. "Don't be ridiculous."

"I mean it, Dad."

"Then you're just being your usual stubborn self."

"I came by that honestly."

Simon sighed, then said in a hostile tone, "I take it, then, that the answer's no."

"That's right. Whether or not you take my work seriously is your problem, but I'm dead serious about it. Even as we speak, I'm waiting to hear from the Visions Card Company. They're very interested in my work.''

"It's that cowboy, isn't it?"

Kelly prayed for patience. "That 'cowboy,' as you call him, has nothing to do with my decision. Obviously you didn't hear a word I just said."

"I heard you, all right, but I still think you're making excuses. And when it comes to that cowboy, you'd best listen to me. You're from two different worlds and a collision is inevitable. You mark my words."

Refusing to trade any more barbs, Kelly said with as much politeness as she could muster, "Thanks for calling, Daddy. Good luck with the party."

Long after the dial tone buzzed in her ear, Kelly continued to hold the phone, her stomach churning, feeling as if she'd been on a roller-coaster ride.

Tucker would make her feel better, she assured herself with a smile, especially when he kissed her. Now that was a roller-coaster ride she would definitely enjoy.

Kelly had just turned the sign to Closed and was about to walk out when the phone rang again.

"Hello?" she said a trifle breathlessly, positive that this time it would be Tucker on the other end of the line.

"Ms. Warren, this is Martha Havard from Visions."

Where the hell was she?

Tucker glanced at his watch for at least the tenth time. It wasn't like Kelly to be late. At first he hadn't been concerned, thinking she might have gotten held up at the hospital. But he'd called there, and Claire had told him that she hadn't seen Kelly since early that morning. Then he'd called the house and the shop, but he'd had no luck either place.

The fact that she was over an hour late and he didn't know why made him crazy. And mad. He didn't want to care. He kept telling himself that he *didn't* care. But he knew he did, and that was the problem.

If he continued to see her, he would be in a heap of trouble. Crusty's words gonged like a warning bell inside his head. *Them kind of women is poison.* His friend was right, and she would break his heart, too, especially if her old man had any say in the matter. Why, Simon would have a stroke if he thought... Thought what? That she might marry him?

Hell, he was losing his freakin' mind! He hadn't even slept with her, and here he was thinking about marriage.

"Crusty!"

Crusty hobbled over to the bar where Tucker stood. "Yeah, boss?"

"Mind things for me, okay?"

"Sure. Is something wrong?"

"Maybe. I don't know."

"Anything else I can do?"

"Nope, but thanks anyway."

"Whatever you say, boss."

Tucker felt Crusty's eyes follow him out the door as he headed into the sweltering heat toward his truck.

The loose caftan felt good; it didn't touch her anywhere. And it was cool. Today the mercury had hit the hundred mark, and even though dusk had fallen, the heat index hadn't. Thank goodness for air-conditioning, Kelly thought as the East Texas heat and humidity made for a combustible combination.

It wasn't the weather, however, that had drained her. She leaned against the cushion on the chaise longue in the living room, and when she did, tears trickled down her face. Pulling a tissue from her pocket, she pressed it against both eyes.

Visions had turned down her sketches. She still couldn't believe it, despite the crushing weight on her heart. She'd been ecstatic when Martha Havard had identified herself, only to sink into a pit of despair moments later.

"The powers that be were split," Martha had said. "And because your sketches were slightly offbeat, the tiebreaker went against you." She had paused, then continued. "I hope you won't let this discourage you. There are other companies who will be interested in your work. I'm only sorry it wasn't us."

Kelly had managed to thank her and hang up before the tears came.

Now, as she got up and walked outside, she drew a deep breath and prayed for a numbness that wouldn't come. She felt like a failure, wallowing in her own self-pity.

Kelly didn't know what alerted her that she was no longer alone. Maybe intuition, or maybe she heard something. She twisted her head and watched as Tucker climbed the steps onto the deck.

"Why the hell didn't you show up at the club or answer the damn phone?" he demanded without preamble.

"I—"

His quick approach cut off her words. "What's wrong?"

Kelly caught her lower lip between her teeth and bit down on it.

Kelly swallowed the lump in her throat. "Visions... turned me down."

"The card company?"

She nodded.

"The hell with them. They're not the only game in town, are they?"

"No, but—"

"Forget the buts." He took her arm and pulled her to him. "Come on, let's go inside and get you some wine and me a beer. That'll make us both feel better." Once they reached the kitchen, he paused, leaned over and kissed her on the tip of the nose. "Besides, you know I can't stand to see you cry."

The concern in his voice and eyes proved Kelly's undoing. She crumpled inside like a discarded rag doll, which was exactly what she'd been wanting to do since the call. Tears blinded her, and she began to shake all over.

Tucker placed his hands on her shoulders. "Kelly, please... don't."

She lifted her face, and in that precise moment her heart almost leapt out of her chest. Concern shone in his eyes, but so did something else, that same something she'd seen when he'd whispered those naughty words.

"What can I do to make you feel better?" he asked in a guttural whisper.

"You—" Again she stopped, unable to go on.

"Tell me what you want." His knuckles moved down the sides of her neck before stopping at the V in her caftan.

"You can . . . can hold me." Kelly's voice was shaking, too, but she couldn't help it. Emotions she'd never experienced were charging through her. She wanted to run, yet she knew it would take an earthquake to move her.

Tucker's features tightened. "I can't just hold you. I want more. But then, you know that."

Kelly couldn't say anything as anticipation and fear waged war inside her. She could only look at him with her heart in her eyes.

"Oh, Kelly, Kelly," he groaned, and fastened his lips on hers. As always, his kiss robbed her of both her breath and her sanity.

Helplessly, she clung to him in wild abandonment while he slipped a hand between them and eased her zipper down just enough to release her creamy, burgeoning breasts. He pulled back and drew in his breath, but that hesitation was only minuscule. Dipping his head, he circled a nipple with his lips.

"Oh, Tucker," she whimpered, striving to maintain her balance.

He seemed to sense her loss of equilibrium. Using his free hand, he reached around, cupped the cheeks of her buttocks, then braced her between his legs.

When Kelly felt him, hard and pressing against the confines of his jeans, her breathless excitement turned into an aching need.

"See what you do to me? See how much I want you?"

If he expected an answer, Kelly couldn't give him one. She was powerless to speak as his mouth continued its assault on each nipple in turn, now moist, rigid and throbbing.

"I want you, too," she finally managed in a broken whisper.

With their lips locked, they fumbled with their clothing, desperate to feel skin against skin.

Later, Kelly realized that the thought of making love in the middle of the kitchen floor had never crossed her mind. But when Tucker slid his tongue along her body, then knelt on one knee, she had no choice except to give in to the weakness in her legs and sink down with him.

His tongue pressed into her navel, even as he eased her onto her back. But it was when he transferred that hot tongue to the curls at the apex of her thighs that she both squirmed and moaned his name.

"Tucker, Tucker, Tucker."

"Let it go, baby. Enjoy it," he whispered, sounding almost frantic himself.

She dug her fingers into his hair and rode the waves of pleasure before finding the strength to touch him.

"Oh, Kelly!"

His deep-throated groan caressed her ears as he moved on top of her, parted her legs, then entered her with swift, torrid assurance.

Her eyes widened as he filled her completely.

He paused, his own eyes glazed with passion. "Am I hurting you?"

"Yes . . . no."

"You want me to stop?"

"No," she gasped, sinking her fingers into his buttocks, urging him higher inside her.

Moments later they both cried out, their hearts and bodies peaking in unison.

Long after their release, they remained joined as one.

Chapter Ten

Kelly opened her eyes and realized that she was in her bed, only she didn't remember when she got there. She remembered *how,* though. She smiled a contented smile as she shifted her gaze to the pillow beside her. Tucker's deep brown eyes were fastened on hers.

"Hi," she whispered.

"My, but you're lazy," he whispered back.

"What time is it?"

He looked beyond her shoulder. "Your clock says midnight."

"No wonder I'm lazy." She scooted closer to his warm body and gave another contented sigh.

"Are you all right? I mean...I didn't hurt you...." His voice seemed to fade before it strengthened again. "You're so tight, I was afraid..."

She placed a finger across his lips. "I'm fine, believe me, despite the floor."

He chuckled. "You noticed you didn't get the top, after all."

"Thanks." Kelly's face reddened, despite the intimacies they had shared.

Tucker's chuckle deepened. "You bet. Hell, even *my* tough knees will never be the same."

She laughed, until she felt his fingers trail up and down her back. Then she shivered, wanting him all over again, which brought a flush to her face. After the episode on the floor and the several other encounters that had followed, how could she possibly want more?

"You haven't been with a lot of men, have you?"

"How did you know?"

"For one thing, your tightness. For another..." Tucker paused with a frown. "I guess my gut instinct just kicked in and told me so."

"You're right on both counts," she responded softly.

"Have you ever been in love?"

"I thought I was once."

"Charles?"

"Horrors, no! He was before Charles, and though the chemistry was there, we couldn't get along. We argued all the time about everything. We were both too immature, especially me. So I broke it off."

"I see."

"Turnabout's fair play you know," she said, circling his navel with a long fingernail.

He groaned. "If you don't stop that, I won't be able to answer your questions."

Her hand stilled, and she grinned. "Right now your answers are more important."

"Aw shucks," he drawled.

"What about *your* marriage? I have to say, I was shocked you'd ever walked down the aisle."

"I didn't. We got married by a justice of the peace."

"Funny."

He grinned, then sobered. "From the get-go, it was a match made in hell. We also argued—about money and about my work. She hated me being gone all the time."

"What ended it?"

"I got home early one Friday, and guess what?"

"She was with someone else?"

"You got it."

"I'm . . . sorry," Kelly said, hearing the pain and bitterness in his voice.

"Don't be. The guy she was getting it on with was much more her type than me. In the end, I was more relieved than anything. Except for Nancy, that is. She and I had a special relationship. But you get over it and move on. *Life* goes on. And I have to say that all was not lost. It taught me a lesson I'll never forget."

"And what is that?" Kelly asked with a sinking feeling in the pit of her stomach.

"That hearth and home ain't all they're cracked up to be."

Kelly didn't respond, fighting not to take his comment personally or let it upset her.

"I'm sorry about your sketches getting turned down," he said, changing the subject.

"Yeah, me, too."

"Well, it's their loss. Someone else will take your work, you'll see."

"I know they will, because I'm not giving up."

He kissed her on top of her head. "So, in other words—'Visions eat my dust,' right?"

She smiled. "I couldn't have said it better."

"I know how you feel."

Kelly raised herself enough that she could look into his eyes. "What do you mean?"

"I just learned that a new club's opening on the other side of town."

"So?"

"I'll lose a bunch of customers."

"I don't see why."

"Well, I have to admit that your lessons will help to hold 'em captive and, hopefully, so will the bull that's about to be installed."

"All right!" Kelly exclaimed, then kissed him. "You won't be sorry about the bull. That other club will eat *your* dust."

"I wish. But unfortunately you don't know how small towns work."

"Just wait and see if I'm not right."

He ruffled her hair. "Okay, you're on, only this is one bet I hope to hell I lose."

Kelly snuggled closer. For another long moment they were quiet, trying to sort out their thoughts and make sense of what had happened, what *was* happening, between them.

"You're not sorry, are you?"

Kelly didn't pretend to misunderstand. "No, are you?"

He sighed. "Yes and no."

"I'm not sure I like that answer."

"Even if it's the truth? Our being together has its share of built-in complications, you know."

Kelly waited for him to elaborate on those complications, but he didn't. Of course, he didn't have to, not really. It didn't take a rocket scientist to figure them out.

As Simon had said, they were from two different worlds, with nothing in common but their love of dancing and their craving for each other's body, neither of which made for a lasting relationship.

Too, there was Simon's pompous displeasure hanging between them. And she couldn't forget Tucker's caustic statement that hearth and home weren't all they were cracked up to be.

"While I agree there are problems, I don't want to stop seeing you."

"Me neither."

"So what's the game plan?" Kelly asked in a small voice, somewhat fearful of the answer.

"No game plan. For the moment, let's just enjoy the ride and not worry about the final destination."

She grinned coyly. "Do you mean that literally, by any chance?"

His eyes glittered with sudden passion before he leaned over and tongued a breast. "What do you think?"

Kelly answered with a moan as his hand slipped between her legs, testing the warmth there, as if to make sure she was wet and ready.

Then, with a groan, he lifted her, never taking his eyes off her. She gasped as he eased her down onto him.

"Oh, Tucker," she cried, beginning to move.

"Yes, oh, yes . . . don't stop. . . ."

She didn't.

That night set the precedent for the following weeks. They simply couldn't get enough of each other. Kelly was happier than she'd ever been in her life, even when she was pelted with unexpected trouble.

Because now she had Tucker for strength and support. He was beside her when her grandmother suffered a setback and had to be placed in a facility that provided around-the-clock care. He was there when the roof on her shop leaked and she lost a large portion of her inventory. And he held her when another major card company turned her down.

Still, he had never told her that he loved her or even hinted at a future. While their lovemaking was wild and passionate and all-consuming, Kelly continued to sense his aloofness, which both angered and hurt her.

Deep down she feared it stemmed from their backgrounds, or perhaps the fact that he'd been burned when it came to marriage. Still, she wanted to literally chisel away at that barrier. She wanted *all* of him.

The phone jangled beside the bed. Thinking it was probably Tucker, she picked it up on the second ring.

"Good morning."

"Ah, your phone demeanor's improving, my dear."

"Hi, Daddy."

"Somehow I sense you're disappointed again."

"That's not true," she said, though a bit too quickly to be believable.

"Well, no matter. How 'bout us getting together today? It's Sunday, so you have no excuse."

"Oh, Daddy, I'd love to, but I have work. Besides, you should spend it with Grandmom. She misses you."

Simon sighed. "You're right. Maybe I'll take her for a drive."

"She'd like that."

He didn't say anything for a moment.

"Daddy?"

"I'm still here. Look, you aren't still seeing that cowboy, are you?"

She sucked in her breath, then let it out. "Yes."

"Damn it, Kelly, you know—"

"I'll talk to you later, Daddy," she said in a firm voice, then hung up.

She had barely placed the receiver back on the hook when the doorbell chimed. "Good grief," she mumbled, tossing back the covers and grabbing her robe.

"Who is it?" she asked from the hallway.

"Guess."

She unlatched the door and jerked it open.

"Hi," Tucker said, looking her up and down.

"Do you like what you see?" she asked huskily.

"You know I do. Only I want you to put some clothes on."

Her eyes widened. "You do?"

"Yep. I wanna show you something."

"What?"

"It's a secret."

Chapter Eleven

"Cat got your tongue?"

"I guess it has. It's just too beautiful for words."

Tucker shoved his Stetson back and gave her an incredulous look. "You're serious, aren't you?"

"Not only is it beautiful, it's peaceful, as well."

When they'd left the house, Kelly had had no idea where Tucker was taking her, what his secret was, but she hadn't cared. As long as she was with him, nothing mattered.

She had to admit, though, that after thirty minutes of traveling, her curiosity had been piqued, especially after he turned onto a country road, then onto a tract of land filled with huge oak and pine trees. He hadn't stopped the pickup or said anything until he'd parked under one of the big oaks at the foot of a hill.

"I have to tell you, I'm shocked," he was saying. "Most women from the city don't like the country."

Kelly slapped him playfully on the arm. "Well, for starters, I'm not most women."

Tucker collared her around the neck and gave her a warm kiss. "You're right. You definitely march to a different drummer."

"Are you complaining?" she asked above the rapid beat of her heart.

"Hell, no. I like my women bitchy."

She elbowed him in the side this time. "Watch your dirty mouth."

He kissed her again, grabbed her hand and started up the hill. When they reached the top, he pulled up short, then smiled down at her. "The view's something, isn't it?"

"Mind-boggling." Kelly's voice was filled with awe.

And it was. Beyond the hill, which was covered with tall, magnificent trees, was a pasture littered with a colorful array of wildflowers that she itched to paint, only she knew she couldn't do them justice. In the middle of that beauty was a pond. Kelly looked on as the clear water sparkled like diamonds in the sunlight.

"Mind-boggling. That's a good word for it," Tucker said at last, awe in his voice, as well.

And something else, something Kelly couldn't identify. "So, whose place is this?"

"Mine."

Her eyes widened. "Yours?"

"Yep. My uncle left it to me."

"That's great."

"I thought so, too, since it's the only thing he ever gave me that's worth a damn."

Kelly heard that same bitterness in his tone and realized again how very differently they had grown up—she with all of life's amenities, he with none.

"And you love it here, don't you?"

"Does it show that much?"

"Yes," she said softly, her gaze lingering on him. "There's something in your voice, something I don't hear except when...when—" She broke off, embarrassed by the train her thoughts had taken. Her face turned fiery red.

Tucker's eyes twinkled. "Except when what? When I make love to you?"

"Yes," she said in a strangled tone.

"You're right. When I'm here, I get the same high as when I'm buried deep inside you."

Kelly felt the fire in her face travel down her body and settle between her legs. "You certainly know how to push my button," she whispered.

They stared at each other, their emotions out in the open. Tucker was the first to turn away. "I have plans for this exact spot, a big house, but only if—" He stopped and looked at her again, a bleak expression on his face.

"Only if what?" she pressed, sensing that something was hanging in the balance, something so fragile that if it weren't handled with care, it would shatter into a million pieces.

"Only if you'll share it with me."

She didn't move. She almost didn't breathe. "Is that your way of saying you love me?"

He winced openly, then said gruffly, "Yes, I guess it is."

"And I love you."

"You do?"

She laughed and launched herself into his arms. "Of course I do, you big idiot."

He pushed her back slightly. "When did you know?"

"For a while now."

He threw back his head and laughed out loud, then lifted her off her feet and swung her around and around. Finally they landed on the ground, still laughing, with Kelly splayed on top.

Pushing herself up enough so that she could see into his eyes, she whispered, "I do love you."

He pulled her face down to his. "And I love you."

Tucker frowned. He'd been doing book work all morning, and with each minute that passed, his mood darkened. Boot Scootin' was floundering. He couldn't gloss over that fact; the unvarnished truth was before his eyes.

No matter how much he juggled the figures, they remained the same. Oh, the club wasn't about to go under, but he didn't even want it to hiccup. The mechanical bull had been installed and had been a hit, as were the dance lessons.

But his competitor, who was now open, also had gimmicks: a restaurant, which offered barbecue, and the financial means by which to draw big-name country bands.

Tucker had a couple of ideas brewing that just might hold all his patrons, or at least most of them. One was a tight-jeans contest. Another was a dance contest. But before he made firm plans, especially concerning the latter, he wanted to bounce them off Kelly.

Ahh, Kelly. The best thing that had ever happened to him, he told himself, smiling. Even now, two weeks after the fact, he still couldn't believe that she loved him.

And though he was secure in that love, he often wondered if he could hold her. He would have liked to think he'd come a long way since his first marriage, that he'd dropped the excess baggage he'd held on to for so long.

Still, he had doubts. Kelly had always had the best of everything. He couldn't provide for her on that level, though he hoped one day he could. But until then, would she be content to live within his means?

He suddenly felt confident that she could. That was why he was going to ask her to marry him. With her at his side, nothing was impossible.

A knock on the door suddenly interrupted Tucker's thoughts. He peered at his watch and hoped it was Kelly stopping by with lunch, as she often did, having begun closing the shop for an hour at noon.

Tucker plopped down his pencil and eased back in his chair. "It's open," he said in a soft, lazy tone.

The knob turned, and Simon Warren crossed the threshold.

Tucker shot straight up in the chair and narrowed his eyes on the man he considered to be his archenemy.

"I hope you don't mind the intrusion," Simon said, not bothering to extend his hand.

"I don't reckon it'd make any difference," Tucker drawled. "Seeing that you're already here."

Simon stepped closer to the desk, his mouth drawn in a hard line. "You can stuff that good-old-boy garbage, Garrett, because it's wasted on me."

Tucker stood, towering over the man. "Mmm, sorry to hear that."

"Look, I didn't come here to dance around the mulberry bush."

"Now that's a fitting phrase," Tucker said, drawling again, determined that this son of a bitch wasn't going to see just how much he wanted to lean across the desk and put a permanent dent in his smug face.

"You think you're smart, don't you?"

Tucker didn't bother to respond. Instead he was thinking that he would have Crusty's backside for letting this man inside the club. But he knew he wasn't being fair; hell, Crusty wasn't his keeper.

"Well, let me assure you that you're not," Simon hammered on. "Not if you think I'm going to stand by and let you marry my daughter."

Tucker lifted his eyebrows. "I don't think you have anything to say about that."

"That's where you're wrong." Simon's tone was nasty. "I love my daughter and want what's best for her."

"That goes for both of us."

"If that's the case, then stay away from her."

"'Fraid I can't do that. You see, we love each other. And if she'll have me, I plan to marry her."

Simon's face turned red, then gray, then white. "I'll see you in hell first. No way is my daughter going to marry a two-bit, penniless—"

"Whoa, now, I wouldn't go stepping too deep in that pile of manure, if I were you."

Tucker never raised his voice, but the dangerous coldness in it seemed to have the desired effect. Simon clamped his mouth shut without finishing his sentence.

"I think you'd better leave before we both say and *do* things we'll be sorry for."

Simon reached inside his suit pocket and pulled out a checkbook. Leaning over, he placed it on Tucker's desk. "All right, I get the picture. So, how much will it take for you to disappear from Kelly's life? A hundred grand? No. How about I make that two—"

Tucker reached across the desk, latched onto Simon's tie and jerked him upright. Simon's eyes bulged, and he cried out, but Tucker wasn't listening.

"Keep your stinking money! I don't want it. And it's only because of Kelly that I'm going to let you leave with your teeth intact." He let go of Simon, then, after straightening his tie and patting him on the shoulders, added, "Now you've had your say, like a dutiful daddy, so I suggest you get the hell out of my place and don't come back."

The sunlight streamed through the window and created shadows on their naked bodies.

Two weeks had passed since they had confessed their love, and Kelly felt certain that her feet hadn't touched the ground yet. In fact, she'd talked about Tucker so much that her grandmother had lovingly threatened to stuff a rag in her mouth.

But Kelly's desire to wallow in her happiness burgeoned, especially now, after they'd just finished making love during her lunch break at her grandmother's house. Still wrapped in each other's arms, they lay naked and exhausted.

Earlier, their lovemaking had bordered on the sweetly savage. Kelly couldn't seem to get enough of him. Every time Tucker touched her, her insides turned to putty, and she was so malleable he could do anything he wanted with her.

While that excited her, it also concerned her. She feared she loved him too much and that something would happen to part them before he asked her to marry him.

"God, I don't ever want to lose you," he whispered, as if he had read her thoughts.

She heard the desperate note in his voice and gazed at him through puzzled eyes. "Why on earth would you even think something like that?"

He didn't respond for the longest time; then he said, "Your father came to see me."

Kelly bolted upright, then peered back down at him. "Why?"

"Guess."

"But . . . but . . ."

"Stop stuttering. I knew where he was coming from. He wants what's best for you, only I'm afraid I didn't handle him with the the respect he demanded."

Kelly smiled. "What did you do, belt him one?"

"Almost," Tucker admitted sheepishly.

"I wish I could've been a fly on the wall."

Tucker's face was sober. "He only wants what's best for you," he repeated.

"Like hell he does! He wants what's best for him, and that's to control my life—just like he's always done."

"Simmer down. Maybe he has a point when it comes to me."

"What's that supposed to mean?"

Tucker shrugged. "I'll never be able to give you what you've been accustomed to."

"But I don't care about *things!*" Kelly shouted. "I only care about *you.*

"Hear me out, okay?"

She glared at him but kept silent.

"The new club has complicated things. It's going to take longer than I thought to pay off the bank note on Boot Scootin' and build the house. So—"

Kelly scrambled off the bed, cutting him off in midsentence.

"Where are you going?"

"It's a secret," she flung over her shoulder.

He snorted. "Not for long, I'll bet."

She faced him and placed her hands on either side of her waist. "Okay, smarty, what does that remark mean?"

He grinned.

Her heart turned over simply because he was once again his old self. Damn Simon! How dare he connive behind her back to separate her and Tucker?

"I've never known a woman yet who could keep a secret."

She made another face.

He laughed. "Gotcha. Right?"

"The last laugh'll be on you. Just wait and see."

Kelly felt his eyes on her as she reached for her purse.

"Mmm, did I ever tell you that you have the sweetest butt I've ever seen?"

She swung around and laughed. "You're perverted."

"I know."

Kelly laughed again, reached in her bag, pulled out an envelope and strutted back to the bed.

He looked at her, a puzzled expression on his face.

"Go on," she urged, her heart in her eyes. "Take it. It's yours."

"What? I mean—"

"Shh. Just open it and all your questions will be answered."

Lowering his head, Tucker ripped open the envelope and began to read.

Kelly felt her excitement mount; in fact, she was downright giddy.

When she didn't think she could stand the suspense a second longer, he raised his head. She caught her breath.

A dark scowl had twisted his features into a menacing mask. "What the hell is this?"

Chapter Twelve

Kelly's stomach lurched. Still, after taking a steadying breath, she managed to say, "It's…it's your bank note. It's been paid off. You know that."

"You're damn right I do!"

Kelly flinched visibly, both stunned and crushed by his attitude. She opened her mouth to defend herself, but she couldn't say anything.

Tucker had no such problem. "Just who the hell do you think you are? My savior?"

Hot fury charged through Kelly. "What if I am? Would that be such a crime?"

"You're damn right it would be!" He reached for his jeans and stepped into them.

"But why? I don't understand why you're so upset." Kelly stood helplessly and watched as he zipped his jeans. Then, suddenly feeling self-conscious at her own nudity, she reached for her T-shirt and slipped it over her head.

"The club is *my* problem, that's why."

He was staring at her once again, his features so hard and cold that he appeared a completely different person. Kelly backed up, shivering inwardly. Yet she felt compelled to try to diffuse his temper so that she could reason with him.

"I understand that, but—"

His bitter laugh cut her off. "Oh, I don't think you do. Otherwise you wouldn't have interfered in my business."

Kelly's face lost its remaining color, but she jutted her chin. "I don't see it as interference. I see it as a gesture of love."

For a moment he seemed taken aback by her words, but then he said, "Let me put it this way. I don't want your father's money—now or anytime."

"Simon had nothing to do with this. The money I used to pay off the club was mine from a trust fund that Grandmom started when I was born."

"I don't want *your* money, either. Can't you see that? Sooner or later I would've paid the note off myself. Granted, the club's in a bit of a slump right now, but it's a hell of a long way from going under."

Kelly extended her hands. "I realize that. But like I said, what I did was a gesture of love, nothing more, nothing less."

"I don't see it that way. Like I said, I don't want your money. Not now, not ever."

"Because I love you, what's mine is yours," Kelly said in a soft, pleading voice, feeling as if she were in a fight for her life.

Tucker simply looked at her with contempt. "You can't buy me, Kelly. I'm not for sale."

"Why...why, you...you pigheaded, ungrateful—" Tears clogged her throat, and she couldn't go on.

"I'll accept that," he said in an unemotional tone.

She looked him up and down, her contempt matching his. "Well, isn't that big of you!"

"Go get your money back. Tomorrow."

She laughed without mirth. "You really are a piece of work. It's your pride, isn't it? You think more of that than you do of me."

"Pride has nothing to do with it," he shot back.

"Oh, yes, it does. It has everything to do with it. What you are, Tucker Garrett, is a bitter bastard who can't see any farther than his nose."

"What I think you're saying is that we're through. Right?"

"That's right!" Kelly stormed.

"Fine, then I guess I'd best get the hell out of here."

With that he crossed to the door and jerked it open. The slam, when it came, jarred the house.

Kelly stood unmoving. Then, with a cry of despair, she sank into the nearest chair and buried her head in her hands.

"Ms. Warren?"

"Yes," Kelly said hesitantly, not recognizing the voice on the line.

"This is Velma Pritchard from Simply Cards. I'm calling about the sketches you sent us."

"Yes."

"We'd like to buy them and any more you have to offer."

Kelly's jaw dropped. "You would?"

Ms. Pritchard laughed softly. "Yes, indeed. At your convenience, I want to set up a meeting to work out a contractual agreement."

"That's great. Any time's fine with me."

That conversation had taken place a week ago, and Kelly should have been on top of the world. After all, she had reached her goal. She had sold her designs to a top-notch company that treated her like a queen.

Instead she'd never been more miserable. She missed Tucker, missed him so much that at times she felt she couldn't stand the pressure on her heart. And it wasn't just the hot sex she missed, though that was certainly a factor. She missed Tucker himself—his lazy drawl, his cockiness, his agility on the dance floor. God, she missed everything about him.

In the wake of his loss she moped. She binged on work. She binged on exercise until her muscles trembled. She binged on food until she felt as if she would explode. Most of all, she cried.

Nothing, however, relieved the pressure inside her. If only she could understand Tucker's reasoning, maybe she could make sense of it all.

That thought was very much on her mind when she walked into her grandmother's room.

"Are you sick, sweetheart?" Claire asked, her keen eyes sweeping over Kelly.

Kelly leaned over and kissed her grandmother on the cheek, then settled into the chair opposite her. For a moment neither spoke as they looked out the big window and watched a squirrel nibble on a hickory nut.

"It's lovely here," Claire said at last.

"I'm glad you like it."

"The house is yours to do with as you see fit."

Kelly was taken aback. "You mean, you want to live here permanently?"

Claire smiled. "As a matter of fact, I do. I have all the comforts of home, plus someone to see after my every need."

"Not to mention that some of your oldest and dearest friends are here, as well."

"That's right. So, you see, I'm content and happy." Claire paused. "Or at least I would be if I weren't so concerned about you. And your father."

Kelly reached over and squeezed Claire's hand, then shifted her gaze. "Don't worry about me. I'll be fine."

"You're a terrible liar, Kelly Warren. Always have been and always will be."

Kelly swung back around, her face flushed. "I can't put anything past you, can I, Grandmom?"

"No, my dear, you can't. But then, anyone with half a brain could see that something's terribly wrong. I suspect it has to do with Tucker. Am I correct?"

Kelly nodded, shifting her gaze.

"I thought so. Simon said you weren't seeing him anymore."

"He's right," Kelly said flatly.

"Is your father to blame for the breakup?"

"No. Although he did go behind my back and tell Tucker to leave me alone, which was stupid. But Tucker handled Daddy just fine."

"So then it was something else." Claire reached for Kelly's hand and held it.

"Oh, Grandmom," Kelly cried, misery welling up inside her. "I shouldn't be burdening you with my problems, not in your condition."

"That's utter nonsense. Right now my heart's in good shape. Better than yours, I'll wager. But it wouldn't matter if it wasn't. I'm here for you—always. So tell me what's going on."

As if a dam broke inside Kelly, the words tumbled from her lips. When she finished, her grandmother didn't say anything. She just handed Kelly a tissue instead.

Only after Kelly had mopped the tears from her face did Claire speak. "You should remember, dearest, that it's not the destination that's the important thing, but rather the ride, which is to say, the satisfaction of getting there."

Kelly blinked. "Excuse me?"

"You heard me. Just think about what I said, then apply it to Tucker."

It only took a moment of quiet thought for the light to dawn. Suddenly Kelly sat up in her chair and scooted to the edge. "What you're saying is that I did to Tucker what I would have killed Daddy for doing to me."

"Exactly."

"If Daddy had gone, say, to Visions behind my back and bribed them to take my designs, which he could very well have done, I would have felt cheated, because he would have robbed me of achieving success on my own." Kelly paused while her eyes filled with tears again. "Which is what I did to Tucker. I robbed him of his opportunity to reach his goal."

"I couldn't have put it better myself."

"Oh, Grandmom, I feel so stupid, so ashamed for being so blind."

"Don't. What you did came straight from the heart. It was a mistake, but one made out of love."

"Do you think he'll forgive me?"

Claire smiled. "Well, you won't know till you ask, that's for sure."

Kelly stood and again kissed Claire on the cheek. "I guess I'd best go find out."

Claire's eyes sparkled. "I guess so."

Kelly dashed to the door where she turned and cried, "I love you! And thanks."

Tucker's belly was level with a snake's. He'd tried to rebound, but he couldn't. Even now, as he walked through the club on his day off, nothing about him seemed to function. He paused and leaned against the bar.

Sunlight streamed through an open blind and rippled across the tables. After a moment his gaze wandered onto the mechanical bull, then back to the dance floor where he and Kelly...

"Don't!" he muttered harshly. She was the last person he wanted to think about. Unfortunately, she was all he *did* think about.

He ached for her, not only in his groin, but everywhere else, as well. He wasn't worth a damn to himself or anyone else, as Crusty had so aptly phrased it this morning.

"Whatever's gnawing at your gut, son, I wish to hell you'd take care of it."

"I don't need your smart mouth," Tucker had countered.

"No, but you damn sure need my advice."

"Oh, really?"

"Yeah, really. The club's bounced back, but I have to say, it's not because of anything you've done. You've been drunk the better part of the week, so how would you know?"

"I see the books," Tucker had said, gritting his jaw.

Crusty had sneered. "Why the hell don't you admit you can't live without her and go get her?"

"It's not that easy. I made an ass out of myself."

"Now why don't I find that hard to believe?"

Tucker had thrown him a go-to-hell look.

"Okay, so that was a smidgen outta line." Crusty had limped closer. "As long as you know that, why don't you fix what's broken?"

Tucker had frowned. "I don't know if that's possible. Like I told you, I screwed up pretty bad."

"Well, just think about it," Crusty had said. "I'll see you tomorrow."

Once he was alone, Tucker had paced the dance floor, his bleak thoughts dogging his every step. Hell, what did it matter if he was a kept man? Wasn't that preferable to a broken heart? It wouldn't kill him, or at least, it hadn't so far. She hadn't redeemed her money, which meant the club was still his, free and clear.

No one had ever done anything for him in his life, until Kelly. And what had he done? He'd flung both her love and her generosity back in her face. And for what? His pride, as she'd said, pride that in the scheme of things didn't mean a damn.

Yeah, he was a fool, all right. Maybe, though, it wasn't too late for this fool to make amends.

Tucker strode to the back door of the club and jerked it open, only to freeze. Kelly was standing on the porch in front of him. He blinked, thinking he was hallucinating. When he realized he wasn't, he held his breath while his eyes devoured her.

"I'm so sorry—" Tucker began in a voice that sounded like a croaking frog.

"Me too," Kelly whispered, one lone tear trickling down her cheek.

Tucker opened his arms. "Come here."

With a cry, Kelly dove into them. He kissed her cheeks, her nose, her lips, her neck, while she clung to him.

"I'm sorry, so sorry," he said, his tears mingling with hers.

"Me, too. I love you too much to ever hurt you or embarrass you."

"I know," he said against her lips. "And I love you."

"So what now?"

"Will you marry me?"

"Only if you'll promise never to leave me again."

He kissed the tears off one cheek and stared deeply into her eyes. "Believe me, I'll never leave heaven a second time."

"Well, Mrs. Garrett, how do you like being married?"

"Mmm, I don't know, since I've only been that way for an hour."

Following the service and reception in the small church, with only Simon, Claire and Crusty in attendance, they had gone straight to her grandmother's house, where they planned to live until they built their dream home on Tucker's land.

During the week of the wedding, they had talked endlessly about their future, which included not only a home on top of that hill, but children, as well.

Even Simon, thanks to Claire, had faced the fact that Kelly had a mind of her own and was going to do what she thought best. But clinging to that independence didn't mean that she didn't love Simon or want him to remain a part of her life. She did.

Moments before the wedding, she'd put her arms around him and whispered, "I've never been happier, Daddy. Be happy for me, too."

Simon had merely shaken his head, smiled, then hugged her. "I know when I'm beat." Once they'd pulled apart, he'd faced Tucker and held out his hand. "I'm sorry."

"So am I." Tucker had taken his hand and smiled. "And if I don't make her happy, you'll have every right to kick my backside."

Simon's mouth had twitched. "Count on it, son."

Now, as she felt Tucker nibble on her neck, Kelly sighed contentedly. "I ought to be mad at you, you know."

"How's that?" He didn't stop his nibbling.

"Because you made me get my money back at the bank."

"Only you're not mad, at least, not anymore."

"No, you're right, I'm not. I understand. But the money's there, if you need it."

Tucker quit nibbling and looked at her. "I know," he said with a catch in his voice. "And that's one of the reasons why I adore you."

Her eyes misted, and she smiled.

"I think the others wanted us to hang around for a while." He started nibbling again.

"I know they did."

"Well, too bad. I wanted you all to myself."

She tweaked one of his button-hard nipples. "I think that was fairly obvious from what you whispered to me during the service." She pulled the other nipple and ignored his yelp. "The very idea of jockeying for position."

Tucker grinned as he covered a breast and thumbed her nipple. "You couldn't wait, either, though. Could you?" he whispered, his eyes glazed.

"No!"

"I love you."

"And I love you."

"So, what's it going to be?" he asked, his hand dipping between her legs, searching, teasing. "Top or bottom?"

"Surprise me," she whispered.

And he did.

* * * * *

A Note from Mary Lynn Baxter

Since I was a young girl, books and reading have been an important part of my life. Only after I read all the "goodies" in our public library did my mother encourage me to buy Harlequin Romances, then thirty-five cents each. (Wow!)

Those reading years became the stepping stone for my later opening and managing my own bookstore. Eventually, though, I craved a new challenge. Never in my wildest dreams did I think that challenge would be learning to write.

Now that I've become the writer I longed to be, I never stop thinking about my craft, which is what led me to write "Boot Scootin'." I love to country/western dance. Every Friday night my husband and I go to a club and "polish belt buckles." It was during one of those Friday nights that I asked myself why not write a story about the Western dance craze that's sweeping the country?

Instantly, the idea for "Boot Scootin'" was conceived.I enjoyed every day that I worked on it. I sincerely hope you, as a reader, experience that same enjoyment.

Happy boot scootin'!

FANCY'S MAN

Ann Major

This book is dedicated to the people who helped me
write it. I owe them all a big thank-you.

First and foremost: To Joe Knolle, my birthday mate. He
and I were born on the same day, the same hour in the
same town. He is a fellow sailor and a real-live dairy
farmer who spent a lovely spring afternoon showing me
and teaching me about his dairy farm. Thank you, Joe.

To Isabel Swift, Marcia Book Adirim and
Tara Gavin for their help.

Prologue

*M*ore. More. More.

Those three little words summed up the beautiful, world-famous fashion designer, Fancy Hart, better than any of the hundreds of articles that had been written about her. For no matter how many goals Fancy had achieved, no matter how many new glories she had won, none of them had ever been enough.

Until now.

Until Jacques had walked out on her a year ago, screaming that she worked too hard and was no fun. Until her talent had seemed to vanish overnight. Only then had the craving that from the cradle had compelled her to impress and dazzle the world left her.

She hadn't missed Jacques, but she, who had been driven by talent and ambition so long, felt empty and lost without them.

Life had seemed simple when she had rushed through her twelve-hour workdays, her shows and interviews and Jacques's incessant parties like a well-trained rat in her glittering maze. She had been busy, busy, busy. Too busy to think or to feel. Too busy to consider that there might be more to life than constant klieg lights, gorgeous fabric and a packed calendar. Too busy to realize that she had never loved Jacques, that he had only been part of her scene. Too busy to realize how profoundly lonely she was. Arrogantly, she had told hundreds of reporters that living well was a matter of deciding what one wanted and then working very hard to get it. Foolishly, she had believed it.

Her problem wasn't so much that she had failed.

It was that she had succeeded.

With her Titian hair and pale complexion and size four figure encased in her elegantly stylish black dresses, she caused a stir wherever she went. She was so beautiful and rich and famous, so brilliantly talented, that everybody believed she had been born that way.

Everybody believed she was happy and fulfilled. And the reason they did was because Fancy wanted them to.

Fancy had always been good at getting her own way.

Much too good.

At a mere thirty-two years of age, her designs were renowned on two continents. She was the sole owner of the Fanta-Sea Fashion Inc. Her creations were worn by chic royalty and wild movie stars as well as by staid presidents' wives. Not only did Fancy have glamorous offices in New York, but in Paris, too. She was now divorced from Jacques Decaz, one of France's richest and most dashing playboys. Her personal residences included a magnificent, twenty-room co-op overlooking Central Park, a plush apartment on the Rue du Rivoli and a Basque-style villa on the Gironde in France.

In short, like so many others before her, she had won the world and lost her soul, and, thereby, the talent that had made her stellar success possible.

But unlike so many others, she had a quirky, perverse streak that made her almost willing to give up the dazzle, if only she could reclaim her soul.

But how?
No clear path presented itself.

There was an emptiness in all her relationships and a loneliness in her frenetic activities.

She hated where she had come from—small town Texas.

She hated where she was—upscale, ruthlessly social New York and Paris and the precarious fashion world where one badly received collection could spell doom.

For the first time in her life, Fancy, who had always had all the answers, didn't have a clue. For a year she had drifted through her grandiose apartments filled with priceless antiques, feeling lost and empty. She felt worse when she lifted pencil to pad and found her mind was blank. It was as if she were trapped in an emotional vacuum. Sometimes at a party she felt like a bug in an airless bottle, cut off from her old friends by an invisible glass wall. She smiled more, gave interviews more, partied more and worked more maniacally than ever before, hoping that her passion for her life would return. She made thousands of sketches, but her designs lacked the sizzle that had made her famous.

Totally blocked, Fancy was forced to devote herself to publicity and the financial and social aspects of her business and to rely on her fashion assistants and upon her new partner, the frequently hysterical but extremely talented Claude DeMott, to create the product that had made her so famous and so rich.

Not knowing what to do, she continued to drift, trapped on that gilded stage she had chosen to make her life.

Until the shoot at her villa on the Gironde.

Until Jim's phone call.

Until that raspy, macho drawl from the past brought back forbidden memories of the tall, dark cowboy she had left behind. Until she at last sat down and sketched something that thrilled her—his face. Until she began to remember sapphire-blue fields shimmering with wild bluebonnets. Until she began to remember wide Texas skies and stars and fireflies spattering the warm summer night darkness.

Jim's whisper had shivered down her spine, and she had felt alive. Only then had Fancy remembered their terrible parting; that moment she'd taken the fatal first step upward. She had twisted off his engagement ring and tossed it at him, saying she was going to New York and not home with him to Purdee. He had thrown the ring back at her even more violently, yelling that if she walked out, she couldn't ever come back. She had gone home and sobbed till dawn, and the next morning she'd stubbornly set off for New York. She had put her talent before love. It had been that first step away from him, that seemingly tiny step that had made her die inside even as it led her ever upward to dazzling professional heights and profound emotional despair.

But not even after his call did a clear path present itself.

For Fancy had lived so boldly she had burned her bridges. She didn't believe in looking back, or going back. She was a creature of the present and the future, who believed she had to find a way to go on.

But how?

Chapter One

Flamboyant scarlet clouds streaked the horizon and the moist air smelled faintly of rain.

Beyond the dark shade of the murmuring pines and Fancy's elegant, white stucco villa with its rough wooden beams, the turquoise Gironde was dotted with tiny *optimistes* and *pinasses,* those oyster fishermen's wooden boats that Americans find so picturesque. Some distance from the narrow golden beach, a fleet of Dragons were out for a regatta.

Usually Fancy looked forward to spending June in Royan, France, before the high season with a dozen or more glamorous houseguests. But today, although she had only been there a week, she was already wishing she were back in New York.

She had grown bored with her guests and had loaned them her red Mercedes limousine and driver. She had commanded her haughty French chef, Albert, to pack them a picnic basket stuffed to the brim with several delicacies he was so famous for in Paris: *escargots de Bougogne*—snails with garlic butter—and *paupiette de saumon et langoustines au vin de Sancerre*—Salmon and crayfish rolls braised in Sancerre wine—just to mention a few, along with several bottles of her best St. Emilion. Fancy had waved goodbye as they had set off without her for the great dune at Pyla, assuring them that she simply had to stay home and work.

But then, without the distraction of her guests' superficial gaiety, Fancy felt even more bored and alienated as she chased Claude, her new partner, down the drive to the back of her villa to watch the shoot. There she stood for hours, holding a hand over her eyes and squinting into the reddening sun, studying Alain, the notorious Parisian photographer in pretentious black whom Claude had insisted they use. Sometimes Alain hung from a tree or from her balcony like a monkey to get just the right angle; sometimes he threw himself prone on the sand, shooting upward.

Alain worked desperately with his great Amazonian models and his cameras during those long hours to get the shots he wanted before his precious light faded. Alain's work was extraordinarily controversial and too erotic for some of the tamer American fashion magazines, too erotic for Fancy's taste, but Claude had been determined that this shoot be as boldly different as their clothes. Claude had sold her on Alain's *outré* vision, on his use of the blue-green end of the color spectrum instead of the more popular orange tones. Alain's assistants were shouting and dashing down the craggy limestone cliffs to the beach, adjusting a white silk scarf, changing a model's earring, retying a white balloon and arguing with Claude.

Claude, with his great tuft of dyed red hair and baggy overalls and high-tops, looked more like a mad clown than a fashion designer. He got more and more excited as the day progressed. He kept clapping enthusiastically while he ordered everybody about as he tracked up and down the beach after Alain and the models. Suddenly Claude began to shout at Alain, and

Fancy decided she'd better calm Claude before he got too demanding and Alain marched off in a huff.

Inside her villa, her telephone rang.

Fancy frowned when her secretary, Maigret, came down the stone steps in a rush, yanking the antenna out of a cordless phone. Fancy had told her to hold all calls.

"Fancy, *j'avais peur de vous déranger, mais*— I was afraid to bother you, but—"

"*Merci.*" Fancy took the phone. "*Allô?*"

"*Fancy?*" came a man's deep, huskily broken Texas drawl.

Fancy shuddered on a wave of emotion so strong she could almost reach out and touch it. Her hand went to her hot throat when *he* said it again, only softer, throatier—sexier.

Again *his* slow, melodious voice rocked through her like an electric shock. Just as years ago the feather-light touch of his calloused fingers had had the same effect. It had been a long, long time since she had felt such a visceral, sensual thrill.

"It's me—Jim." His husky tone deepened, if that were possible. There was an echo on the line, so that his voice seemed to repeat itself.

Fancy tensed as her too fertile imagination conjured memories and feelings from the past when she had been much less the sophisticate…and much more the primitive. Almost she felt the heat of his brilliant dark eyes sliding over her body. Almost she tasted his perfectly shaped, hard mouth, that mouth that had been so warm and kissable, so talented when it had skimmed across her skin exploring her intimately—everywhere.

Shivering, she struggled to sound calm. "Yes, I know," she whispered, startled when her own voice broke, betraying her. He had struck a chord. Deep within her bones, within her heart, within her highly imaginative, romantic soul. It was as if some part of herself still belonged to him. As if she were again the high school bookworm, too shy and tongue-tied to speak when he, the popular football hero, said hello to her.

"I'm afraid that I have bad—" His reluctant voice died away, then echoed and died a second time.

There was an endless silence.

Then the quiet sounds of the Gironde washed Fancy—the delicate rustling of the quivering pine needles in the breeze seemed vaguely ominous, the soft murmur of the waves caressing wet sand, dangerous.

And suddenly her heart began to throb in slow, staccato-sharp beats. She clutched the phone till her fingertips ached. "Is it . . . Mother?"

"She fell . . . off her roof. I found her a little while—"

"No!"

"There was nothing anyone could have done. Hazel died instantly—like she would have wanted to," he went on bluntly. But his deep voice was as kind and concerned as it had been that long ago day when he'd pulled Fancy from her wrecked car and saved her life and thereby caused her to fall in love with him.

Fancy, who never cried, sobbed quietly.

She remembered her mother in her kitchen making blackberry jelly, deftly filling canning jars and setting them in the window where the bottles sparkled like dark amethysts. Fancy had loved following behind her mother as Hazel walked the rows of her garden in her broad-brimmed straw hat, tenderly plucking a ripe tomato or viciously squashing a plump green caterpillar. Her mother had been so strong and vitally alive. Fancy had assumed she would live to be a very old lady. Her sudden death seemed unbearable.

A long time later he said, "I'm sorry. I wish it wasn't me telling you."

"No. I—I'm glad...*you* called and not somebody else.... Mother loved you so much. I—"

Fancy stopped short of mushily admitting that once she had loved him, too. "Thank you—Jim."

"Just let me know your flight into San Antonio, and I'll send my pilot to pick you up."

"I wouldn't dream of troubling—"

"But I insist." His voice had hardened, and she remembered how tough and implacable, how infuriatingly difficult, he could be. The simplest decision could become a contest of wills, and unlike most men, he was not intimidated by her.

"I'll have one of my assistants call you," she murmured coolly, impersonally.

"Fine." He was even cooler.

He barked out his phone number. Then he was gone.

So, he was still proud—insufferably, arrogantly proud. And he still had a temper.

But Fancy held the receiver, feeling shivery and bereft and somehow hurt by his rejection.

Her mother was dead—her difficult mother who had never understood her, but who had always been there for Fancy like an unseen anchor.

And strangely, what Fancy ached for more than anything in that moment of dark grief was Jim's tender, consoling voice again, or better than that, his arms around her, holding her close, making her feel that she didn't have to face it alone.

Which was ridiculous. He meant nothing to her now.

Still, she couldn't seem to forget his call.

Unbidden came memories of Jim's dark, chiseled face. He had been huge and broad-shouldered, and so virile and strong that his body had seemed sculpted of bronzed muscle. Whenever she had compared New York men to him, they had never been as tough or as real—inside or out—as he. They were too well educated, too refined. Their hands were too soft and their minds were so alike that all their ideas seemed to come from the same place. Fancy had thought she hated arguing with Jim, only to be surprised that she had missed the challenge.

Jim had been movie-star sexy—with his black hair waving across his dark brow. And he had known it. Still, she'd been secretly thrilled when his sultry, whiskey-colored gaze followed her instead of another girl, even though those had been the times when she'd insulted him the worst.

By the sixth grade he'd already had that entrancing aura of forbidden male power about him. By high school, every girl had wanted him. And why not? He was a man in every sense of the word.

He was every woman's secret dream.

He had been tough, but gentle, too, pushing her so hard only because she had pushed him.

For ten years Fancy had suppressed her memories of him. But the instant he had drawled her name, she had remembered everything—all the fun they had had just being together, even when she'd hated being stuck in Purdee. She remembered that day she'd waited for him in the forest wearing nothing but a thin blanket of sweet-smelling wildflowers. His golden eyes had dilated with passion when she'd winked up at him and whispered happy birthday. He had removed the flowers stem by stem with his teeth, letting his lips brush her skin, but not kissing her until every single blossom was gone. Then he had teased her until she was wild with desire. He had been wonderful to her...and she had been terrible to him.

A tear of regret beaded her lashes. She had loved him, truly loved him, but since she had grown up with him she hadn't realized how extraordinary a thing such a love was, how extraordinary *he* was. Foolishly she had believed love would be an easy thing, but it hadn't been for her. The memory of no other man had lingered through the years. He alone had been special, only she hadn't known it or wanted to admit it—*until now*.

He had loved wide open spaces; she, the excitement of the city. She had been the intellectual, the reader of fine books, the listener of fine music, the pianist, the conversationalist; he, the lover of animals and children and lazy afternoons paddling down some river or fishing or hunting. He hadn't had to talk much; he'd kept a lot of his feelings to himself.

Their conversations had been like a game of Ping-Pong. He would talk about what he was interested in and she about what interested her. Even though they had talked at each other, they had listened, too, and, most of all, they had cared. Even if he hadn't said he loved her as readily or easily as she might have liked, he had sparked something inside her. At least he hadn't ever been a phony like so many of the people she knew now, gushing when he didn't mean it.

She felt the vertigo of an endless need for this thing of great value that she had so heedlessly cast aside to chase her ambition. Then, profound disillusionment as she realized she had achieved everything she had ever dreamed of and more. And that maybe even though everybody called her a winner—her career would never be enough.

For a year she had wanted to feel something other than loneliness. Now she almost wished she felt numb and indifferent again like a bug in a glass safely shielded from the real world. Instead the glass walls had shattered, and she felt stranded and alone and exposed. She felt a vague longing for this man she had once loved, for that special time when she had been young, when she had believed she could have it all.

Most of all, she wondered what he was like now. She knew his wife had died. He would probably come to Hazel's funeral. What if...

Fancy blushed and pushed her ridiculous fantasy aside. She couldn't possibly be such an idiot to think her reaction to his voice meant anything.

She would go back for her mother's funeral, clear out the old house, call a Realtor and leave. With her new collection to get out, all she could stay was two days—at the most. She would avoid Jim as she had all the other times when she had returned to Purdee.

Except that first time when she had gone back to see if he still cared and he'd run off and married Nottie when he'd heard Fancy was in town.

The shadows from the pines behind her villa were falling thicker now. A slight chill was displacing the balminess of the afternoon. She caught the fresh, damp scent of impending rain, felt the first chilly sting of a drop hitting her wrist and then another pricking her cheek.

She stared at a piece of driftwood the waves had washed up. It seemed to Fancy that her life had rushed past her, carrying her along in a swirl, and then, suddenly when she least expected it, she felt stranded.

At the villa next door two little black-haired boys were throwing a stick to a miniature poodle. The dog would wag his tail as they shouted in French for him to pick it up. Then their mother came out on the terrace to call them inside, and the children and dog came bounding into her arms. An older lady with silver hair and lots of diamonds joined the group. For an endless moment they all clung lovingly, the children babbling, the poodle barking, the women smiling. Then the little boys pulled from their pockets treasures they must have found on the beach, and sand flew everywhere. The women praised everything, raving especially about a broken boomerang.

"Regardez! C'est merveilleux!"

Fancy remembered how her own mother had begged her to stop working so hard, to settle down, to give her grandchildren like Jim's rambunctious twin sons who came over nearly every week to roughhouse with Hazel's golden Labrador retriever.

Jim's motherless sons.

An odd little hush caught at Fancy's heart.

They could so easily have been hers.

In the next instant she pushed the foolish maternal inclination out of her mind. She didn't know the first thing about children. Nor did she want to.

With an effort Fancy forced her attention back to Alain. He was running up and down the beach shouting impatiently to his towering models in their short, white silk dresses, shouting, as well, to Claude to get out of his way. Alain threw himself onto the sand and beckoned with a dramatic flourish of his long fingers that the women move in close. Then he ordered them to stand above him. He tilted his camera back at an obscene angle, so that he got more leg and thigh than dress.

That wasn't the kind of shot that Fancy wanted.

Claude was jumping up and down in a rage, his orange-red hair bouncing like a pom-pom.

Fancy knew she should supervise Alain and calm Claude. The old, know-it-all, want-it-all Fancy would have rushed down to the beach and reminded Alain she was paying his exorbitant rate because she wanted photos she could publish in a fashion magazine, not a girlie magazine. The new, vulnerable Fancy was too preoccupied with her own destroyed emotions and strange fantasies to make a fuss.

Out of the corner of her eye Fancy saw the grandmother and mother carry their little boys into their villa.

Fancy felt a crushing loneliness, a bewildering emptiness. And soon, she, who until today had prided herself on almost never crying, could no longer make out Alain's dark figure or the girls' paler ones through the blur of her tears.

"Fanc-e-e-e—" Claude screamed maniacally, hopping toward her when she turned away. "Fanc-e-e-e—"

But she no longer heard or saw anyone on the beach.

The shoot was forgotten.

The damp air felt so thin she could barely breathe.

She sank down on the steps, trying to remember the last time she had seen her mother.

Chapter Two

His black eyes narrowed, Jim King frowned as he peered sheepishly down into Hazel Hart's elegant coffin. He felt a vague twinge of guilt, partly 'cause he knew everybody in the funeral parlor probably attributed his uneasiness entirely to grief. They were all feeling sorry for him, figuring he was noble and high-minded. Not that he wasn't glad they weren't on to him, not that he wasn't glad they couldn't see what was really eating at him.

Hell, no! He wasn't so much sad as he was mad. And scared. Mad as a hornet at old Hazel for being so stupid. And scared 'cause Fancy was back in town. He was cursing his fate and thinking he was the unluckiest bastard in the whole state of Texas. And it wasn't easy to hide such raw rage and terror behind a somber mask everybody would take for grief.

His tall, lean form slumped lower over the coffin. His tense, arrogant face darkened.

Hazel, you crazy old coot. What in the name of creation made you think you were spry enough to go up on your roof to replace that shingle the squirrels had chewed a hole in? Why didn't you ask me to fix it the way you nagged me into doing everything else? How could you go and break your scrawny neck—the day before we finalized the sale of your farm?

He had warned her about feeding squirrels and wild critters after a squirrel had gotten inside her house, eaten holes in her sofa pillows and made a helluva mess. He'd helped her chase the little cuss outside and offered to blow his head off with his shotgun while the brazen rascal had fluffed its tail and munched a potato chip on her porch, taunting them. But Hazel had nearly had a heart attack at the thought.

Hazel's eyes remained stubbornly closed, her mouth pinched and uncharacteristically serene as she lay stiffly upon the white satin pillow in that elegant coffin that had cost way more than she would ever have approved Fancy spending. Some cadaver-faced mortician that hadn't known Hazel had kinked her hair up real tight and dabbed on too dark a shade of lipstick, so that she looked more like one of those uptight, gossipy old church biddies than the free-spirited old reprobate she'd been. Somebody had chosen that black lace dress with pearl buttons, the one you couldn't have stuffed Hazel into on a bet when she'd been alive.

Jim knew where that dress had come from. Her daughter, his old flame, Whitney Hart, who everybody called Fancy, had sent it to her on Hazel's seventieth birthday two months ago.

Hazel had said grumpily, "Now why does Fancy keep on sending me funeral dresses when all a body needs is one?"

They had been sipping lemonade together on her shady veranda with Hazel's dog, Yeller, panting up a storm as they'd discussed what to tell her hired hand, Pablo, to do about her ornery bull, Buster. Buster kept busting out of his fenced pasture either so he could terrorize the city slicker who had leased Old Man

Lowery's place or to pester Jim's dairy cows in the north pasture.

"Fancy always did like fancy things. Which was why she left me."

"I used to think she'd smarten up."

Jim had propped his high-heeled cowboy boots up on Hazel's railing and leaned way back in her swing, lazily stretching out his long legs. He'd pulled his Stetson low over his forehead. "She's done okay." That was an understatement if ever there was one for Fancy's meteoric climb in the fashion world. "The dress will look okay."

"If you're a fool who puts looking good over feeling good, which you and me both know you don't, Jim King."

"You could wear it to church or to a party or to something fun," Jim had suggested, ignoring Hazel's shrewd glance when he'd complimented Fancy. Hazel hadn't cottoned much to Fancy and him breaking up all those years ago, and ever since Nottie's death and Fancy's divorce, Hazel had started hinting that he should take his boys on a vacation to New York.

"Fun." Hazel had snorted. "I hate the word. It's the most overused word in America. I mostly go to funerals anyway." Hazel had stuffed the dress back into the box and gone to see about Buster. Jim had set down his lemonade and followed her.

Alive, Hazel would have yanked a brush through those corkscrew gray curls just to muss them up. She would have exchanged the dress for a pair of old jeans and a cowboy shirt.

Even to Jim, who was as peeved at Hazel as a body could be, it didn't seem right for her to be buried like this for all eternity—not looking a thing like herself.

Once again Jim's resentment toward Hazel—for dying on him way before her time and before he'd finalized the sale of the land he'd been leasing from her—overpowered any sympathy for how Fancy had prettied up the hardheaded old cuss for burial.

How could Hazel have done this to him?

How could she have left him to cut a deal with Fancy on his own, especially now, when he felt so bothered about the fact that both of them were single again? When the mere sound of Fancy's honeyed voice two days ago on the phone had made him restlessly think about how alone he felt, made him wonder if she ever felt like that, too?

Jim had started remembering stuff he didn't have any business remembering—and that had started him fantasizing. He'd started imagining how it'd be, seeing her for the first time at the airport. Then he'd felt so odd, almost sick to his stomach, when Fancy's assistant had called and said Fancy wouldn't be wanting him to meet her plane, that she'd rent a car and drive down on her own. Finally he'd decided that was best after all. The less they saw of one another, the better.

Yes. Just the thought of seeing Fancy in person in front of the whole town after they'd avoided each other for ten years made him start to sweat under the armpits of his long-sleeved shirt and black wool suit. It was plain crazy the way knowing that impossible, high-flying redhead was single and home for a spell made the knot of his silk tie tighten all by itself like a hanging noose, and he could hardly breathe. She was bound to show up at any minute. Hell, he was under enough pressure trying to act sad and not mad, without having to contend with Fancy.

How could one woman fill him with such dread?

The red roses that lay on top of the coffin gave off a powerful, smotheringly sweet smell in the close little funeral parlor. There was an extravagant overabundance of lilies and chrysanthemums, and suddenly Jim was remembering how Fancy had always loved flowers.

For no reason at all he remembered that spring afternoon on his twenty-first birthday when she'd left a note and a red rose on the seat of his car. The note had said to meet him at their special place down by the river. And he'd found her there—naked as she smiled up at him from under a blanket of wildflowers.

He remembered how soft and wild she'd been, trembling a little when he'd touched her, her mouth tender and sweet like rose petals warmed from the sun. He'd kissed her, savored her, his tongue exploring every part of her till she was all hot and quivery and wet as she'd arched herself up to him. He remembered the way their bodies had fit so perfectly, the way she'd clutched the small of his back and promised she'd never, ever stop loving him, the way they had come to a peak in perfect harmony. Once hadn't been enough that day. Or most of the other days or nights she'd let him have her.

The truth was he'd been so hot for her he'd never been able to get his fill of her. Nor she of him. When she'd left him for good, yelling she loved him but not nearly enough to bury herself alive in Purdee, Texas, for the rest of her born days, and set off for New York, never answering his letters or saying she was the least bit sorry, he'd thought for sure he'd die of a broken heart. But he hadn't died; he'd just learned that love could be a contingent thing, and he'd formed the habit of keeping a lot more of himself to himself, so there hadn't been all that much left over for Nottie.

And here Fancy was single again and haunting him all these years later when memories of making love to her were the last thing he needed or wanted. Especially since he was going to have to see her and make small talk with her in front of Gracie. He had to act like Fancy was nothing to him now. But how could he act like she wasn't when he kept thinking about lying naked with Fancy, when he kept worrying that Fancy or Gracie—or both—might see it in his face?

Suddenly he wished he hadn't let Gracie talk him into coming. But Gracie had said that in a town the size of Purdee, people would really talk if he didn't go.

So Jim prayed Fancy had gotten wrinkled or maybe fat since her husband had left her. Or maybe she'd be weak-willed and pliable and in no way an interesting challenge. Jim prayed he'd look at her and feel nothing but a sense of relief and closure. On that happy thought, Jim was about to move away from the coffin and tell Gracie he was going outside to check on Oscar and Omar, his notorious twins. They were only in the fourth grade, but to hear the school people talk, a stranger would have thought they were as bad as a band of old-time outlaws, that the kids came to Purdee on school days to deliberately prey on teachers and on the weekends to terrorize storekeepers.

A door opened behind Jim.

The steady buzz of small talk died. Suddenly the room felt smaller. The lush, unwanted memory of Fancy's slim, opulent body and her sparkling eyes after he'd lifted those wildflowers stem by slender stem and begun to kiss her pale, warm throat and then her honeyed mouth sprang vividly into focus again.

Jim King neither saw her nor heard her, but he knew the exact instant Purdee's most famous former citizen stepped into the funeral parlor.

She had always had some special something.

He felt the electric pull of her presence pulsing through every pore of his body as she walked hesitantly toward her mother's coffin to join him there. All eyes turned to her and stayed glued on her.

All eyes but his.

A suffocating band seemed to close around his heart, and he was too damned scared to look—even to check her out on the desperate hope that she'd gotten fat and ugly.

Too damn scared she was as pretty and sexy and as boldly one-of-a-kind as ever.

Fancy had been his girlfriend in high school and his lover in college. More than his lover. His life. His everything. Not that he'd let on to her how much he'd loved her. He'd been too damned proud.

He backed slowly away from the coffin as he felt Fancy's tall body carve its way through that silent, crowded room and approach him.

It had been ten years since the day she'd broken up with him because he'd decided not to follow her to New York, but to return to Purdee and take over his father's and his grandfather's farms. He'd gone into dairy farming and gotten respectably rich. He owned five thousand acres of green pastures and more than a thousand purebred jersey cows. He had his own plane and a landing strip. He'd married pretty Nottie Jenkins and been widowed two years ago. After a decent interval the whole town, even Omar and Oscar, had conspired to find him a new bride, every man, woman and child convincing him that sweet Gracie Chapman, Purdee's new vet, was just about the next best thing to perfect for him.

Gracie had the same kind of affinity for animals Jim had, and he'd been thinking about asking her to marry him until he'd stopped by Hazel's and found Hazel crumpled under her ladder with her neck broken. He was still in shock, but everybody knew, himself included, it was just a matter of time before he popped the question.

So, with his dairy business prospering and a happy future with Gracie and the boys in the works, why couldn't he turn and look at Fancy, smile at her smugly even—or at least casually—as if memories of her lying naked beneath him in a springtime forest didn't haunt him, as if the cruelty of their last night didn't drag at him? As if he thought things had turned out best for both of them.

But he felt clammy, and he couldn't turn around.

It had always been like this whenever Fancy came anywhere near—this crushing, overpowering sense of unwanted physical awareness of one for the other. Like they were the only two people in the room. Like they were the only man and woman on the entire planet. And he didn't welcome being overwhelmed by anything—especially not his own emotions.

After she'd moved to New York, he'd never felt passion like that again. Not for Nottie, his petite, dark wife who'd tried so hard to please him. And not for sweet, golden Gracie, who made even more of a fuss.

But he was getting older. And smarter. Way too smart to get involved with Fancy again. A man who was tied to the land needed a certain kind of wife. Someone sensible and manageable who wanted to cook and keep house. Someone who could see the point of spending money to trim a mare's hooves but wouldn't want to waste either the time or the money on a professional manicure for herself. Someone who was firm and maternal with children, someone who could deal with a rowdy set like his boys. Not an internationally successful, fashion designer like Fancy who had once told him the last thing she'd ever want was to be buried alive on a farm and raise a houseful of children.

Fancy was, even before her stunning successes in New York and Paris...well, way too fancy for him. She always had been, and she always would be. She was as extravagant and showy as he was down-to-earth, hardworking and thrifty. His land was something he'd care for and then pass on to his sons; her land probably meant nothing to her.

Maybe she'd been born a farmer's daughter, but even then she had dreamed of bright lights and limousines. Of professional men, men who were as high on themselves as she was on herself. Book-smart men or worthless, superrich playboys like the jerk who'd divorced her, men who made their living charging obscene amounts of money for nothing more than their opinions. Or men who got through life on charm and were as phony and chock-full of bull droppings as high-flying Fancy.

"Gracie Chapman meet Whitney Hart," Waynette Adams said in a tittering gush behind him.

It was just like Waynette to make the most of the inherent drama by introducing his current squeeze to his old flame.

"Gracie moved to town a few months after Jim's Nottie died two years ago."

"How nice," Fancy murmured politely, "for everybody...if you like it here."

"Oh, I just love it," Gracie drawled Texas-style, making the word *just* go on forever.

Jim's broad shoulders strained the itchy black wool of his suit as he struggled to ignore the three women standing beside Hazel Hart's coffin. He ran a hand through his thick, black hair, closing his eyes and trying to endure Waynette's eagerness to put her gossipy spoon in his soup and give it a stir.

"Just call me Fancy. Everybody always does, sooner or later," Whitney continued in that deep, cultured, sugary voice that got to him.

Other groups of people had resumed talking.

Everybody but him. He should join Lionel Adams who was over by the wall ranting about the inflation in feed prices, but Jim felt too trapped and edgy. Why couldn't he turn around and go through the polite motions expected of him? All he had to do was put his arm around Gracie and say hello to Fancy like he would have if she'd been anybody else, but who she was.

"How long will you be staying, Fancy?" Gracie asked.

"A day or two. I just have to decide what to do about Mother's farm."

"Do you plan to keep it or sell it?" Waynette asked.

"Mother's death was so unexpected. I really hate to think of selling, but I'm afraid I don't have a lot of choice—"

"Well, it just might interest you to know the talk is that Jim King has had his heart set on buying it," Waynette said, thrusting her spoon in Jim's soup a little deeper. "Why, his place is as big as a ranch, and he's got all those cows. He's been leasing grazing rights from Hazel for over a year now. You might ask him."

Lordy, Waynette, you're some meddler.

"Jim? Really? Selling to him wouldn't be nearly as bad as selling to a stranger. Is he here?" Fancy asked a little breathlessly, her bright head turning.

As if she wasn't as aware of him as he was of her.

Jim almost felt the exact moment when her sea green eyes bored through his back and jump-started his heart.

"Right over there," Waynette said.

"Jim, dear—" Gracie called sweetly.

People kept coming and going through the doors of the funeral parlor, and the air-conditioning was fighting a losing battle with the Texas heat.

Fancy wanted to sell the Hart place, and he wanted to buy it. But suddenly Jim didn't much care. He felt like he was roasting alive. His silken noose of a tie had tightened around his neck and was damn near choking him. He couldn't talk about the farm now. Not till he felt easier and more relaxed about Fancy. Nor did he feel able to get his first eyeful of Fancy right in front of Gracie, either.

No. He had to get outside and calm down first. So when Gracie called to him again, he turned and waved at her, pointing toward the door and mouthing the names Omar and Oscar. Gracie frowned, but by that time Jim had bolted toward the door before she could protest.

But just as suddenly that sugary-sweet voice called his name, electrifying him the same as it had on the phone.

Which made him move even faster—to escape.

It was just like Fancy to sprint after him so fast she got there before him. As fluid as a cat, she sprang lightly in front of the glass storm door, blocking his path.

Which meant he almost slammed full-force into the very woman he'd been running from.

He struggled to catch his breath.

Instead he inhaled her perfume. As always, she smelled of flowers—like she'd been lying in a bed of 'em—the way she had *that* day.

"Jim," Fancy whispered, "long time, no see."

Like magnets, his whiskey-colored eyes were drawn helplessly to her upturned face. He saw the loneliness in her luminous gaze. But he saw, as well, the silent invitation of that soft, half-parted, red mouth.

And the minute he saw her eyeing him like that, he knew his instinct to run had been right. Because that keen, lost, interested look spelled trouble for them both.

She was still beautiful, incandescently beautiful.

A chunky collar of gold flashed from her ears and throat. She was so dangerously elegant and lovely in that plain black dress, she scared the hell out of him.

Most of all, he kept thinking about the fact that she was single....

Chapter Three

Why did Fancy always have to push him onto center stage? Jim thought desperately, awash with a mixture of confused emotions: embarrassment, fear, yearning, guilt, dread and fury that she was about to make a scene in front of everybody.

Fancy damn sure hadn't gotten fat. No, she was as skinny as ever, as fashionably handsome, too, with her flame-dark hair and sad green eyes. Beautiful enough and conceited enough to want to tease him like this, maybe just so she could test her power over him.

Jim glanced at her wet mouth again, its shape so artfully lined in red, the full bottom lip glossed a lighter shade. He was suddenly conscious of the accelerated beating of his heart.

Frantically he forced his gaze from her lips. Outside, Omar and Oscar had forgotten they were at Aunt Hazel's funeral and were supposed to be on their best behavior. They had stripped out of their coats and ties and shoes and socks for a rowdy game of hide-and-seek in the parking lot with their friends and a couple of dogs.

Omar was stuffing handfuls of rocks into his trouser pockets, which were bulging as if they were about to pop their seams. But the worrisome question was—what did Omar want those rocks for? The boys had cost Jim trouble and money last summer when they'd skimmed so many rocks across the city sewage pond they'd clogged up the entire system. Yesterday they'd gotten him into trouble with the authorities again by using the school bus for target practice.

"Jim—" Fancy whispered again, forcing his attention back to her.

Just the way she said his name, sweet as sugar and soft as velvet and yet determined, too, made him forget the city council meeting when the whole town had decided he had to pay for the damage his boys had done to the sewage system, made him forget to say something about buying her farm.

Jim wished she'd move out of his way, but Fancy stayed right where she was—directly in front of him, so he'd have to touch her to get past her. Sunlight shone from behind her, lighting up her slender curves like an angel's aura.

"Everybody thinks I came over to talk about selling you Mother's farm, but..." Her voice was dark and cool now, her pretty red smile very dangerous. "But I came over because I wondered if you ever remembered how it was with us?"

As if he could ever forget—no matter how damn hard he tried.

He jammed his fists into his pockets and stared at her stubbornly. Which was a mistake because she laughed a little—nervously, though.

A spray of scarlet roses and snowy lilies were pinned to her prim collar against her slender, white throat. He remembered kissing that throat and how warm and satiny her skin had felt. Suddenly the memory of that wanton spring afternoon when she'd worn nothing but flowers and given herself to him as a birthday gift hit him again full-force. He just kept looking at her as if he'd gone daft.

"Yeah," he said bitterly. "I remember..."

"I couldn't ever forget you, either—no matter how hard I tried," she said softly, a sad note in her voice. "So, I've decided maybe I should just stop trying, Jim."

If ever a woman meant trouble....

He knew he should run, and yet he sensed some new, almost desperate, vulnerability in her.

He remembered how shamelessly she'd chased him in high school. How easy he'd been to catch. How their relationship had always been a contest of wills.

He kept staring at her till a rosy blush suffused her cheeks, till he was almost sure he was blushing an even darker shade of pink than she was.

He forced himself to remember how easily she'd discarded him when he'd served her purpose. His expression hardened.

"I wasn't sure you'd come to Mother's funeral because in all the times I've come home, you've never once dropped by even to say hi," Fancy said. "And I knew you visited Mother nearly every day. I know you were avoiding me."

"I *was* married."

"So was I." Some sadness flared and then died in her eyes. "I was sorry about Nottie dying."

He couldn't very well say he was sorry about her rich husband running off, so a silence fell till he finally managed, "I'm sorry about Hazel, and, er, Gracie said it would look bad if I didn't show today."

Fancy smiled ruefully. "I forget how it is in small towns. Everybody's always watching and judging everything and everybody."

"Like now," Jim said, eyeing Gracie and Waynette uneasily, hoping Fancy would take the hint and get out of his way.

"Waynette's still the same old busybody, but I sure like your Gracie. She's sweet. And I'm grateful to her for making you come because you're the one person I truly wanted to see."

Fancy's words, soft and flirtatious, offered so freely and so warmly, only increased the strain he felt.

"Those other times when I was home, I didn't want to talk to you, either, Jim. Now I do."

Oh, boy. Here we go again.

"What for?" he muttered. "You told me once that I was a shortsighted hick to settle for Purdee. You sure thought you had me pegged."

Her eyes wandered up and down his tall, male frame in a way that made him even edgier.

"Well, maybe I wasn't as smart as I thought," she said silkily. "Or maybe I just said that so you wouldn't fight too hard to keep me here. I think I was scared it would have been pretty easy for you to change my mind."

"Well, we'll never know."

"You never were one to chase after a girl. But you look good, Jim. Like you're made of nothing but muscle now. I thought maybe you were scared to see me because you'd gotten bald or paunchy."

The last thing he wanted from her was a compliment. "I never was much to look at, either."

"I seem to remember that every girl in the county was chasing you—before I got lucky."

"Because I was a talented quarterback."

"You had other talents I admired more."

He drew a raged breath. "That was a long time ago. A lot of water has gone under the bridge."

"For me, too." Again he caught that sad note in her voice.

They stared at one another. Suddenly he wondered how many men she'd slept with besides the one she'd divorced. Did she remember him as some clumsy hick compared to her more elegant lovers?

"I was hoping you'd gotten fat," he said savagely.

"Maybe I was hoping the same thing about you. So—maybe I'm disappointed, too." But she smiled in a way that said she wasn't.

With her red hair pulled back at her nape and her severe black dress that emphasized her femininity, Fancy looked so sleek and ravishing his pulse started pounding. Her breasts were fuller. She was more voluptuous. Sexier. And, of course, she knew it.

In elementary school days she'd been a prissy-looking stick with her thick braids and weird lace dresses. Then there had been that third-grade Easter party out at Hazel's farm when it had rained and Hazel had tried to make Fancy wear jeans like the other kids instead of a favorite lace dress, and Fancy had gotten so mad she'd stormed down to the party stark naked.

Naked—that got his mind on the wrong track. Just for a moment he imagined her without the elegant black sheath—without a stitch.

His eyes burned hungrily into her. He saw her soft, pale body; her heavy breasts, her tiny waist. The alluring vision was so compellingly vivid, he felt a swift, stirring need to touch her, to taste her, to see if the reality could hold a candle to his imagination.

But instead of lifting his hand, Jim looked away quickly, desperately, so Fancy couldn't read him and suspect. His stern, tanned face got grimmer as he pretended to study the rusting door hinge.

"You didn't used to be so stuffy and serious," she whispered. "So impolite . . . to old friends."

"This is a funeral." His voice was hard. "Your mother's."

"She wouldn't have minded you being nice to me, Jim."

"Maybe I mind."

"I don't see why we have to hate each other just because we were once—"

He wished she didn't always have to speak her piece out loud.

But Fancy, who was as mule-minded as ever, never had avoided speaking or doing the outrageous. "Lovers."

Her husky word hung there between them like a dare for the longest moment, conjuring visions of her body in the forest on that bed of flowers, of her long legs wrapped around his, of the unforgettable glory of taking her and savoring her. Again, her tight black dress seemed to dissolve, and he was almost blinded by her beauty.

"I don't hate you," he muttered savagely.

"You sure don't want to be around me."

"That's different from hating." His voice had deepened ominously.

"Does that mean you're scared of the feelings you might still have for me?"

Why did she always have to push him?

"I don't have feelings for you, girl!"

She studied him. "Good. Then things won't get complicated. You and Gracie and I can be friends. And as a friend, you won't mind my telling you how sorry I was about the way I jilted you when your daddy died and you had to come home to help your mother."

The genuine regret in her beautiful, sea green eyes made him feel soft like he'd better bolt outside right away or be sucked into something that was a whole lot stronger than he was.

"Everybody says you've done very well," she continued.

"Money always did make a difference to you, Fancy."

"Not so much anymore. Not ever with real friends."

"Stay away from me, girl. You and me—we can't ever be friends."

"Then what can we be?"

Ignoring the challenge in that, he leaned toward her and cracked the storm door so that he felt the warm, sultry outside air. Oscar and Omar were dashing around the parking lot hollering like they were chasing a gang of outlaws.

"You're still angry because I didn't believe you'd ever amount to anything. Don't you see, I should have said I was sorry years and years ago," she whispered. "Because I was. But I was just too stubborn."

Jim turned back to her. Did she think all she had to do was apologize and everything would be just like it was before? It wasn't that easy. The hurt had been eating at him too damn long. Besides, there was Gracie. "Look, I've gotta go," he said abruptly.

"Sure."

He opened the door wider and the sunlight lit up her red hair.

Desperately he said, "Gracie and me—we're getting married, you know."

"Of course you are, Jim."

"Oscar and Omar are just crazy about her."

"But how do you feel?"

Five minutes ago that would have been a whole lot easier to answer, if he were the talkative type. But in the heat of that moment all he could see, all he could feel—even though he didn't want to—was Fancy's heart-shaped, white face, her long, silky red hair and her soft, voluptuous red lips. She was single and so was he. Suddenly all he wanted to know was if she still tasted sweeter than honey. If her hands would still be as hot and silky and expert if they roamed his body. If it would still be as much fun to fight and argue about everything in tarnation.

"As if you care how I feel," he growled in a low whisper.

An exciting tension coiled around them.

An easier woman wouldn't have risked rejection.

"Oh, but I do," Fancy said boldly.

Her teasing words burned through him like acid.

"I'm crazy about Gracie, too," he thundered defiantly, stunned he'd admitted such a thing out loud.

The funeral parlor had gotten deathly quiet, like a field full of rabbits when the hawk swoops low. Fancy's hair seemed to catch fire; her face went white.

Dozens of silent eyes watched them. Dozens of ears pricked when he raised his voice.

"I hope you'll be very happy, then. As your friend—that's all I'd ever want for you, Jim."

"That's a barefaced lie if ever I heard one, Fancy Hart! And every eavesdropping busybody in this funeral parlor knows it."

There was an audible gasp from his spellbound audience.

Without thinking, he grabbed Fancy and pulled her against his hard, male body. His big, work-toughened hands were sandpaper rough against her silk sheath. "Like I said, you and I can't ever be friends!"

"No," she whimpered, whether in agreement or denial, he didn't know.

All he felt was the searing imprint of her soft breasts as they flattened against his muscular chest. All he knew was that this was where she belonged. Where they both belonged—forever.

The heat of her seeped into him, devouring his resistance, and he knew then that he shouldn't have touched her. Just as he knew he should let her go, but her delectable, velvet-soft body slid against his, fitting perfectly the way he'd known deep in his soul it would, and his iron arms couldn't stay the wild need to crush her even tighter as if merely holding her had aroused all the old hungers.

Fancy's green eyes grew huge. Even though his long, rough fingers were tightly clamped around her arms, she neither cried out nor struggled against him. Maybe she knew that to do so would have been useless. Maybe she just didn't want to do anything that might make the scene worse. But probably what she'd wanted all along was to rile him so he'd do something crazy and wild like this.

So he'd touch her. So she'd show the whole town what a hypocrite he was. So he'd give in to the urge to lift her flaming hair from her nape and press his mouth there.

He was panting hard to fight worse impulses.

"Jim—" It was Gracie's quiet, nagging voice behind him.

The whole town was watching, listening, gaping. The gossips would buzz about this for days.

He didn't give a damn.

"Jim, you'd better let Fancy go and see about your boys," Gracie said a little bit louder although her tone was still hushed. "Omar just bounced a pellet or something off Waynette's station wagon."

"He what—" Waynette yelped, making a beeline for the door.

Slowly the red haze of emotion clouding Jim's brain cleared and he unclenched his fingers from Fancy's soft arms. His big hands fell weakly to his sides. But the thrilling shock of having held her stayed with him.

He knew he was way out of line. But he couldn't apologize. Not when it was all he could do to breathe. Not when fighting with Fancy felt a whole lot better than making love to any other woman. Not when what he really wanted was more of her.

Suddenly it had all been too much for him—his anger over Hazel's death, his strange, unwanted feelings for Fancy, her saying she was sorry about the past when he knew damn good and well she wasn't.

Something had burst inside him like a dam, and the flood of emotion seemed hell-bent to destroy everything in its path.

He took a deep breath and then jerked at his tie. Maybe if Fancy hadn't spoken to him, he would have regained his composure.

"Are you okay?" Fancy whispered huskily, touching his arm, causing that unwanted electricity to leap between them again.

"As if you care," he snapped, beyond control again, furious at her for showing him up for the fraud he was. "When did you ever give a damn about anybody's happiness but your own?"

Gracie gave a sharp little cry and ran toward him. Fancy's pale, beautiful face shattered as he roughly shoved the door open and pushed past her.

Again their bodies brushed against one another, only this time she jumped back self-consciously as if burned. He knew he'd hurt her. Maybe he'd hurt Gracie, too, but he couldn't deal with either woman right now. Or his rowdy sons. Or the town.

He had to be alone.

He stomped across the porch, down the concrete stairs, ignoring his twins' exhilarated war whoops as they dashed recklessly between the cars in the hot, dusty parking lot. He ignored Waynette who was yelling after him to do something about Omar who was chucking rocks madly. He hardly noted that it was Fancy who went down to discipline his kids.

Like Hazel's maddened bull, Buster, set on a rampage, Jim galloped past his sons toward his pickup.

But once Jim was speeding down the highway in Old Blue, his farm truck, and yanking his tie loose and unbuttoning his stiff collar, he felt no better.

Without a second thought as to what Gracie would say later, he pitched the silk tie onto his dash into the dusty mess of oil cans and screwdrivers and wrenches he stored there.

It wasn't much use to run very far. Not when there was nowhere to hide. At least not from the thing gnawing inside him.

He hadn't wanted Fancy to come back. He hadn't wanted her single again so his secret fantasies could take hold and start pestering him again.

He pulled off onto the shoulder of the road and stopped. For a long moment he stared unseeingly across Melvin Schindle's green pasture. Then Jim leaned over the steering wheel and squeezed his eyes shut.

Fancy. Dear God. He groaned aloud.

She had felt so treacherously good when he'd held her close.

Just looking at her had brought the old hunger back, as though she'd never been gone. He wanted to feel her velvet skin beneath his hands again. He wanted to crush his mouth to her lips; he wanted her naked and twisting under his body.

For ten years he'd buried himself alive—marrying the wrong woman, having kids right off, buying land, cows, buildings and sophisticated equipment. He had new barns, new bulldozers, tractors and an irrigation system. Last of all, he'd built a mansion on top of a hill with a view of his broad, rolling pastures.

But it was just like Hazel had said. "You just work all the time trying to prove you aren't the no-count hick Fancy said you were. She's doing the same in New York—she's durn near killed herself to prove she was right to leave you behind."

Hazel had been wrong about Fancy, but she'd been right about him. He'd never gotten over Fancy. He'd only pretended. The first time she'd come back to Purdee after jilting him, he'd gotten so upset he'd run off and married Nottie just to prove to everybody, especially Fancy, that he was over her.

Now, seeing Fancy again, holding her... She was the blinding flash that changed everything. She was the "road not taken" that had always haunted him. She was the microsecond disaster that shattered his safe little world. She was the head-on collision. The bad C.A.T. scan. The long-distance phone call in the middle of the night. Like a dangerous rush of an addictive drug, she could seduce him away from right and reason.

If he got tangled up with Fancy, he might as well throw his whole life in a manure heap. Because she wouldn't want more than a fling. But just a time or two in her bed would be enough for her to reset her hook fatally deep in his heart.

Then came the horrifying thought that he wasn't the most important component in this equation—*Fancy was.*

Hell, if Fancy had him in her sights, it was probably already way too late.

If Fancy didn't get the hell out of town in a day or two, he would lose Gracie and the fragile happiness he'd worked so hard for.

Chapter Four

"So when are you going to ask Fancy if she'll sell you the farm?" Gracie demanded, and not for the first time.

"When I feel like it," Jim said, hunkering lower.

"Okay. Okay. I'll stop. You win."

"Good."

Silence. After a long, uneasy moment, Gracie went to the sink again and washed two apples.

Jim guiltily slumped behind his morning newspaper and tried to hide from her, but that only made the pitter-pat of her practical, soft-soled heels pad with more determination as she moved back and forth across the linoleum of his huge kitchen, opening cabinets, noisily wrapping and stuffing sandwiches for the twins into their lunch pails while pouring milk into their thermoses. She'd been badgering him for nearly an hour while she'd tidied up the house and cooked breakfast.

This was the first morning Jim really wished the twins hadn't pulled that damned-fool stunt of pinging rocks at the school bus last Friday till they broke out the back window. If they hadn't done that, then they wouldn't have been banned from riding the bus for a week and Gracie wouldn't be stopping by every morning on her way in to her clinic to give them a lift to school.

And then *he* wouldn't have to see so much of Gracie.

Not that Jim wasn't grateful to her.

The phone rang, but before Gracie could catch it, the boys grabbed it upstairs on the first ring. It was as though they were expecting a call. Which was suspicious.

"Everybody in Purdee is talking about the way you treated Fancy so badly at Hazel's funeral Saturday," Gracie said, taking a different tack. "And then about the way you just took the truck and ran out on me and the kids. You know, Fancy was wonderful. She fed us supper and then brought us home."

Fancy again. "I'm surprised to hear Purdee's prodigal daughter knows how to cook."

"I imagine she's terrific at most things she tries. The boys had a really great time with her. And they were so *good.* She knew just what to say. You know, she said Hazel would have wanted them to have Yeller."

"Well, you can tell Fancy from me that I already told them they *can't* have Yeller," Jim snapped.

"Why not?"

"Because I said so."

Jim kept his eyes glued to his paper. Fancy had damn sure succeeded in setting him up—big time. Gracie had been on his case ever since the funeral. Not only had Fancy driven them home, she had cleverly offered the twins Hazel's worthless mutt, who had a bad habit of chewing holes in their clothes as well as chasing everything that moved, especially cars and chickens and dairy cattle. Most mornings, like today, the twins got up too late to feed the animals they already had—so the last thing Jim needed was Yeller scratching on the screen and barking at every sunup for breakfast.

"Jim, the way you treated Fancy at the funeral, the way you won't even ask her about buying the farm—"

"Don't!"

"Even the way you are today about Yeller— Well, everybody says you're not acting like yourself at all. You're usually so quiet and sweet."

Quiet and sweet. Maybe he was that way when Fancy wasn't around. But now that she was back, his temper felt like a shredded rope about to rip apart in a dozen places.

"Everybody—" Gracie was saying.

"Everybody being mostly Waynette and Lionel Adams and *you,* I'll bet," Jim stated grimly, flipping a page so hard he tore straight through the column where he was reading about German dairy machinery. "Everybody can be damned! I'm sick and tired of living my life for other people." He looked up from his paper. "Hey—the twins are supposed to pack their own lunches. You're going to spoil 'em. Anyway, you know they like chips and Coke better than apples and milk."

"Maybe the Adamses were the first to talk," Gracie continued. "But more people than just Waynette and Lionel are talking now. More than me." She watched him as she wrapped an apple in cellophane.

"Who?"

"Mostly everybody."

"I would have thought you would explain for me instead—"

"I did tell them you'd been in shock ever since you found Hazel. That you were a little upset about the negotiations to her farm going up in smoke when she died so suddenlike, what with your plans to expand the dairy and all. That—"

"So the talk will die down in time."

"But I know Fancy must feel terrible."

"She's a whole lot tougher than you think. She'll get over it."

"Her mother just died, Jim. I think Fancy's taking it real hard. Least, that's what she's telling everybody. She said she wants to be your friend."

"Do you mean she's sneaking around talking about me behind my back?" he yelled, furious that Fancy had found another way to best him. "Damn it, I thought she was going to leave town right after the funeral!"

"Well, she says she's changed her mind, and now she plans to stay—indefinitely."

"What?" he exploded.

"You just have to go over there and apologize to her, that's all," Gracie insisted as she snapped the buckles on the battered lunch pails, set them side by side on the counter and then poured Jim a fresh cup of coffee. "I know you feel awful guilty," she whispered, pouring very slowly. Their eyes met for an instant, and he felt himself blush, thinking for sure she saw through him.

"You won't be yourself until you go over there," Gracie continued to nag gently. "I'm tired of you sulking and moping."

Jim looked up and stared at her bleakly.

Is that what she thought he was doing?

He hadn't held her or kissed her once since the day of that funeral, and she was a pretty little thing with her soft golden hair and big, shy brown eyes that always followed him so adoringly. But her looking at him that way made him feel even guiltier because he didn't return her feelings. He couldn't fool himself anymore that she even came close to stirring his blood as if there were a hot current going through it, the way Fancy could without half trying.

Gracie was so sweet and kind, so sedate and ladylike. And so damnably talented with his cows. Usually she was easy and pliable—agreeable, just what everybody had told him he needed. She'd cook every night, too, which was important to a man who did hard, physical work all day.

"Do you have any idea what made Fancy decide to stay?" he asked, knowing that the only hope was for Fancy to go back where she came from. So maybe he could set to work forgetting her again.

"Well, for one thing, she wants you to make a decision about that farm. Which means you've got to go over there and apologize, so you two can get down to business."

He thought of Fancy, beautiful and soft and all alone at Hazel's. She was all those things and yet tough and a challenge to him, too. Just the thought of her gave him a buzz.

If Gracie loved him, why didn't she sense the devastation that threatened them?

He felt so tense he wanted to stand up and shout some sense into her head.

I'm afraid to go over there, woman. I'm afraid to even talk to that mule-minded witch. Because I have

*feelings for her that are way more powerful than any
I've ever felt for anybody else—including you.*

But the last thing he ever wanted to do was hurt
Gracie. Especially since she was so good to his boys
and they were so crazy about her. So he pushed his
chair back and rose, forcing himself to pull Gracie
gently into his arms.

"Now don't you go messing up my lipstick,
Jim—"

Slowly he lowered his lips to hers, determined once
and for all to banish Fancy from his mind.

But he found Gracie's lips stiff and primly childish,
and he didn't relish the kiss much himself till he forgot himself and fantasized it was Fancy he held, Fancy
he kissed. Fancy, who had always been so hot and wild
and willing. But his hungry kisses were too much for
Gracie, and she pushed him away.

"We'd better not get carried away."

"For a vet, you're awfully prudish."

"Jim."

And he hated himself for wondering how Fancy
would respond if he went out to her farm and tried the
same thing with her. 'Cause he knew, and it got him
hot.

"Maybe it's time we *did* get carried away," he
growled. "That's what people planning to marry each
other are supposed to do."

"Was that a proposal?" Gracie whispered, looking
startled.

He felt just as surprised and put off by the idea as
she, but before he could answer, Omar and Oscar
came galloping down the stairs like a pair of wild
broncos busting out of their rodeo chutes.

"'Bye Dad!" they shouted, grabbing their lunch pails. "Dubs on the front seat!"

"It's my turn!"

"Mine!"

They were wrestling each other to get out the screen door first, lunch pails banging.

"Hope she didn't pack grapefruit again," Omar yelled, slamming the screen door.

"Or yogurt."

"Yuck!" said Omar.

"Dad, Fancy just called. She said we could come over and pick up Yeller anytime."

Fancy, calling, pestering, pushing. Jim saw red—great fiery tongues of rage seemed to devour everything in the kitchen.

Thankfully Omar and Oscar were dashing down the drive before he could grab them by their collars and snap out a nasty comeback.

On her way after them, Gracie called back to Jim from the door, "Now promise me you'll go over to Hazel's today and make up with Fancy."

"Why don't we go over together—this afternoon?" he offered weakly.

"Because I think this is something you and Fancy need to work out alone."

Jim stared hard at Gracie's sweet, innocent face. A good woman had to be the dumbest critter alive. Would she be so insistent that he see Fancy—*alone*—if she knew how just the thought made his chest quicken and his blood heat?

Jim hesitated and then nodded grimly, his unspoken promise making him wonder if his fate wasn't sealed. Feeling doomed, he stomped out onto his wide veranda, which was cluttered with bicycles and bats and footballs. He watched her as she coaxed the boys out of fighting over the front seat and into their seat belts before driving them down the long, sandy driveway in her practical little Japanese car. Omar was leaning forward from the rear seat, chattering eagerly to her.

His kids adored her—even if she packed apples and grapefruit and yogurt in their lunches.

But how do you feel? Fancy's question, haunting him again.

Not so good. Guilty as hell, in fact. Because he knew too well what Nottie's death had put them through, how truly impossible they'd been till he'd started dating Gracie. Guiltier still when just remembering how Fancy had looked in that tight black dress made his loins clench.

Jim had dozens of chores to take care of. There were water tanks to check to make sure the pumps hadn't malfunctioned. Lactating dairy cows needed a lot of water, and they could get into serious trouble in less than twenty-four hours without it. He had a huge herd, which meant he had to see to lots of pastures and lots of tanks. He needed to drop by the office and check on Sudi and Marna, his secretary and accountant. Then his nutritionist was coming at ten. After that, he had appointments with two of the world's leading veterinary specialists who did nothing but fly around the world checking on newborn dairy calves. He had a couple of calves with respiratory problems he was worried about. Then, Tubby, his foreman, had been pestering him to get started on vaccinations.

But instead of getting down to work as he should have and concentrating on something to take his mind off his troubles, Jim studied the great, blue, cloudless sky and sank lazily onto the shady steps of his veranda and thought about the one person he shouldn't have—Fancy.

Chapter Five

Back in high school, Fancy Hart had never been anything but trouble. At least, that's how she'd been with Jim.

When other girls had chased him, Fancy had constantly pointed out his shortcomings. Yet this skinny nerd with long, red braids and fancy dresses with whom Jim hadn't had a thing in common had finally gotten to him the way the other girls hadn't. Even though Fancy had acted stiff and proud and snotty, like she was way better than him and everybody else, she'd had some lonely, vulnerable quality that had eaten clear to his heart. She was always picking fights with him, yet he always ignored her insults and instead acted gallantly by making the other kids leave her alone—when he could hold his temper.

Fancy hadn't ever been popular with them the way he'd been, maybe 'cause she'd been a spoiled, only child, maybe 'cause she'd been a voracious bookworm, maybe 'cause she'd dressed differently, but mostly 'cause she hadn't cared much about fitting in.

When the other kids had been raising rabbits and pigs and calves for their agricultural clubs, she'd been practicing the piano and reading encyclopedias from cover to cover. She was always prancing across the school stage with her nose in the air, seizing all the awards at the honor assemblies. A time or two she'd even picked him out of the audience and smiled grandly down at him just to taunt him as the principal handed her a prize.

Then there was the way she rode. Everybody else wore normal jeans and boots and cowboy hats, and they rode Western style. Fancy prissed about in jodhpurs and riding boots and bragged about her English riding lessons. That's why some of the kids took to calling her Fancy Pants, which got cut short to Fancy.

During recess the other kids got hot and dirty playing football or soccer while she curled up in the shade in her prim dress-up dresses reading fat books with no pictures like *The Three Musketeers*—books that weren't even assigned in school. Or she drew sketches of models in dresses. She'd even sent sketches to New York and once or twice bragged about the prizes she'd won.

She'd made the best grades in school. She wasn't even dumb in math and science the way girls were supposed to be. Jim hadn't been too good at anything except football, but she hadn't set any store in football players. She was always bragging, especially to him—as if he'd cared—that one day she was going to leave Purdee and be rich and famous, that she was never, ever, coming back.

When she was sixteen and made straight A-pluses, her parents had given her a cute little English sports car, and that had made her snottier and more impossible than ever. One day, after she'd had it about a week, some of the rowdier boys had played a prank on her the last period of school.

Her car was so small, it had been easy sport for ten of the biggest football players to heave it up the gym stairs, while she and the other girls were showering after Phys. Ed. After the last bell, she'd come racing outside in one of her white dresses with her red braids wrapped around her head. Two starched white bows were in her hair.

The sight of her car at the top of those stairs had brought her to an instant, horrified standstill. All the kids laughed at her when her eyes filled with angry tears.

She'd whirled around. "Which one of you big stupid football jerks did this?" Then she'd looked straight at Jim, zeroing in, like she knew for sure it was him. Which made him blush hotly. Which made her doubly sure. "You're the dumbest player of all, Jim King!"

Which made everybody roar louder 'cause it hadn't been Jim. When everybody looked smug and nobody answered, she got so flustered she dropped her car keys.

Bo Bo Johnson, Jim's best friend, had grabbed them and dangled them above her head. "Who's stupid now?"

"You are! You big... retarded—"

"I ain't retarded, 'cause I got your keys, Fancy Pants." Bo Bo had tossed them over her head.

Then the other boys had started throwing them back and forth, whooping and jeering at her frantic efforts to catch them. Finally, when she'd gotten red in the face and had ripped the sleeve of her dress 'cause she stretched her arms too high, Jim had thought the game had gone too far. So he'd jumped in front of Bo Bo and caught her flying keys.

Not that she'd thanked Purdee's star quarterback for his trouble. No. She'd come up to Jim warily, as if she thought he'd throw them over her head like everybody was shouting for him to do. But she'd stared up at him, her eyes red and her face almost ugly from crying, and he'd sensed her loneliness, her alienation. So instead of throwing them, he'd gently placed them into her outstretched hand. For an instant her hand had lingered in his and he'd felt crazily drawn to her...like there was a bond between them.

Then Bo Bo had let out a groan, and Fancy's fist had curled over the keys, her nails digging into Jim's palm as she glared up at him and spat contemptuously, "I do hate you! Worse than anybody else. Because you carry on like you're somethin' because all the girls chase you. You're nothing but a big, dumb football player. You're even dumber than Bo Bo."

"Hey, I didn't have anything to do with your dumb car," Jim had howled, enraged.

Then he had lunged for her, but she'd gotten in her car and would have slammed the door on his hand if he hadn't snatched it back in the nick of time. He stood there staring at his fingers, knowing if she'd had her way even unintentionally, his hand would have been crushed, and he might never have thrown another football.

Furious, he'd watched as she'd driven off, each wheel bumping clumsily down those steps and then hitting harder over the curb.

Angrier than he'd ever been at any girl—even her—he'd hopped in his truck and chased her. When she'd caught sight of him in her rearview mirror, she'd stepped on the gas.

Which had just made him madder. So mad, he'd stomped down harder on his own accelerator.

When she turned onto a back road to shake him, he knew he had her. 'Cause no little prissy bookworm with nerdy braids could know the back roads around Purdee the way he did. He spent a lot of his nights driving over them with Bo Bo. They'd drive for hours and then pull off and drink beer and talk dirty about girls.

The road was sandy, and she was driving too fast. He should've slowed down himself, but he was so furious he wasn't thinking straight and so he forgot about the bad patch where the dirt and sand were thick and deep.

That's why what happened had been all his fault.

When he rounded the turn, she was already in a skid. He slammed on his own brakes just as her cute little red car flipped and rolled on top of itself into the ditch.

His last terrified thought was that she was dead for sure. Then his forehead slammed hard into his steering wheel.

For a long moment he was too dazed to move. The first thing he saw when he opened his eyes and peered through his own blood was Fancy's long red braids hanging out from under her car.

One of the little white bows had come undone and was fluttering. He couldn't see the rest of her.

Lordy.

If she was dead, it was his fault, and he didn't want to live, either. He thought of how she was Hazel's only child, of how everybody talked about how old Hazel had lost all those other babies that had come before Fancy, that that was why plain, sensible Hazel had spoiled Fancy like she was a princess.

Jim nearly fell when his ankle crumpled painfully as he stumbled out of his truck. It was all he could do to hobble toward Fancy. But he forgot his own pain because the sight of those red braids that were always clean and bright lying limp and dull in the dirt with their ribbons curling in the wind terrified him.

His blood rushed so fast he was afraid he'd faint.

One of her tires was still spinning when he got to her. The smell of gasoline made him sick to his stomach.

"Fancy?" he'd whispered, frantic to get her out before the car blew up.

No answer. Just the big, empty sky and the silence.

Peering under the car, he saw her bunched up in an unnatural-looking, lifeless ball.

He drew in a deep breath, scared to try to move her, and scared not to.

Gently he leaned down and put his hands on her shoulders and pulled her body out from under the car.

Her eyes were closed, and she felt limp and boneless—infinitely fragile. Not at all like her usual impossible, mule-minded self. With a trembling hand he touched her face. He didn't think he'd ever felt anything so soft or warm as her cheek. He wondered why he'd never noticed how pretty she was.

'Cause she was so weird and mean to him all the time, that was why.

"Fancy!" he yelled.

She just lay in his arms like a rag doll, her smooth complexion pale and waxen. Her lips were chalky.

He began to shake and hug her close, shouting her name. But she didn't move or moan or anything. He didn't think anybody could be so pale and so quiet and still be alive.

Then he saw the blood all over the front of her white dress and, remembering what old Coach Hanks had taught him in health class about arteries and stopping the flow of blood, Jim laid her down on the ground and began to yank the tiny white buttons of her bodice open.

Even stained as it was with blood, she had the prettiest, laciest brassiere he'd ever seen. He was a rat to even notice such a thing, to notice how full and pretty and pert her breasts were, especially at such a time, when maybe she was dying. He ripped off his own shirt to staunch the flow of red ooze that seemed to come from a jagged cut above her right nipple.

He wished a car would come by. Anybody.

The cut wasn't all that deep, and the blood stopped almost at once. He began to relax a little. Under his hand he felt the soft warm flesh of her breast. For a minute the guilty, forbidden thrill of touching her there disoriented him. Then slowly he grew aware of a steady pulsating rhythm beneath his fingertips.

It was her heart.

She was alive.

He hadn't killed her after all.

He was aware of a hawk soaring high in the vast blue sky. It was the happiest moment of his life.

"Open your eyes, girl," he coaxed in a low, soothing purr.

She just lay there, stubborn as always.

"Damn you, Fancy Hart, quit torturing me and open them now!"

"You don't have to cuss," she purred bossily in a low drowsy tone as her auburn lashes fluttered open. "I don't like boys who cuss 'cause cussin's dumb."

He hardly heard the sting of her words. He was noting that she had the prettiest green eyes.

"You always think you're so smart," he murmured almost tenderly.

"I know I'm a whole lot smarter than you."

"Then why'd you drive off the road, Smarty?"

"Because you were chasing me. Why—you ran me off it."

"Did not!"

But Jim lowered his head guiltily and saw his tanned hand on her white breast. *Lordy.* He swallowed, gulping against the knot of fear clogging his throat. Scared of the truly terrible tongue-lashing she'd probably give him for being fresh, he jumped back. What would she do? Who would she tattle to after she saw he'd ripped her dress to her waist and put his big hands all over her?

"What's the matter?" She surprised him with the softest, most seductive smile. "You look spooked. I thought big, tough quarterbacks were brave. I thought you knew everything there was to know about girls."

"Maybe you shouldn't move or talk," he growled, expecting her to attack him any second.

"Well, I certainly can't lie out here half naked all day, letting you paw me—especially since anybody could come by and catch us."

But when she struggled to sit up, she gave a painful gasp that hurt him nearly as much as it hurt her. Swiftly he leaned down and put his arms around her

to help her. But when he had her sitting up and would
have pulled away, she wouldn't let him go.

"Somebody really might come by and see us like
this," he said in a rough whisper when she kept clinging and pressing herself against him.

She lifted her eyes to his, but she didn't speak for
nearly a minute. "I don't much care," she murmured
boldly, softly, laying her head against his broad
shoulder. "I think you saved my life." Her breath was
like a warm caress. The thick red coils of her hair
tickled his chest.

His mouth went dry as the warmth of her body
seeped into him. He felt her softness molding the
harder contours of his muscular shoulders. He knew
he should get up, but somehow he was losing his will
to do so. He looked down and got an eyeful of breasts
and nipples again.

She was beautiful, so gosh-damned beautiful. And
he didn't want her to be. Suddenly it was all too
much—the fear, the inexplicable, illicit desire for the
most impossible girl in all the world.

"I gotta get you home," he said, his voice coming
out in an awed rasp.

Still she clung, sensing her power. "Not yet. I'm
awful scared." Her voice, usually so sharp, was
sweeter than honey. "Just hold me for a little while.
When you hold me, I don't feel nearly so dizzy."

Nobody had ever made him feel so strong or so
powerful.

She cuddled up closer and sighed trustingly, and he
caught his breath in shaky surprise when her hand
strayed across his thigh.

He was calming down because she was alive, and he was getting excited at the same moment from holding her when she was stripped to the waist, when her fingers moved along his leg. It was turning him on that, instead of blaming him for the accident, she saw him as a hero. She snuggled closer. Her innocent hand roamed with instinctive expertise. All too soon he felt surrounded by a heat wave of their own making.

"I'm sorry I called you dumb," she whispered a long time later. "I've always wanted to think everybody and everything around here was dumb, especially you—because I didn't ever want there to be anything that might tempt me to stay." Through half-closed lashes, Fancy glanced up at him.

His pulse leapt when he saw her gaze lingering on his mouth. "Why not?"

"Because there's more to the world than Purdee, and I want to see it. And the only time Mother or Daddy ever leave the farm is when they need a hydraulic hose or a pulley or maybe a new tractor blade. Their idea of excitement is riding around in our dusty old pickup and eating at Burger Boy."

"I reckon Purdee's not so different from other places. And I like Purdee pretty good."

She kept studying his mouth, and the soft, green fire that lit her eyes seemed wildly erotic. But her voice was mild, sweet, without its usual challenge. "And Purdee likes you just fine, too. But I don't fit in."

"'Cause you don't try to. I like you just fine, Fancy."

"Any girl would do for you," she murmured, licking her lips.

"Not anymore."

"Really?"

"You're something else." He smiled down at her.

"You are, too," she said softly.

He brought his hand to her face and curled a red tendril around his fingertip. "You've got the prettiest hair. It's so soft. In fact you're...real pretty...when you're nice."

"Maybe I was afraid to be nice," she said.

"I kind of liked you...even before you were nice."

"I liked you, too."

It was a strange conversation for him because he didn't usually get mushy with words.

With exquisite gentleness she leaned forward and kissed him, and the sudden, hot sweetness of her soft mouth on his, as well as the little quiver of sensation that went through her when he automatically deepened the kiss, stunned them both into silence. Again he would have pulled away, but her arms had wound around him until they were pressed so tightly together it seemed as if the heat of her body would fuse them into one. When his tongue touched the tip of hers, she clung more tightly in fierce possession. She was a natural at kissing, sighing and moaning, almost purring, right from the first, at least with him, and the kiss went on for a very long time, till he'd hardly been able to breathe.

In the weeks that had followed he had started dropping by her farm after football practice and his chores to see how she was doing. He had even borrowed a book or two and read them all the way to the end just to impress her. But she read a new book herself almost every day, and she was more interested in practicing up on her kissing.

"I can read by myself," she'd said wisely, snapping his book shut one day as she lead him out to the porch swing. Then her lips had claimed his eagerly, breathlessly. "I—I can't do this all by myself. Wouldn't want to, even if I could. Wouldn't want to do it with anybody but you, either."

When she was better, she found excuses to go into town by way of his daddy's farm when she figured he'd be driving the tractor. He would wave, and she'd pull over and watch him.

She made all the other girls seem too easy, too dull.

And it wasn't long before he realized he had made the horrible mistake of falling madly in love with a girl who was as different from him as day was from night, a girl who believed in dreams more than reality, a girl who pined for the moon and the stars when all he wanted was her.

Chapter Six

Hazel's hummingbird feeder swayed in the wind.

Fancy had to be inside the house.

With his fist poised an inch from her front door, Jim stood stubbornly on Hazel's porch. First he would find out if Fancy would sell him the farm. Then he would end this thing between himself and her once and for all.

So, why didn't Fancy make things easy for once and answer the damn door? Yeller had chased Old Blue, barking up a storm till he'd plum near worn his worthless self out. Then he'd wagged his tail sheepishly and settled himself on the Welcome mat in front of Hazel's door like he was still waiting for her.

Jim took off his Stetson and wiped his perspiring brow with his forearm. He'd knocked so long and so hard on her big door he'd durn near taken the hide off his knuckles.

He swallowed a long, impatient breath. Stepping way back from her door, he stared down at the scuffed toes of his high-heeled, mud-caked boots. They'd gotten filthy when he'd fixed a pump that had gone bad in one of his tanks.

He went over to a step and began scraping the dried mud off. Then he went back and knocked again. Finally he peeked under the shades of the tall windows into the darkened house while he fanned himself with his hat.

He walked back and forth and again came to a standstill. From the shadiest part of the veranda, he eyed Hazel's swing, remembering how he'd sat there with Fancy sipping iced drinks, talking and whispering, in between kissing.

The scent of sweet clover, sun-warmed hay and ripening blackberries took the edge off his mood, carrying him back to those happier, carefree days. Maybe Fancy hadn't been all that keen on school sports or socializing with the other Purdee kids, but her book learning had honed a mighty powerful imagination. She'd been curious to see the world and to find out about sex, wanting to try stuff with him that she'd read about in her books. From the start, she'd been hot, and in no time at all she'd gotten a whole lot hotter. And that, above all else, had finally gotten him interested in book reading.

The veranda wrapped the big house on three sides, and he walked all the way around it, calling Fancy's name. Not that he got an answer other than the tinkle of Hazel's wind chimes. But he wasn't about to leave. Not with Fancy's rental car parked in the drive beside Hazel's ancient Dodge.

Finally he gave the front door a shove and stepped inside. Without Hazel to remind him to scrape his boots, he forgot. Then later when he saw the chunks of dirt on the floor and remembered, the empty house was so cool and dark and dead-feeling without Hazel, he didn't figure it much mattered.

Pictures had been taken down from the walls and were stacked neatly. Boxes overflowed with Hazel's jeans and boots and her wide-brimmed straw hats.

His boots echoed on the wooden floors as he walked quickly past Fancy's piano, through the high-ceilinged rooms, pausing in the dining room to lift an emerald green goblet out of a box and hold it to the light. Thunking it with a fingernail, it made a sweet crystalline note. This particular habit of his had always annoyed Hazel who'd come running from wherever she was to snatch it out of his hand.

A curtain fluttered at the window, and for a moment he smiled, suspecting Hazel's ghost. There was a sound outside, and then his attention was caught by the galloping black horse at the far end of the pasture and the beautiful woman with flame-dark hair who was riding him.

Jim set the goblet down on the maple dining room table so hard he nearly broke it. That's when he saw the stacks of fashion sketches Fancy must have made lying beside a newly installed fax machine. Curious, Jim thumbed through six of seven faxes from some hysteric called Claude who kept insisting she return to New York at once. Fancy has made a slashing X through a faxed drawing of a black evening gown with leather bondage straps Claude had signed.

Then suddenly Jim's gaze fell to three very charming charcoal drawings of Oscar and Omar petting Yeller in that patch of primroses down by Hazel's windmill. There was a watercolor of the twins sipping iced drinks with Yeller sprawled across their laps on the porch swing.

Jim lifted the drawings, liking them so much, a lump formed in his throat. Then he tossed them down again, cursing silently. Fancy had gone behind his back and deliberately made friends with his kids. Why had she taken the time? She had said she never wanted kids.

He pulled the legal documents regarding the sale of the farm out of his back pocket, unfolded them and pressed them out flat on the table beside Fancy's sketches of the boys. Then he went outside, angrier than ever. Since he didn't watch where he was going, he ran smack-dab into Hazel's wind chimes. It took him a second to get himself untangled.

It was late afternoon, and the slanting light was tinting the boards a golden rose where it struck the white clapboard house. The long shadows under the eaves of the unpainted barn on the opposite side of the pasture had gone almost purple.

He'd forgotten Fancy's habit of riding at this hour. He sure did like the sight of a pretty woman on a good horse. And nobody in the whole town could ride better than Fancy. Maybe because nobody else had had so many expensive lessons.

Jim walked out onto the field, picking his way along the rutted clay gullies in the middle of the pasture that was choked with thistle. Yeller came chasing after him from around the house.

There were dark cottonwoods and a line of salt cedars on one side of the field and barren dusty countryside on the other. The grasslands that he coveted for his dairy herd lay in a deep violet haze as he strode up the faint rise. High above him, a pair of turkey buzzards soared lazily.

Fancy saw the man and the dog suddenly and reined in her mount. Jim stopped in the middle of the field.

Each studied the other for a long moment under that vast, purpling sky.

He felt a great quiet, a terrible stillness. The dangerous beginning of something new and grand.

Fancy seemed to fill the huge emptiness of the landscape, the huge emptiness of his life. Over English riding boots and jodhpurs, her red cotton serape curled in the breeze, shaping itself in voluptuous folds against her slim body. She carried a riding crop. Her horse was a black aculeo, a small, stocky breed brought to the New World by the conquistadors, and much favored by Hazel.

With a muted cry Fancy struck the horse and galloped wildly—straight at him. Old Yeller took off like a bullet.

Jim's heart quickened, and he would have flinched if she had been anybody else. Instead he stood his ground as stubbornly as she charged toward him.

Even when she didn't draw her reins until the last possible second, even when he was sure she intended to trample him to death, he gritted his teeth and dug his heels in deeper, forcing himself to stay where he was. Finally, when she pulled back hard, her steed skidded flashily to a halt, thrusting its hind legs forward.

She'd always been a spectacular rider—in perfect control. She still was.

But his own legs were shaking, and he was clammy and vaguely nauseated.

Jim felt the horse's hot breath mere inches from his bloodless cheek, and beads of terror trickled down his spine. His heart was racing violently. Deep within him an all-enveloping rage began to build in the aftermath of his fear.

Fancy's dazzling maneuver was a rodeo stunt she'd learned when Hazel had sent her to Peru. Fancy had performed it before, but never quite so dramatically. Never at the risk of his own life.

He willed the wild rush of blood and fear and sickening excitement in his head to lessen a little. But as he stared up at Fancy, he just got madder.

Furious, without thinking, Jim reached up and, grabbing her by her wrists, dragged her down from her horse.

When her boot caught in her stirrup, he pulled harder. Then he yanked the riding crop from her, snapped it in half and threw it on the ground. "What the hell were you trying to do, kill me?"

Her red, perfectly outlined lips curved. She lifted her chin ever so proudly, defiantly. For a long moment she didn't answer. But when she did, her honeyed voice was soft and cool. "Would you have let me?"

"Would you have killed me?"

She stared at him stubbornly and then casually began unfastening her leather riding gloves. "That is the last thing I would ever want to do."

"Then just what were you trying to prove?"

"I think you know," she whispered huskily, putting her slim, soft hands on either side of his flushed face. "I had to know how far you'd go to prove yourself to me. I had to know if you're still the same macho idiot I fell in love with."

"And?"

"You're even *worse* than before. You stubborn fool, you should have run from me."

So—she'd been teasing him, goading him into losing his temper, playing with him, like he was still her toy. "You always could bring out the self-destructive worst in me." He jerked her closer. "I almost feel like killing you myself."

"I don't think our needs are nearly so simple."

"What do you mean?"

"Why did you insult me at my mother's funeral and then drive off like a coward?"

Coward. His lips thinned at her taunt.

"Gracie sent me over to apologize for that," he muttered.

Fancy's mouth curved. "That's not why you came."

"You always think you know everything," he said.

"I know what I know. You're the one who's afraid to admit the truth."

His eyes narrowed. "Which is?"

She pressed her body into his. And before he could argue or push her away, her lush mouth was on his, hot and seeking and ravenous and so wonderful, that all his arguments were shattered by the wildness of the emotions her exploring lips aroused.

"I have missed you, missed this," she murmured hungrily a long time later, not seeming to mind the stubble of his hard cheek against her smooth skin, not seeming to mind that he smelled faintly of sweat and mud and his dirty cattle tank.

He was so shaken by his unwanted desire for her that he was in no shape to say much. On a raw, husky note he said, "You left me, damn you. If you missed me so much, why the hell did you stay away?"

"Well, I'm sorry for that and for everything else." She tried to kiss him again. "But I'm here now."

"Not good enough," he muttered, pushing her away. "Besides, we both know that nothing on earth could keep you here for long. Go back to New York, Fancy. The sooner, the better."

The way she looked at him then—like her soul was in her wide, green eyes—shook him. "You're just as stubborn about thinking you know everything as I am." Her voice was unnaturally quiet, and somehow that shook him, too. "Look, I've got to see to my horse—cool him down."

Jim was nearly sure there were tears in her eyes when she turned away, nearly sure her slim shoulders trembled as she made the low, strangled whistle that brought the aculeo galloping obediently back to her.

Jim watched Fancy lift her slim fingers to secure the stirrup iron at the top of the leather strap beneath the flap. She stroked the black muzzle and then gently picked up the dragging reins and led the animal toward the barn. There was a defeated slump to her shoulders that he'd never seen before.

This might be just another ploy. Still, he thought about Hazel dying, about how Fancy might really be lonely out here with no friends, about how hard it was going through her mother's things, about how he should say something sweet to comfort her. But he was too afraid of his other more dangerous feelings, afraid that somehow she'd lure him into admitting what he didn't want to admit.

So instead he said coldly, "If you decide to sell the farm, I left the papers in the house. Hazel already agreed—"

"I'll take a look at them and let you know…later," Fancy murmured, but her voice was dead, as though she was fighting as hard as he was not to feel.

Was he just some game to her? Or did a woman like her have real feelings?

He wanted to go to her so badly, he felt his heavy muscles pulling under his skin.

He kicked a dry dirt clod in disgust. Then another while he fought to remind himself that he had to end it now, that she had been the biggest mistake in his life, that he would forget her in time if she sold out and left.

"And another thing," he called after her, causing her to turn. "I'm not taking your Yeller."

"Omar and Oscar want him."

"Don't try to come between me and my kids."

"I wasn't," she pleaded softly. "I—I just wanted to meet them. They remind me of you—at the same age. You used to run wild and act tough, just to get everybody's attention, before you took up football."

"You stay the hell away from them."

Her face went so blank and white even her eyes seemed to lose their color.

She chewed on her lip as if she wanted to say something. Then she just watched as he turned grimly to go.

But with every triumphant step he trudged away from her, his boots sank more heavily into the hard earth and his mind grew gloomier. His heart sputtered so jerkily he felt an almost wild tearing in his chest.

The wind chimes were tinkling sweetly from her veranda when he swung wildly around again.

But she had already vanished behind the big, old, tumbledown barn that he'd been nagging Hazel forever to make Pablo fix. For once Buster was nibbling grass contentedly in one of the work pens.

Jim felt all alone. Fancy had set him free. He hadn't let on how much he still felt. He could go back to Gracie, to their perfect life.

But as he stared wildly up at the vast, darkening sky, contemplating their future, never had he felt so empty and hopeless.

Time as he knew it had stopped. Desire for Fancy raced through his veins and licked along his nerves, filling him with an unbearable pain. The years of his life seemed to stretch before him. Without Fancy, some part of him would die.

How could he marry Gracie when all he could think of was Fancy?

He was mad, insane to do it, but he cupped his hands and yelled Fancy's name to the sky. To the world. Again and again, and the wretched, agonized cry that seemed torn out of him vanished on the warm wind.

Fancy had won. He had lost.

But he would hold her naked body in his arms and sink his rock-hard body into hers one more time. He would kiss her, taste her. He would devour her so thoroughly she would carry the hot imprint of his hard mouth on her flesh forever.

In the next instant he was moving blindly up the slight hill, despising himself as he stumbled across the uneven, dry furrows. When he saw her walking the horse in the back paddock, he sank to his knees and

watched her, only getting up again after he saw her
lead the aculeo into the darkness of the barn.

If she had been bad for him before, she was worse
now.

His kids' happiness was at stake as well as his own.
Their whole lives hung in the balance.

But he had to have her—no matter what it cost him.

Chapter Seven

"Fancy—" Jim called hoarsely as he entered the barn.

He remembered the spring afternoon he and Fancy had played in this barn after milking time. They'd chased the chickens around the yard, and then they'd started chasing each other. He'd caught her in the loft, and they'd made love that first time there.

Jim swallowed, fighting the sudden constriction in his throat, fighting for every raspy breath.

He knew he should go.

But he stood without moving and let the cool dark quiet of the barn close around him. After the brightness of the sun, all he could see were the odd shapes and lopsided shadows of the stacked hay bales.

Then the aculeo snickered and stomped from the corner stall, and he heard Fancy crooning soft words of comfort. Jim called to her again, but she just hushed up completely like she was scared to answer him back.

He stormed toward the stall and then kicked the door open so hard it banged against the wooden wall. Startled, Fancy jumped back as the aculeo side-stepped nervously.

"Easy, easy," she whispered in a low tone, ignoring Jim and concentrating on the skittish horse as she lifted the heavy saddle off the aculeo's back.

Jim strode toward her. When he took the heavy saddle, Fancy's green eyes went wide and soft. "I thought you'd gone."

"No, you knew all along you'd win and I'd lose." His deep, hard voice came with difficulty through lips that were as dry as dust.

"No..."

But her whole face seemed to fill with light as she watched him heave the saddle over the top edge of the stall. She said nothing more. She just went about what she was doing as though he weren't there, removing the bridle and then turning on the hose, running the cool water over the aculeo.

"Where's Pablo?" Jim asked.

She cut off the faucet. "I gave him the day off."

As she brushed the horse, Jim crept up behind her, so that when she stepped back a bit with her dripping brush, their bodies touched.

He felt the electricity leap like a silent fire sparking the air between them. He felt the treacherous tingle of it for a long time, singeing him from his scalp to his toes, even when she went back to rubbing the horse. He rocked back on his heels and stood there with his hands in his back pockets, just watching her, his body heating, his jeans stretching tighter against his need as he took in every graceful movement of her slim figure and trembling hands. He was remembering how good she'd always been to her animals.

When she was done, she turned to him breathlessly.

Suddenly the barn seemed too hot—almost airless.

She looked so young and luminous. And not at all like the clever, sophisticated star of the international set she was reputed to be. She seemed more like the girl he had loved, like the girl he'd taken in the loft on a soft spring day.

He felt a dazzling explosion of longing.

Damn her for making him so craven. "I thought you'd never finish," he whispered, taking the brush from her and placing it on a shelf.

"I'm a little nervous," she said in a shy, soft tone.

He laughed harshly—at himself. At her. "Yeah, right, like you're scared, too."

"I am."

"Liar." He took her hand and drew her out of the stall and pulled her to him hard. "I'm the one who should be running for my life." But his hard mouth slanted across hers.

Her welcoming arms slid around his neck, and the moist warmth of her kisses was wild and frantic. His tongue was inside of her, tasting, devouring. Soon she was quivering every time his lips touched her, every time his rough hands caressed her, as though she felt the same, starved longing he felt.

He wanted to hate her. Instead as he shoved her up against the rough, wooden wall, imprisoning her with his heavy arms, he knew that her very existence brought him into being. The barn smelled of hay and the aculeo, but more powerful than that was Fancy's sweet, feminine scent.

For a long time he stood there, kissing her, savoring her with his mouth, stroking her bright hair with his hands. Then he lifted her against his body and molded her to himself so that she felt his masculine need. She was so light, so slim and fragile against his superior crushing strength. He knew it was chauvin-

istic to savor her helplessness, but he reveled in whatever tiny power he had over her.

She cried out when his hands found their way beneath the serape to fondle her breasts. Ripping her
silk-covered buttons apart, he whispered hotly in her
ear that she had the sexiest body of any woman alive,
that he wanted to lick and kiss her nipples and her navel and her womanhood. She gasped. He felt her are-
olae pucker under his caressing thumbs. Her fingers
dug into his scalp.

"You're so good with your hands," she murmured
on a shiver, wrapping her arms around him and hugging him tighter.

Who else had she said such things to? How many
other men had she let pleasure her like this?

His mouth curled in jealous, murderous revulsion
at the thought of other men. Until he remembered this
was not the time to torture himself by dwelling on the
life she'd lead away from him, or on the probability
that she was just doing this because she was bored and
lonely.

His kisses roughened. His tongue was in her mouth.
With his hands around her, he sank to his knees because he no longer had the strength to stand. Then he
fumbled with his belt buckle.

"Not here," she whispered raggedly, slowly pushing him away and leading him to the ladder that went
up to the loft.

High, under the topmost eaves, she drew the serape
over her head and spread it on top of the fresh hay. He
watched, remembering again that first time when
she'd been a virgin.

She'd been so shy, he'd had to undress her.

He wanted her more now than he had then.

Slowly she unbound her hair, and he watched as the hairpins rained one by one to the floor and the gleaming masses of silken tangles danced down to her shoulders.

He felt a terrible ache in his heart, an endless need as he drank in the sight of her. She was so beautiful he hurt.

"Ever since you called me in France, I haven't been able to get you out of my mind." She bent at the waist to pull off a butter-soft riding boot.

It crossed his mind that her damned boots probably cost more than one of his cows. "So you figure this will get me out of your system?" he growled bitterly.

"Is that really what you think?" Her eyes filled with dark pain.

But when she didn't deny it, he guessed, then, that he had her figured. So—she was using him for sex because she was lonely.

He almost hated her because he wanted so much more.

She finished unbuttoning her silk blouse and stripped out of it. Slowly she unhooked her transparent bra. Her breasts swung free, and she looked so cute, wearing nothing except her jodhpurs, he forgot his anger.

Wild heat raced up from between his loins.

He loved her. He had always loved her.

There was no help for a fool like him. She would leave him again, the same as she had before. She'd kiss him and then tell him goodbye with a pretty smile. And he'd be in hell forever.

She slid her jodhpurs down, and he grabbed her before they had reached her knees, tugging them down her long, slim legs.

She tore his shirt off and unbuckled his belt. Next she slid her hand to the zipper of his jeans, and he throbbed at that first light touch.

Then he was naked, too, and her fingers felt cool, so cool against the hard, flaming warmth of his tight skin.

The last rays of the setting sun seeped through the cracks of the barn and made her hair glow like fire. With her pale skin and blazing emerald eyes, she was flawlessly beautiful in the murky half light as he pulled her under him and kissed her mouth, her face, her ears, and her throat, making love to her with hungry, reckless abandon.

He wanted to go slow, but he was panting like a hard-run horse. She was just as silent, just as frantically impatient. They both sought the same goal. He felt like he'd die if he didn't find again the blazing glory he had once known and lived so long without.

And soon, too soon, on that bed of prickly hay, she brought him to the most mutually satisfying climax of his life. He reveled in the hot, sweet taste of her, in the fluid, velvet tightness of her. Her hands dug into his back as she arched forward, weeping and moaning as the tumultuous waves swept her, too.

In a single flash he was whole again. She was warmth and love; life itself. She was everything he had lived without for ten dark years.

Even when it was over, and they were lying in the loft, their fingertips touching, their bodies wet and limp, it wasn't over. Not for him. His entire life had changed as irrevocably as it had the first time he'd taken her here. He couldn't imagine that he could ever survive without her again.

Tears beaded her lashes as she lay on her side in the dark, staring into his eyes. Instinct told him he was getting in too deep, too fast, with a woman who was all wrong. He knew he should maintain some shred of independence and treat her coolly so she would not guess what she meant to him.

Instead he was tender. Instead he helped her dress. When they got to her house, he made love to her again on her antique pine bed that smelled of lavender in a room with yellowing cherry wallpaper and to the tinkle of Hazel's wind chimes. And the second time was wilder and sweeter than the first.

Afterward he slept while she clasped him tightly in her arms and played with his hair. When he awoke to the warmth of her body tangled in his, she said she was hungry and that she didn't have a thing in her kitchen. No way could he take her into the town's only café, Burger Boy. But she acted so helpless, like she'd starve if he didn't feed her, he reluctantly invited her to dinner in San Antonio.

When she smiled and nodded, he called Sudi, who lived in a cottage on his farm, and asked her to watch the twins. Sudi said she'd make sure Tubby saw to the herd.

After that, her phone rang, but Fancy let the machine answer it.

"Fanc-e-e-e . . ." an excited male voice screamed.

Fancy smiled. "That's Claude, my new partner. He goes crazy anytime I'm gone."

When Claude hung up, she took the phone off the hook.

After she showered, Fancy put on a filmy, black sundress that made Jim want her again. Then Yeller chased them through a swirl of shimmering fireflies to his truck. When Jim opened the door, a beer can toppled off the dash. Fancy started laughing as he gathered up the junk from the floorboards of Old Blue— magazines and flyers, old socks, and then his crumpled silk tie—and pitched them all into the back seat. When she brought a trash can, he refused to throw anything away.

"Not even a gum wrapper?" she asked, picking one up off the floor and tickling his nose with it.

Gently he snatched it away. "No. I damn near live in this truck, and I might throw out something important."

"You couldn't find it in all this garbage if you ever needed to. You need a better system."

"Don't boss me, Fancy. Not tonight."

They stopped at the pond so she could pick some of the wild dark violets Hazel had planted there. Fancy carried them to her mother's grave. She told him that Hazel would have liked them being together again. Jim ran his fingers over the engraved letters that spelled Hazel's name on that freshly carved granite marker and studied Fancy's kneeling figure and reflected on that.

Then they were driving through silvery fields of sorghum and cotton in a hushed silence beneath a vast, black sky peppered with white stars. He was dodging rabbits that raced in front of his headlights.

It was a warm, wonderful night. Or maybe it was just the joy he found in Fancy that made it seem wonderful. He was so caught up in her spell, he would have run out of gas if she hadn't pointed to the needle quivering on E. They stopped at a station that was about to close, bought soft drinks, sipping from each other's bottle. They watched crickets swarm up to the lights and laughed shyly over almost nothing. He pointed out the constellation, Orion, and she told him she never saw stars in Manhattan.

"Well, I'm glad Purdee's got something on New York," he had teased.

She had laughed and touched his lips with her fingers and said Purdee had more to attract her than the stars. He had wanted to tell her that the prettiest stars of all were those sparkling in her eyes when she looked at him.

Then once again they were speeding along those familiar, moon-dark, country roads with the same eager excitement they'd felt when they'd raced along them as kids. He pulled her close and laced his long, calloused fingers through hers. She turned on the radio, somehow remembering and choosing his favorite kicker station.

Country and Western music throbbed into the darkened cab, the plaintive melodies echoing the timeless emotions he felt for her. She got real quiet when the next song that came on was the one that used to be their song. She began to sing, about getting married in a fever, and he began to tease her like he used to—'cause, smart as she was, carrying a tune was the one thing Fancy still couldn't do.

Her hair was tangled from their lovemaking, her
face deliciously soft and languorous, her eyes remote
and unfocusing when she pretended to concentrate on
the road or what he was saying. There seemed a fragile dreamlike quality, a tenderness to her mood. The
strap on her sundress kept sliding sexily off her shoulder, and it was all he could do to keep his hands off her
and his eyes on the highway.

By the time they reached the outskirts of the glitter
that was San Antonio and its suburbs, he was consumed by curiosity to know who Fancy really was
now.

So he began asking her questions and forcing himself not to say he couldn't believe people would pay the
outrageous prices she charged for her clothes. The
hardest part was forcing himself to confide in her, too.

She wanted to know about his dairy, about Nottie
and how she'd died. Then Fancy told him about Oscar and Omar sneaking over to Hazel's every day since
the funeral to sit on her porch swing or to pet Yeller
while he moped in front of Hazel's door. Fancy's voice
went real soft when she told him that the twins had
said that they knew how sad and lonely she and old
Yeller felt since their own mother had died and their
daddy had worked most all the time ever since; that
he'd quit taking them hunting or to fairs; that they got
so lonely sometimes they almost wished he'd take
them back to Sunday school.

Jim swallowed a lump at the thought of two wild
outlaws like his Oscar and Omar going over every day
to console Fancy and a dog because they knew about
loneliness firsthand. And he figured, then, that
somehow Fancy had bested him again and that that

damn-fool, chicken-chasing Yeller was as good as his pup. But Jim didn't mind so much about Yeller or even about Fancy making friends with his twins anymore.

He found himself talking almost easily to his glamorous, world-famous career woman, telling her of the happy times mostly on the farm, but of the sad times when Nottie had been sick, too.

Fancy described her own life in Paris and New York. She told him about spending so much time in hotel rooms and different houses that no place really ever felt like home. She told him about how hard it was to keep up the frantic pace of managing a business on two continents, of juggling the money, of enduring the crazy panic of preparing collections and putting on fashion shows. She told him more about Claude, who'd pestered her every day she'd been in Purdee. She described the fight for department store orders, the difficulty of dealing with the jealousies and egos of her assistant designers. She amused him with stories of famous models and flamboyant photographers who too often strove for pictures that would make a name for themselves instead of shots that would set off her clothes to best advantage.

Finally she touched on her bitter loneliness and on the terrifying creative block that had plagued her for more than a year. He began to understand the dark side of creativity, the terror and depression of her own frozen mind when her talent had deserted her and there was the unrelenting pressure to churn out more designs as well as the incessant hype about other designers who seemed to create effortlessly.

"I started off on my knees with pins between my teeth in a fitting room. It took me forever to convince people I had talent. Then I had to build a reputation. After that I had to make the scene—parties, summer weekends in the Hamptons, so the right people would wear my clothes. I worked and partied to the exclusion of all else. I should have stopped and made time for fun, love, marriage or children. But I was hot and scared that to stay hot I had to see and be seen all the time. That's why Jacques walked out."

Her voice grew soft when she said Jim's telephone call about her mother's death had been a wakeup call.

"Maybe you just needed a rest," Jim said at last.

"Or maybe I strayed too far away from the path of my heart. I'm afraid my success has given me more pain than pleasure for a very long time."

"So what do you want in your future?" His question felt charged somehow.

"Sometimes . . . like tonight, I have the wildest fantasy of giving it all up. Of letting Claude run the show—" When she looked at Jim longingly, the muscles in his throat tightened with some fierce, unwanted emotion. "Then Claude makes some crazy mistake."

"You'll never quit, Fancy." Jim's low voice caught.

"I—I'm sure you're right," she said desperately.

But he felt the pull of her hot, troubled eyes on his face again. The pull of his own unspoken needs.

"I feel so good with you, Jim. So...so...incredibly happy."

"Honey, just 'cause we slept together you don't have to pretend tonight meant something if it doesn't."

"So, was it just sex—for you?"

"You were lonely."

"I can't stand it when you think you know what I'm thinking—when I don't know myself," she said with a new edge to her voice. "Why did you sleep with me? What do you feel, Jim King, for me?"

He pressed his lips together and stared into the flying darkness.

"Not that you'd say. You'd rather die first." Her voice trailed off miserably. Still, he felt her watching him as if she were hanging on his answer.

He kept quiet, of course, finally saying grimly, "Honey, I have a life, kids. I can't afford lies, false hopes."

"Well, neither can I."

"I don't want to fight tonight, Fancy," he whispered.

But the old tensions and half truths had crept into the cab. He didn't know what to expect from her, so he couldn't trust her. She hadn't given him much to go on, but maybe he hadn't given her much, either. Still, it was too soon to spit out his feelings. So he pulled her close and said no more. She eased up on him, too—till they got to the restaurant on the river. There they talked again, but about other things. Which meant the tension stayed there between them.

After dinner he would have taken her home but she said she was having too good a time and that she wanted to go slow-dancing the way they used to.

Impatiently he led her through the throng that ambled along the river walk—raucous teenagers in shorts and message T-shirts, kids pitching popcorn to the pigeons under the palms and ferns, fat tourists with

Camcorders, mothers toting babies in carriers, lovers walking hand-in-hand. There was too much jostling and too much noise. The thick black haze of diesel smoke from the riverboats burned his lungs. He had to dodge crowded tables and umbrellas jammed along the river's edge. Jim didn't like the packed, carnival atmosphere the way Fancy did. But then, that figured.

He took her to a nightclub that had once been an old limestone warehouse. There they danced away from the crowded dance floor, wrapped in each other's arms, swaying endlessly on their own balcony overlooking the river. Dancing close got him wildly aroused again, and every time the music stopped he pulled her against the wall and kissed her like some sex-starved teenager. Not that she seemed to mind.

She said she was thirsty, so he bought her a bottle of French champagne. Only, the bubbly froth slid down his parched throat more easily than it did hers, and he drank most of the bottle. Soon he was so high on Fancy and champagne, he recklessly ordered another.

Which turned out to be the biggest mistake of his life.

'Cause while she just sipped a little and dazzled him with her sparkling eyes, he drank most of that one, too.

The next morning he woke up in a strange hotel bed, surrounded by expensive, impersonal-looking, Formica-topped furniture. He felt queasy and sick to his stomach with his eyelids aching hotly the way they did when he was down with a fever.

He got the shock of his life when he saw Fancy, curled up in a warm, naked ball, snuggling against him, and he saw the brand new gold wedding band gleaming on her finger.

Lordy.

He stared so fixedly at that ring it swam in and out of focus.

Then at Fancy whose tangled red hair was all over his pillow.

There was a contented curve to her red lips.

His heart began to bang like a sledgehammer as he remembered the judge and the middle-of-the-night ceremony. And then everything else came back to him, too.

What the hell had he done?

Chapter Eight

When he opened the door, Fancy stirred drowsily. "Jim?"

His name seemed to float away on a hazy wisp of sound as she nervously felt for her new wedding ring to make sure it was real.

He turned back to her, his gray face hard and set in the shadowy light, his eyes unreadable. "It's early. I didn't mean to wake you."

A heavy, dark tension snaked around her heart.

His harsh voice was worse than a thousand bad reviews of one of her collections in *Women's Wear Daily*.

He was sorry about last night.

For a second her mouth was too dry to speak and she could only stare at him. He was so lean and hard-looking, so devastatingly handsome with his tousled, blue-black hair and sleepy, whiskey-colored eyes. She wanted to beg him to come back to the bed, to take her in his arms, to kiss and caress her, to tell her he loved her.

He shoved a hotel key deep in his hip pocket and pushed the door open wider.

"Why are you leaving?" she managed weakly, hugging the sheets closer around her icy body.

He set his Stetson on his black head and then pushed it back to that jaunty angle, the way he always wore it. Only the gesture was wearier and grimmer than usual.

"'Cause I need air, girl.'' His grim, anguished eyes slid over her. "I expect you need to think on this thing, too. I—I must've been plum drunk out of my mind to do such a damn-fool crazy thing as to marry you. And before you go getting yourself all riled up, don't think for a second I intend to hold you to it.''

All riled up. When her heart was flying to pieces. When she was dissolving with pain, and his cold voice and stern face were killing her.

"Then you want a divorce?" she whispered.

For a moment he hesitated.

She held her breath. Dear God, let him say anything but that. Something seemed to break inside her as his forbidding, dark golden gaze slid indifferently from her misting green eyes to the curve of her mouth. Last night when he'd been drunk, her charms had swept him off his feet. But this morning when he was stone-cold sober, the sight of her made his mouth thin with savage pain.

"Sure, honey," he muttered in a low, dead tone. "Whatever you want."

As if he didn't care.

From the river below came a burst of children's laughter.

Fancy looked wildly toward the balcony.

When she turned back, he was gone, the door slamming behind him.

"Jim—" She got out of bed and ran naked to the door. When she cracked it, the long, maroon hall was empty. From around the corner the elevator bell sounded.

"Jim!"

The heavy doors opened and closed, and he was gone.

Had last night meant nothing, then? Worse, did he despise her for it? Not that she would blame him.

She dragged herself to the shower. Hot water blasted her, but she felt cold. So cold. The radiant happiness she'd felt when Jim had eagerly rousted the old district judge out of his bed to sign their emergency wedding license had faded to despair.

She remembered how Jim had playfully set his huge Stetson on her small head before lifting her in his arms and carrying her over their threshold. How he'd smiled when she'd started kissing him as soon as he'd shut the door. How seconds later he'd pulled her down on the bed, teasing, "You're a sex maniac, Mrs. King. Not that I mind. That's why I married you."

He had taken his time once he'd had her naked, waiting until her whole being felt like it was aflame. And knowing that she was his wife as he made love to her had brought her an exquisite joy she had never dreamed possible. Afterward, as she had lain beside him, she had hoped that he had given her a child.

Now as she turned off the water and reached for a towel, she saw the empty bed in the mirror. Loneliness washed over her. She lifted her filmy black dress from its hanger and began to cry as she remembered Jim's eager hands taking it off.

Then she twisted her hair up on top of her head in a severe knot. She applied her makeup with a trembling hand, blushing with shame every time she looked at her pale features.

She'd done everything short of hog-tying him to lure him into her bed. At the funeral she had goaded him into grabbing her to make him look bad to the narrow-minded town. She'd befriended his sons and his naive girlfriend who'd sent him over to apologize.

The rest had been child's play.

All her life Fancy had figured her odds and played her hunches. Usually she got lucky. But sometimes she went too far. She remembered the third-grade Easter party when she'd stormed down to her party naked to get even with her mother. Only her mother hadn't followed her. All the children had started snickering and pointing. Except for Jim, who'd seen through her boldness to her shame.

He'd ripped off his shirt and covered her. Then he'd pitched a football hard into Bo Bo's chest and gotten the kids playing. That was when she had started liking Jim and fighting to pretend she didn't. His seeing through her boldness and rescuing her had scared her more than anything.

Boldness had carried her to the top of her career.

Boldness had made her fling her engagement ring in Jim's face and choose ambition over love.

Boldness had destroyed her.

When Fancy finished at the mirror, and Jim still hadn't returned, she grew frantic. Afraid to leave, afraid to stay, she went out onto the balcony.

Beneath her in the balmy, early morning heat, happy couples were drinking coffee at a sidewalk café beside the sluggish brown river. Fancy scanned the tables for Jim, but he wasn't there.

In a panic she dialed the garage, but the man said Jim's truck was still there. Next she called the front desk and then hung up before anybody answered.

Finally she called Claude.

At her voice, Claude screamed accusingly, "Fanc-e-e-e. Do you know how hard I've been trying to reach you?"

"I'm sorry." She held the phone way back from her ear.

"I need you here! Today!"

"Claude, I—I got married. To Jim."

"You what?" Claude was a New Yorker through and through, and there was profound horror in his hushed question before he lapsed into an addled silence. At last he managed the appropriate cliché. "I hope you'll be very happy."

Happy? Her red mouth trembled and she thought she might cry. She bit her lip. "Oh, yes. Thank you." Finally she asked, "Claude, why did you need me?"

"Oh.... Because... I—I didn't want to tell you like this . . . not over the phone. But I've found the money to meet your price and buy you out."

"Claude, I never agreed to sell—"

"But I can read between the lines. Even before your mother died, your heart wasn't in the business. Now you've married this . . . this farmer. My backers won't move until they meet you. They're in town tonight. Tomorrow they fly to Japan. I'd like to get the ball rolling. If you don't come today, it might mean a delay for months. If they lose their enthusiasm altogether, it means never. And they won't give me the money without a commitment from you."

"Like what?"

"They want you to promise you'll oversee the company from afar, at least for two years. You know I'll let you work as much as you want after that. Fanc-e-e-e, please come."

Claude was offering her a way out of the business; a way to start over. She would have the freedom to do anything in the world she wanted to do. She could be a wife. A mother.

She pressed her wedding band to her lips and whispered a silent prayer. If she agreed, she was probably throwing her whole life away.

"I'll be on the next plane," came her muted whisper. "But I can only stay for a couple of days."

Pacing back and forth in the lobby of her hotel and eyeing her watch dozens of times every few seconds, Fancy was miserably tense.

What was the use of waiting any longer? Jim had been gone for hours. It was pretty obvious he didn't want to come back.

Still, she paced until there was less than an hour before her plane. Only then did she scribble a message for him and race with it to the front desk. Even when she was outside on the curb, she kept fidgeting and scanning the street and the hotel entrances while the doorman whistled for a cab.

When her cab whizzed up, she climbed into the back seat and just sat there feeling forlorn.

The stocky cabbie adjusted his rearview mirror impatiently with a hairy hand and eyed her with contemptuous dark eyes. "Where to, lady?"

She peered reluctantly over her shoulder at the empty street.

"Lady?" The cabbie's voice had roughened with disdainful annoyance.

"Start your meter," she said softly. "But give me a minute."

She stared at the empty sidewalk until it blurred.

He wasn't coming.

"Lady?" the obnoxious cabbie demanded.

"To the airport, I guess," she whispered. "I'm late. I'll pay you double if you hurry."

Just as the cab shot off the curb, Jim bolted out of the hotel garage crying Fancy's name.

A yellow traffic light flashed. Fancy screamed. And the cabbie stomped on the accelerator.

"Stop!" Fancy yelled at him just as Jim lunged in front of the cab waving his Stetson.

"Damn crazy cowboy!" Rubber burned black marks into the pavement as the cabbie furiously jerked the wheel to his right.

There was a soft thud as Jim was pitched lightly across the hood and hurled back to the street. Fancy was thrown forward as the cab slammed into a parked car.

Glass and chrome shattered.

All Fancy saw was Jim sprawled lifelessly on the street.

Dear God! Was he dead?

Sputtering with rage, the short-tempered cabbie sprang out and hauled Jim up by his collar. "Look what you did to my cab!"

A siren screamed. Red lights flashed as a cop on a motorcycle roared up.

The cabbie rammed Jim hard against his cab, pummeling his dark face with his hard fists.

"Hold it!" The cop swung a heavy leg over his bike and swaggered over.

In a daze, Jim began struggling with his assailant. Finally he managed to get in a lick or two. Then the cabbie punched him in the gut.

Jim doubled over. The cabbie opened a knife and sprang at him viciously. "You crazy, son of a—"

As Jim drew back his fist and lunged, the cabbie jumped deftly aside. And the cop rushed full-force into Jim's fist.

Knuckle shattered jawbone. The big officer crumpled over, falling so heavily against Fancy's window, the whole cab rocked. The cabbie pocketed his knife just as another police car raced up and Fancy got out.

The cop lay at her feet. Jim's nose was swollen and his hand looked red and broken. Blood dribbled from his brow. The hulking cabbie smiled at everybody malevolently.

His hand on his gun, the second cop got out of his car.

"Officer, I didn't do nothin'. This damned lunatic in the cowboy hat threw himself in front of my cab! He tried to kill me! Then he assaulted your officer friend here."

"That's not exactly true," Fancy said, her lips quivering. "The whole thing was a terrible mistake."

Jim's burning dark eyes raked her pale face. "Like hell."

"The lady doesn't know—" The cabbie began belting out four-letter words, blaming Jim for everything. Two more cops drove up.

Nobody would listen to anybody.

Least of all Jim, who tore his gaze from Fancy in disgust as two officers jerked him to his feet and manhandled him to the sidewalk. The cop on the ground came to and accused Jim.

Soon there were four more police cars. Jim and the cabbie were spread-eagle against a brick wall. Two officers, their guns drawn, frisked them. Lights were whirling; radios were crackling. Officers were writing reports.

A knot of enthusiastic onlookers had formed to enjoy the drama.

When Fancy asked one of the officers what was going to happen to Jim, he said, "Ma'am your friend here assaulted an officer. He's gotta come downtown."

"Oh, no! You don't mean—"

"I'm afraid so."

"B-before you take him, may I—I speak to him first?"

"Make it fast."

She went over to Jim, who stood taut and unmoving, his fists knotting as if to claw the wall. "Jim—"

He refused to look at her. Cautiously she reached out to touch his arm. He jerked away from her with a snarl. "Officer, the only person I want to talk to is my lawyer."

"This is your fault, too, you know," she whispered. "If you'd come back sooner, if you hadn't lost your temper and tried to hit the cabbie— If you'd let me explain—"

Jim stared stonily past her. "Officer, you'd better get her the hell away from me before I lose my temper again."

"Miss, you'd better leave."

"Mrs." Fancy said, her sad green eyes on Jim's white face.

"Damn you." Jim's drawling voice cracked like a whip. "Not for long—honey!"

One of the spectators laughed. "Some honeymoon!"

Fancy's cheeks flamed. She was so embarrassed she wanted to die.

When one of the blue-uniformed officers grabbed Jim's wrists and roughly cuffed his hands behind his back, she felt his humiliation more intensely than she felt her own.

"Do you have to do that?" she whispered.

But the officer snapped the cuffs tighter and, ignoring her, shoved Jim toward a police car.

"Please, can't you give us five minutes?" Fancy pleaded.

"You heard the prisoner, ma'am. He doesn't want to talk to you."

The prisoner. Dear God.

"But...but he didn't mean it! I'm his wife! We got married last night. When he saw me in that cab, he thought I was leaving him."

Jim stopped and turned, his insolent, hate-filled eyes sliding over her. But he nodded curtly to the men. "I might as well finish this."

"Okay, lady, since you're newlyweds. He's all yours. You've got five minutes."

With the cops and onlookers gawking and hanging on every word, Fancy felt exposed, on trial.

Jim swallowed. "Okay, so where the hell were you racing off to?"

"New York, but . . . I was going for you, for us. Because—"

"Cut the crap. You were running out. When you saw me, you told the guy to speed up."

"No! I was coming—"

"You were leaving me, like you did before."

"No! It wasn't going to be like that. I—I love you."

"I loved you back then, and you said you loved me." His golden eyes narrowed. "But you walked just like today."

"Are you saying you love me now?" she asked softly.

"You'd like that, wouldn't you?" His cold voice was silky; his eyes smoldered. "Me down on my knees, groveling and making an even bigger fool of myself than I already have, so you can stomp all over me, wipe off your feet on me and then walk out again?"

"No." Fancy's blood seemed to cease flowing. "I—I love you."

"I don't believe those words mean the same thing to you they mean to me, Fancy."

"You could have stopped me before, I mean . . . Back then—"

His mouth twisted. "This is the damnedest, longest five minutes—"

"If you loved me so much, why did you marry Nottie?"

"What was I supposed to do, wait forever?" A muscle jerked warningly in his jaw. "I wrote you. What the hell does any of it matter now?"

"You sent me postcards that were so impersonal I couldn't even be sure they were from you. You never once said you cared."

"Damn it. Maybe I would have if you'd ever answered."

"All you ever wrote about was the drought and your cows."

"I never was good with a pen and a piece of paper the way you were. I'm sorry if cows were all I could think to write about. I was going broke." He paused. "Go back to New York. Go on with your life like last night never happened. 'Cause as far as I'm concerned, it didn't."

"But I want last night. I want more than last night—"

"I don't give a damn."

"Jim, please—"

Ruthlessly he cut her off. "What kind of marriage do you think we'd have when we both want such different things? I've got kids and cows. You want New York, glamour, fame. I need space. You need people. There's no place for me in your life, and there's damn sure no place for you in mine—"

Her gaze fell. "So you don't want me? Except for—" *Except for sex,* she thought dismally.

"It wouldn't work, Fancy. Why torture ourselves?"

She started to plead. Then she remembered that arguing with Jim never did any good when his mind was made up.

So she was silent. She knew he was so physically attracted to her, she could probably find a way to persuade him in bed. But how long could she keep him? Six months? And could she make him happy?

If she left, he would forget her in time. He would marry Gracie the same way he had married Nottie. Maybe he would be happier.

She didn't want New York anymore. Somewhere along the way, she had achieved everything she had ever wanted to. She wasn't the nerdy kid in need of applause. Now all she wanted was someone to share her life with.

But it was too late. He couldn't believe her.

So she had to let him go.

More than she wanted Jim, she wanted him to be happy.

"Take care of yourself," she whispered softly, removing her wedding ring and holding it out to him.

"Keep it," he muttered tightly, fiercely. Then he turned away.

She blinked back tears as an officer put a hand on Jim's dark head and shoved him into the back seat of a patrol car.

As the car raced away, her eyes followed it until it vanished.

But Jim never once looked back at her.

Chapter Nine

New York was not the same.

Fancy was miserable as her limo sped through the heavy traffic of the early evening to Claude's party in his loft in Soho.

For Fancy, Manhattan had become a city of strangers. Even her own life seemed like a stranger's now. Although she was still the fashion columnists' darling, all her favorite glitzy haunts were alien and unwelcoming. The streets she had once loved seemed skyless and bleak, even on a sunny day.

She was back on her glittering stage, but like a bad actress in a second-rate play, she was just going through the motions. Only this time she wasn't numb to the pain. Without Jim, she was filled by strange needs and doubts.

Fancy would have given anything not to attend Claude's party tonight, but she didn't have that choice.

It was close to ninety degrees, and the city was steaming. Although Fancy had been back from Purdee for nearly a month, she couldn't tolerate the heat. It made her nauseous and irritable.

Nor could she tolerate the hectic, electric pace, the incessant parties, the constant flights to and from Paris. She found it hard to concentrate, impossible to care about her work. And yet she drove herself harder

than ever. Otherwise she would have gone crazy longing for Jim.

He hadn't called. She would have sold her soul for
a single postcard about his cows.

Her friends and employees assumed she was griev-
ing for her mother. Only Claude knew why she raced
for her phone every time it rang. Only Claude knew
why her voice became listless and sad when the caller
never turned out to be the husband she longed for.

Fancy's driver turned onto Claude's block, and she
sighed when she saw the crowds teaming in front of
the mammoth red doors of his building. His tiny
street, which was in the process of being renovated,
was jammed with shops and popular cafés. But the
crush of people packing the sidewalk was there for
Claude's party.

Floodlights lit Claude's building. Strobe lights pul-
sated from behind his tasseled Victorian shades above.
Rock music throbbed. Blinking red lights ran up and
down his fire escape.

Tonight was important, and Claude, determined to
provoke hype for their upcoming collection, had gone
all out—inviting retailers, journalists, socialites and
supercelebrities. Once, Fancy had been star-struck that
so many famous people admired her talent and bothered to come to her parties. Tonight when her driver
opened her door and dozens of flashbulbs bleached
the night shock white, she wished they'd all stayed
home.

Someone shouted her name. When she tried to see
who it was, another flash exploded. Then a woman
jammed a microphone in her face. As Fancy stepped
out of her car, a white piece of paper pelted down. In-

stinctively she dodged and the deliberately aimed missile hit the toe of her glittering black shoe. She squashed the bit of trash flat as she glided from her car across a length of red carpet toward the building's canopied entrance.

An endless stream of guests, many of them celebrities in their own right, were coming and going from Claude's building. Fancy wished she were one of them and that she could leave whenever she wanted. She would have gone home now. But this was her party, too.

"Ms. Hart—"

It was the female reporter again. Fancy had made herself glamorous in a black-and-gold, Renaissance-inspired ball gown with layer upon layer of ridiculous black tulle for a skirt. Her forced red smile was as dazzling as the borrowed diamonds at her throat and ears as she concentrated on the reporter.

"Ms. Hart, is it true that you got married in Texas and that you ran out on your bridegroom?"

Fancy went white. She had expected questions on the collection that was to be shown tomorrow. All she could do was stare blindly, unable to speak for the wild emotions ripping her apart.

Then a paper airplane whizzed down from Claude's balcony and struck her right between the eyes.

Fancy grabbed the thing and read the clumsily lettered message on its crumpled wings: "Look up, Fancy!"

Rubbing her brow, she lifted her eyes.

"You missed, but I got her!" Omar shouted triumphantly. "Hey, Fancy! We're up here! On Mr. DeMott's balcony!"

The airplane fell through her fingers. Fancy screamed as a red-faced Oscar with raised fists flew out of the window at his brother. When Omar deftly leapt aside, Oscar would have sailed off headfirst had not Claude jumped and grabbed his ankles.

Upside down, Oscar yelled and flailed like a maniac. Claude was yelling just as hysterically.

There was equal hysteria from the press below.

Light bulbs popped. Video cameras zoomed in on Claude's orange tuft of hair as he saw Fancy and shouted down to her, "Fanc-e-e-e!"

"Hold on! I'm coming," she cried, pushing her way through the throng as Claude pulled Oscar to safety.

But there was such a terrifying crush, she couldn't have moved if a big yellow dog hadn't howled when he'd heard her voice. At the dog's low growl, bodies parted in a wave. In the next instant, Yeller yanked his leash loose from a doorman and galloped straight at her.

"Yeller," Fancy said softly, sinking to her knees to stroke his furry head.

She looked past the dog and saw a tall, dark man in a black Stetson standing by the doorman.

Slowly she got up.

The noise seemed to die away. All she could hear was her heart as she slowly walked through the flashing lights toward Jim.

He had come.

"Jim?" Her voice was unsteady as she searched his dark face. "What . . . Why are you here?"

His grave, carved features were filled with warmth and tenderness. "Yeller got to pining something fierce for you."

"Just Yeller?"

"Well, maybe . . . I missed you, too," Jim admitted gently.

"You didn't call or write."

"I was trying to be strong," he continued in that same quiet tone. "Besides, you didn't think much of my postcards."

"What about Gracie?"

"It's all over between us. She was very understanding. You see, she had us figured from the first." He paused. "Are we going to stand in the middle of this circus and talk forever?"

Wordlessly she shook her head.

"You are extraordinarily beautiful," he said, "even in that absurd dress . . ."

In the next moment she was in his arms and he was lifting her high into the air and letting her down so he could kiss her. His mouth felt so hard and wonderful, Fancy forgot that he'd insulted one of her designs.

"Ms. Hart, is this your husband from Texas?" demanded the woman reporter.

"It had better be," someone quipped.

The battery of exploding flashes started Yeller barking again.

But all Fancy felt was the warm pressure of Jim's mouth parting hers. When his rough hands drifted over her bare shoulders, the tingling pleasure of his touch made her moan and wrap her arms tightly around him. He lifted her again and swung her around and around, so that the city seemed to whirl like diamond-bright dazzle.

She didn't even hear the doorman when he started yelling. "Ms. Hart, you've got to tell your cowboy buddy we don't allow dogs in the building. If he doesn't take his animal and clear out, I'm calling the police."

But Jim heard. "Not the police," he murmured with dry amusement, releasing her. "I'll go quietly, sir." He paused. "Fancy, I guess...like always... we're making one helluva scene. I'd better get Oscar and Omar and clear out of here."

Her heart filled with fear. Was Jim going to leave her again? She pulled at his arm, forcing him to face her. "But, why did you come?"

"'Cause I couldn't stay away," he said simply.

"Do you love me?"

Flushing darkly, he scanned the crowd. The woman reporter zoomed in closer with her microphone. At a loss for words, he turned helplessly to Fancy.

"Do you love me?" Fancy demanded.

"Do I have to say it to the whole world?"

She nodded stubbornly.

He rolled his eyes and then closed them. But he took her hand and obediently sank to his knees. He spoke so softly she could barely hear him. But there was warmth in his voice and a tender smile on his lips as he said, "Of course, I love you."

"Now we can go home," she whispered happily.

"What do you mean?" he murmured as she pulled him up.

"I mean forever. I want to go back to Texas with you and Omar and Oscar."

"What about all this? What about your career— New York?"

"I can't be happy here without you. I want to be your wife more than I want to be anything else."

"Even in Purdee, Texas?"

"Anywhere. I love you. I always have. And I always will. I finally know that all I want—is to be with you."

He stared into her eyes.

Neither of them spoke again. Neither of them moved. Her heart was thudding with slow, expectant beats. Gently his calloused hand cupped her chin and he brought her lips to his again in the gentlest but most possessive of kisses.

Then Omar and Oscar started pelting the crowd with more paper airplanes. "Hey, Omar, got any water balloons?"

"Nope, just three subway tokens."

Claude came bouncing down the fire escape. "Fanc-e-e-e... What am I supposed to do about those two wild hellions? They're making airplanes out of all my napkins."

Yeller barked enthusiastically at Claude.

Fancy took a quick breath, grabbed Yeller's leash and handed it to Claude. "Those hellions...are my twin sons now. And this is their father, my new husband."

"Nice to meet you," Claude muttered grimly. "But what am I going to do with all of them?"

Fancy waved up at the boys. "Claude, you're having a party. The boys seem to like you. Yeller likes you, too—" More airplanes rained down. "They look like they're having a good time. Be an angel and entertain them...just for a little while."

"No! Fanc-e-e-e..."

"I'll consider it my wedding present." She patted his hand. "Now, Claude. Remember, our backers said I was the boss. You have a great night! And, don't you let anything happen to my...precious sons and to our family pet."

When Claude opened his mouth to protest, Yeller took off after a poodle on the opposite side of the street, jerking Claude after him.

Fancy chose that moment to escape. Racing with Jim to her limousine, they were soon speeding through the village on their way to her uptown co-op.

"Do you mind telling me where we're headed?" Jim asked as he lifted his lips from her throat.

"I think we deserve a little time alone...together," she said. "If you know what I mean?"

Gently, without speaking, their lips met. They didn't stop kissing until her driver pulled up in front of her building. They separated only long enough to run through the lobby and take the elevator upstairs to her elegant, marble-walled apartment with its wrap-around terrace that overlooked the park.

Then they were naked in each other's arms again, sinking down together upon the burgundy-colored Aubusson carpet that covered the herringbone-patterned parquet floors of her living room.

"You lied about there not being stars in New York," Jim said huskily.

"What?" she breathed, not understanding.

He smoothed her bright hair from her feverish forehead with his hand. "The most beautiful stars I've ever seen are shining right now in your eyes."

"Say it again," she whispered.

He understood her perfectly. "I love you," he murmured.

"Again."

"I love you."

"There," she smiled. "That wasn't so hard."

"Something tells me it's going to get easier 'cause I'm fixing to get a whole lot of practice saying those three little words over and over," he murmured.

"And a whole lot of practice doing this over and over," she purred, stroking him.

As he covered her, the love that bound them together seemed a circle of golden flame—unbroken, endless and eternal.

Fancy gave herself joyously, completely, to the one man she'd loved for almost her whole life.

Epilogue

Fancy sat hunched at one end of the heavy mahogany table that she'd littered with wadded papers and stacks of finished designs. From the kitchen came the sounds of laughter and the redolent odor of baked lasagna.

Her pen flew impatiently across the last sheet of paper, and she breathed a weary sigh of relief as she added a sash with a huge bow to the low-cut, sequined gown she'd designed.

She threw her pen down. That was it. She was through. At least, for now.

She got up slowly. In her black T-shirt and tight jeans, with her hair messily tied up in a ponytail, such glamorous gowns seemed to belong to a faraway fantasy world. A world she had once inhabited. In a week she had to fly to New York for a few days.

But she didn't miss that other life. Not when she was head-over-heels in love with the real-life man of her fantasies.

She'd even trained him to cook. And he did okay as long as he stuck to warming leftovers and frozen dinners in the microwave.

The phone rang, and Jim cried from the kitchen, "Fancy, could you catch that? Anyway, it's probably Claude again."

She rushed into the kitchen.

"Fanc-e-e-e?" Claude screamed out her last syllable.

The twins were quietly, excitedly, hovering over their baby sister's bassinet with a bottle. Enchanted with her big brothers, Maddie was smiling and cooing up at them instead of sucking.

"She likes me most," Omar declared conceitedly.

"Then why's she's looking at me, dumbo?"

"'Cause you're not holding the bottle right, stupid. See—it's falling out of her mouth."

"That's 'cause she keeps pushing it out with her tongue."

Fancy forced her attention back to Claude. "I'm through with all my designs, and I'm fixing to fax ya'll everything."

"You're even beginning to sound like a Texan," Claude grumbled.

"That's what I am now."

"I hope that cow man appreciates you. Especially since I'm having to do without you here in the fitting room. I don't see how you stand the loneliness and the isolation down there."

Fancy stared at the three children and then at Jim. "I don't feel lonely," she murmured with a smile. "Not anymore."

"Dinner, honey," Jim drawled proudly as he removed the lasagna from the microwave.

"I finished my designs," she whispered to him as she hung up the phone. "So I don't have to burn any more midnight oil."

"Which means it's your turn to get up with the baby," Jim teased, setting the lasagna square in the middle of the table.

"Is that all it means?" she whispered huskily into his ear.

A smile played at the corners of his hard mouth. His whiskey-colored eyes darkened as he lazily pulled her into his arms.

"Don't look! They're about to do it again, Omar," Oscar muttered.

Fancy felt moisture sting her eyes as she kissed her husband gently on the lips. She had the man she loved. She had a real family. Life was often hectic, even more so than New York. She was still working for Claude, and with the baby and two mischievous boys, there were a lot of twelve-hour days.

The townsfolk said that she seemed to have a way with the boys, although it wasn't Gracie's way. Maybe Fancy didn't pack their lunches the way Gracie would have, but she hadn't run an international business without figuring out how to motivate and channel people's energy constructively. She saw to it that the twins took care of their animals and their little sister. And people didn't dread the boys coming into town anymore. Not when the boys were always dutifully helping Fancy with the baby. Not when they were either loaded down with the baby's bags or racing methodically up and down the grocery aisles filling Fancy's cart with groceries.

Fancy felt happier and more challenged than she'd ever been in her life. And she might have gone on kissing Jim forever, if Yeller hadn't smelled lasagna and started barking at the screen to get in. If the twins hadn't dropped the bottle and the baby hadn't started to cry.

"Later," Jim whispered, as they both rushed to get the baby.

* * * * *

A Note from Ann Major

I was thrilled to be asked to write a story for a *Summer Sizzlers* edition.

For me, summer has always been a time of freedom and infinite possibilities. As a child I ran free and wild. We had a farm and I would plant cotton seeds in my flower beds. I would catch bees and butterflies in bottles and then let them go.

We didn't have television or air-conditioning, so I didn't come home until the sun had set on those long summer evenings. And then I would go out again and chase fireflies and look up at the stars, and take in the summer smells of new-mown grass as I hoped that some friend might drive by with an idea for adventure. As a teenager I would go out in my sports car to a drive-in and drink cherry Cokes and then drive round and round through that drive-in with a girlfriend, honking at the other kids.

As an adult I have always taken off a lot of time in the summer to play with my own children, to travel, to visit relatives. It is a time to reexperience youth, to remember.

Old songs come to mind, old jokes, playfulness, a carefree regression to other summers, to other relationships.

And so it was that I came to write a book about a hot Texas summer and an even hotter, rugged Texas outdoorsman and the glamour girl who left him behind for something that seemed far better— fame and fortune in Manhattan—only to discover the emptiness and loss in a life without love.

Summer has always been a time for reflection and renewal. A time for fun. And most especially of all—a time for passion and love.

CHARISMA

Laura Parker

Chapter One

Friday, at last!

The air crackled and snapped with uncorked energy as a jumble of financial analysts, secretaries, bondsmen and stock-market personnel poured from their offices in the heart of Manhattan's financial district. The wicked slant of the summer sun drove its chrome-edged light through the canyons of lower Manhattan, inspiring dreams of a long lazy weekend at some New Jersey, Long Island or Connecticut shore.

One man stood out from the crowd hurrying home through the heat of the late-June afternoon. It was not only because his hand-tailored suit revealed a physique formed by discipline. Nor was it his striking, prematurely silver-white hair with pewter undertones. It was his unsurpassing aura of authority. Everything about him said exacting, hard to please and that there was only one way to do things—his way. Some admired, others envied his cool unruffled exterior. Everyone knew who he was. This was Nick Bauer.

Representing the financial interests of three of the city's largest corporations, Bauer could, with a nod, underwrite a new park, float a city bond or secure the financial viability of a political campaign. What he could not charm and cajole out of his allies and opponents, he often rammed down their throats with a combination of stinging wit and overwhelming intelligence. Many curried his favor but none made the mistake of thinking they had him in their pockets. To his face they called him tough, brilliant, a legal wizard. Behind his back they called him the "Ice Man."

The double lines across his patrician forehead indicated his mood on this particular afternoon. One line meant he was thinking deeply. Two meant those thoughts were not pleasant. When Nick Bauer was not happy, there were usually dozens of people in his wake nervously nibbling their fingernails.

As he reached the curb, his chauffeur stepped forward to open the rear passenger door of his Mercedes limousine for him. "Good evening, Mr. Bauer."

"Hello, James." The deep lines on Nick's face relaxed. No matter how hard the day, the sight of James always made him feel better, more at ease with the world. "What's our schedule tonight?"

"Cocktails for the sponsors of the new show at the Guggenheim," James answered quickly. "Dinner at the Tavern on the Green with Ms. Ralston. Then, late drinks with the Evanses at Essex House."

Nick stepped into the cool, dark creamy leather interior, saying, "Who the hell are they?"

"The Memphis Evanses," James supplied.

"Right." Nick waited patiently until James had slid in behind the wheel before pushing the intercom button. "Take the slow route uptown. I need the peace. And then I'm going to need the specs on the Dillinger project for the Evanses. Don't suppose you have them filed under your cap?"

James smiled into the rearview mirror. "I spoke with Ms. Roberts. She'll have them to you by car fax before you leave the reception. There's iced banana-mango tea ready and a hot towel in the warmer."

"Ever efficient, James."

Nick chuckled as he stripped off his signature dark sunglasses and reached for the tumbler of pale pink liquid waiting for him. For years he had used a stiff drink to soften the ragged edges of his hard days in preparation for his equally demanding evenings. Once James started working for him, he found himself being offered instead a glass of freshly brewed herbal tea when he entered his limo. At first he had balked at the New-Age overtones of the suggestions, until he found that a warm towel draped for a few minutes over one's face did do wonders for the disposition. The portable foot massager James later introduced was equally effective.

After a sip of the refreshing tea, Nick shut his eyes and draped the warm scented towel over his face. For a person in his position, downtime was rare. James knew how to make it precious.

"Sir?" came the sound of James's voice over the intercom.

"Hmm?" he murmured contentedly from beneath the towel.

"I just want to say how much I've enjoyed working for you."

Nick frowned. Those words were not a good conversational opening. He peeled down a corner of the towel. "What exactly do you mean?"

Smiling brown eyes met his for a fraction of a second in the rearview mirror. "This is my last day."

"The devil it is!" Nick snatched off the towel and slid forward on the leather seat; the twin horizontal lines between his brows deepened. He had checked his calendar only yesterday and knew he had two weeks left in which to plan his strategy to keep James. "No one said anything to me about this."

"Mr. Bauer," came his driver's patient reply, "two weeks ago you said you thought it was a good idea that I take a vacation."

Nick scowled. "Of course. We've always had that understanding. You want time off, you've got it. You took a full month in January to study for the state bar."

"Yes, and thanks to you, I passed."

"No need to thank me," Nick muttered. He had also helped secure the job that was taking James away. Yet, when he had written that character reference last February, the thought of losing his driver had seemed too distant a prospect for him to worry about. "But what's this about a change in plans?"

"No one expects a man in your position to concern himself with minor staffing problems, Mr. Bauer. But in order for me to take a vacation before I begin my new job, I must do it now. Resignation or time off, it comes to the same thing."

The unruffled response took the umbrage out of Nick. He slumped back onto the leather seat and began toying with the window button. "I don't like this." He knew he sounded petulant, like a small child robbed of a toy, but that is how he felt. Like a willful child, he had retreated into the mind-set that if he did not acknowledge this, it could not occur. "It'll be impossible to replace you."

"I doubt that, sir. Ms. Roberts has already screened three replacements. The paperwork's done. Everything's in order. You'll scarcely notice I've gone."

Nick smiled, a rare trace of amusement that softened the hard lines in his elegantly molded face. "Will my new chauffeur be as pretty as you?"

James again met his gaze via the mirror as they sat waiting for a light to change. "I couldn't say, sir Are you looking for another female driver?"

"No." Nick looked away. *Female driver.* If that's all she was, he would not be feeling now as if he were being abandoned. It was not supposed to happen like this. He had spent six years learning how to live with his emotions in deep freeze. So why was he drumming his fingers impatiently on the burl wood console? Because he could not imagine life without the elusive woman who occupied the front seat. "I'm going to miss you, James."

"And I you, sir. You've been a good employer."

"Is that all?"

He felt her deliberately hesitate as she braked to turn right, sending the limo into the interminable hell of stalled uptown traffic. He knew she was trying to decide how to handle the moment. No one was better than James at subtly evading a subject she had no wish to discuss.

When her gaze came back to meet his in the mirror, her delicate brows were arched in question. "I beg your pardon. Did you say something, Mr. Bauer?"

Nick laughed but the sound of it was not pleasant. "Dear discreet James. Will you insist to the final hour that we remain formal?"

He saw her eyes crinkle in humor. "My name's Eva, sir."

"Yes, I know." As if he needed to be reminded! He replaced his shades, afraid of what his gaze might reveal.

For months, visions of Eva James had been keeping him company during restless nights. Throughout the week he watched the back of her head of soft coppery waves push from beneath her cap, listened to her slightly husky, yet soothing voice and daydreamed. He had almost come to relish the speculations of what it would be like to touch her peachy skin, to nibble the delicate curve of her neck, or suck the lobe of her right ear. The delicious erotic daydreams took him out of himself and his careworn world.

Yet, if sexual attraction was all there was to it, he would soon have gotten bored with the game. He had a self-imposed rule about not dating his staff. For that reason, and others, he had never made so much as a pass at her. Well, if one did not count the kiss on New Year's Eve. But he had drunk a great deal and she seemed to think that explained everything. It did not. That kiss had done nothing to lessen the attraction. He had wanted her then, and he still did.

No, it was more than sexual desire, this yearning that had become as normal as drawing breath. For nearly a year, the subtle attraction had been smoldering between them like the elements of spontaneous combustion. He knew it. She knew it, too. It was only her reserve that had stopped him. Something intriguing lay beneath the surface of Eva James, something engrossing, a furnace burning. Yet, he suspected, she would walk out of his life without a backward glance, unless he stopped her.

"Will you really miss me, Eva?"

"Certainly." She paused to honk at a courier on a bicycle who nearly sideswiped them. "Clerking in a stuffy law office in Albany won't be nearly as easy or as interesting as driving one of the city's leading personalities around town."

Nick smirked. For all the enthusiasm she had spared that declaration, she might as well have been comparing working for him to a visit to her dentist. "I meant me, Eva. Will you miss *me?*"

"Of course, Mr. Bauer." He saw a flash of mischief in those pansy brown eyes that momentarily regarded him. "It's common knowledge that half the single women in the city are in love with you. Most of them want to marry you, the rest just want to sleep with you."

A low sexy smile eased into the chiseled corners of his perfect mouth at this admission. "Which half are you in?"

He heard her soft laughter in chagrin. "What does it matter, when we're all doomed to disappointment?"

Nick did not answer. She was referring, of course, to his reputation as a man who attracted women by the dozens but who most often slept alone. She, on the other hand, freely admitted she was looking for a relationship with a future. The truth was, anytime a woman he was dating started making nesting sounds, he ran for the nearest exit. But there were reasons, good solid reasons.

Six years ago, his life had been shattered when he had miraculously walked away from a plane crash that had killed his wife and four-year-old son. The reverberations from that tragedy had produced two results: he never flew anymore and his hard-won peace of mind was founded on his decision to deep-freeze his emotional life. He had affairs, not relationships, with women. They were brief, intense and perhaps ultimately unsatisfying but safer than the alternative. With his emotions frozen, there was no gain but there was also no danger of pain.

Then Eva had come into his life with her quiet genuine warmth. Long hours in one another's company on road trips to D.C., Boston and Chicago had cemented their friendship. Whether she knew it or not, little by little she had burned a path through to his emotional core. Slowly, unwillingly, he had begun to wonder if it was possible to love again.

Nick slumped down in the seat, feeling the instinct for retreat creep over him. Those were dangerous thoughts. Very dangerous.

The fax machine came to life on the console beside him. A few moments later the specs for the Evanses began spewing out, just as Eva had promised.

In the front seat, Eva James told herself to concentrate on the late-Friday rush-hour traffic but she could not, not when her whole interest was focused on her passenger.

He had raised the barrier of his dark glasses and the taut lines of his face might have been carved from ice for all they offered of warmth and emotion. But she had seen his eyes earlier and they had reflected a weariness that lengthened the long vertical slashes carved beneath his cheekbones and made even his finely shaped mouth seem cruel at times.

How often she had longed to smooth those lines from his face with her fingertips, to brush the thick silver hair at his temples, to soften and warm that hard mouth with her kisses.

Eva sighed and smiled. Her thoughts were so clichéd they were embarrassing. But there it was. In spite of self-awareness and her best intentions, she had gone and fallen for her boss.

The first time she saw Nick Bauer, she thought of that line about men who seem too good to be true. He had stood with his back to windows that framed him in the skyline of Manhattan. When he turned toward her, the lenses of the aviator-style dark glasses he wore bounced off sunlight as golden glints. Behind those glasses his face looked hard, impenetrable. Then he had removed them before extending his hand to her in greeting. That bittersweet chocolate glance had nearly buckled her knees. No wonder he most often kept the barrier of the glasses in place. Those unexpectedly expressive eyes revealed the soul of the passionate private man behind the tough public image.

She had known better than to let her reaction show. She needed a job more than she needed a man, and besides, Mr. Bauer was *definitely* out of her league.

He had at first balked at the idea of hiring a woman chauffeur. He said having an attractive woman at his beck and call seemed a kamikaze declaration in the face of political correctness. But she could not afford to be refused. She had pleaded her case like the law graduate she was. Why, she had asked, should it be more PC for a man to have the job—just because he was a man—when she was capable, already hired by his staff and needed the salary while she studied to pass on her second attempt at the New York State Bar Exam? She could do the job. All she asked was the chance to prove it. He had given it to her.

As his chauffeur she had learned firsthand what the women in his life were like. They were supermodels, society hostesses, trust-fund babies and young business tyroettes, all with their minds firmly fixed on success and its benefits. Being seen with Nick Bauer was a definite perk. His elusiveness made bedding him tantamount to winning the sexual lottery. He knew it. They knew it. And so she watched and listened as he played the odds in his favor. Yet he seldom took advantage of the often blatant offers that came his way.

The surprise was that his image was not all it seemed. People thought Nick Bauer had everything, anything he wanted, whenever he wanted it. They saw only the exterior of the powerful charismatic sexy man. They did not see his loneliness, or his sadness. Only she had caught glimpses of his bleak expression as he sat alone in the dark quiet of the limo, protected for a few minutes from the clamoring, yammering whirlwind that comprised his life. And her heart ached for him.

The blast of half a dozen horns alerting her to the signal change snatched her out of her reverie. She pressed the gas pedal only to jam on the brake as a cab, blaring a warning, scooted past her front bumper to wedge itself into the narrow inch or two of space that she had left between herself and the vehicle in front of her.

"Sorry, sir," she said in apology for the jolt she had given her passenger. *Get a grip!* she commanded herself. She didn't want Nick Bauer's last memory of her to be a bill for the damage she had caused in an accident.

"Find a quiet street and pull over, James," came the reply over the intercom.

"Yes, sir." The order surprised Eva but she did not question it.

It took a few minutes to maneuver them out of the main traffic and locate a relatively empty side street in Greenwich Village where she could double-park. She looked over her shoulder. "Anything else, sir?"

She saw him nod. "Yes. Come around here."

She did so, opening the rear door for him but he merely signaled her with a finger. "Step in and close the door."

They had often sat working on her exam in the back seat but it had been a while and she felt a little awkward now as she sat down opposite him. "What do you need, Mr. Bauer?"

"A moment of your company."

She suddenly felt vulnerable as his dark gaze searched her face. He reached into the fridge and withdrew the bottle of champagne that was part of the standing order that it be kept chilled. "I thought we should toast your last day." The warmth in his gaze increased. "We're friends after all, aren't we?"

"Certainly," she replied crisply, hoping her smile did not look as foolish as it felt on her face. It was absurd that her pulse was galloping and that her mouth felt trembly.

She tried to think practically as he untwisted the wire holding the cork in the bottle. She told herself not to read anything personal into his actions. He was being kind.

She watched him pour the pale golden liquid into one of the limo's crystal flutes. The surface foamed up and the hissing bubbles made a festive sound. When he was done he glanced at his wristwatch, which cost more than her used car. And then he was looking at her again and she forgot to be careful about how she looked at him. "We've got a minute before we must go on but there's something I want to say."

He picked up the two glasses, handing one to her before he touched the rim of his to hers. "To the future, Eva."

"Thank you, sir," she answered in a husky voice, falling back into the formality they always maintained.

"I don't want to lose you, Eva."

She glanced up from her champagne to his face. There was something new in those telling eyes, something more than warmth, something richer than humor and more lethal than charm. She saw in those oh-so-secret dark depths the embodiment of her most cherished daydream: the heat of desire. "What can I do to make you stay?'' he added in his compelling baritone.

Something made her hesitate, something she could not put a name to. It was the same sense of self-preservation that makes a person hesitate to cross the street the moment the light changes only to feel a second later the breezy wake of a vehicle that has run the red. This was crazy. Impossible. She was days from moving out of town. Once before, she had jumped feelings-first into a relationship and lived to regret the resulting bad marriage. One big romantic mistake was all any person was entitled to. Oh, but it was tempting. *He* was tempting. An indulgent smile hovered on his handsome mouth. "Well, Eva?"

She choked on laughter inspired by her own embarrassment. "Please, Mr. Bauer. Let's end our relationship on the same friendly basis we've been dealing with all year."

One deep line appeared on his brow. "Why?"

"Because," she answered with heartfelt honesty, "the alternative is unthinkable." A heartbeat pause. "Isn't it?"

She saw his eyes narrow in surprise. "Is it?"

The words were little more than a snarl. His hand snaked out and gripped the back of her head at the same moment he leaned forward and engulfed her mouth with his.

It was not the most romantic kiss she had ever received but it was the most potent. He devoured her mouth, licking, kissing, nipping her sensitive lips with his teeth, seeking her response as if his very life depended on their connection. She did not dare touch him, could not push him away or even cling to him. She could only register his hunger by the heat of his kiss and the pressure of his fingers on the back of her head. And it was enough and not nearly enough. He wanted her. She wanted him. It was perfect.

"Come up to my apartment with me tonight," he said breathlessly and then chuckled at his own daring. "We'll find out what's possible."

She pulled a little away. "Mr. Bauer—"

"Nick," he corrected, and leaned forward to kiss her again but she shrank away because it was all happening too fast.

The instant it happened, she knew she had made the wrong move. The light went out in the those richly alive eyes and the mouth that had been so persuasively on hers only moments before flattened to a hard angry line. "Is that your answer?"

"I—yes." She did not know why she said it. Perhaps it was the fact that they were being observed by a couple sitting on their stoop. Or perhaps she knew him better than he knew himself. She did not doubt his desire, only the outcome once it had run its course. She could not do that to herself.

She backed away from him and shook her head. "You need a new chauffeur, not a new bed partner." She sounded so calm, so unmoved, when in reality she could scarcely keep from reaching out to draw his mouth back to hers.

The twin lines appeared on his forehead. "I see. I'm sorry." He did not sound sorry. He sounded furious.

He slid back onto his seat and she heard him hiss a vulgarity as he splashed champagne on the seat. He drained his glass in one long icy gulp and then his gaze came back to her face. This time his gaze was as cold and smooth as an oil slick in the North Atlantic.

"I don't know what I was thinking." He reached forward as though he wanted to touch her again. At the last moment he seemed to think better of it and left the gesture unfinished. "I am sorry, Eva."

"No harm done." Eva handed him back her untouched glass. "I really couldn't drink anyway. I'm driving." Before he could stop her, she swung open the rear door and exited.

All the way uptown she felt his eyes on the back of her head. She was almost surprised her hair did not begin to smoke, so intense was his gaze. Yet he said nothing.

When she finally pulled up before the Guggenheim the silence between them seemed ominous.

As she reached to turn off the engine, he moved to the seat directly behind her and touched her shoulder. She glanced back to find his face only inches from hers. His expression was serious, the stark planes of his face strained by some emotion he was keeping under close guard.

"Look, I owe you an apology." His voice was low, subdued.

"There's no need." She tried to smile but it did not quite make it. He was too near, his warm breath fanning her cheek.

Nick searched her face, looking for some clue to her feelings, but all he saw was great wariness. "Good."

He moved back to his original place. It was better that they had not made a mistake. But better than what? he thought bleakly.

"I'll be back in exactly twenty minutes," he said tersely when she had come around to open the door for him.

Eva did not meet his gaze. "Certainly, Mr. Bauer."

He stepped out and snatched off his sunglasses. An instant later she felt the pressure of his fingers framing her chin to lift her head to meet his gaze. It was dark and hot and strong as black coffee. "My name's Nick, Eva. Nick."

He turned and walked away with the easy energetic stride of a man half his forty years.

She took a deep breath and squared her shoulders. She tried the philosophical approach. She was about to exchange a chauffeur's cap for a business suit, the front seat of a limousine for an air-conditioned office in a prestigious law firm. She had worked hard for the opportunity. But, before that, she had a ticket for ten days in Cancún: sun, sand and exotic nightlife. It was just the break she needed. Perhaps then her body would no longer ache from being in close—but not close enough—proximity to Nick Bauer. Maybe her nights would no longer be haunted by images of his face when he thought no one else was looking. Or maybe she would one day wake up and realize she had been a fool to turn her back on her chance to know what it was like to be with him, if only for a night.

"Boss a bit touchy tonight?"

Eva smiled at the man in uniform leaning on the bumper of the limo ahead of hers. Bob was one of the many drivers she had gotten to know over the past year. "No more than usual," she answered in what she hoped was a supremely casual voice as she strolled over to him.

Bob frowned, his cap dipping lower over his forehead. "Never heard it said Mr. Bauer used macho tactics on his female employees."

"He doesn't," Eva snapped, automatically defending Nick even though he had, strictly speaking, been wrong. She produced a faint smile with effort. "My fault."

Bob grinned. "You're going to be missed, kid." He nodded down the long line of limousines on the block. "For looks, the rest of these guys can't hold a candle to you. Of course, without you around, I'll have a better chance to win at poker." On long cold winter nights, an impromptu game in the backside of a limo had been one of the ways drivers wiled away the hours between jobs.

They both glanced around simultaneously as a traffic cop pulled up alongside Eva's limo and began making belligerent noises about parking regulations.

"See you on the other side," Eva said with a wave as she headed to move her vehicle so as to avoid a ticket.

Exactly twenty minutes later Nick appeared at the curb where she was waiting. He was not alone. Two young women in cocktail suits with thigh-high skirts flanked him.

"The ladies need a lift uptown," Nick offered by way of explanation as Eva opened the door. He sounded testy.

"Certainly, sir." She was not surprised. She had ferried many stranded women of assorted ages in the past months. Sometimes they had a real destination, sometimes not. Even so, she just missed slamming the door when the last leggy inch disappeared inside.

What had she expected? A declaration of undying love? No, this was better. But her thoughts were as bitter as five-hour-old coffee as she moved behind the wheel and heard frankly sensual laughter from his two guests in the back seat.

For a second she met Nick's gaze in the rearview mirror. It was as slick and deceptively dangerous as black ice. He wasn't called the Ice Man for nothing. He was hard to handle, and so cold, he seemed hot. If she had been the least bit less careful, she would certainly have gotten burned.

Chapter Two

"He fired all three?"

"No, of course not." Even over the phone Ms. Roberts's tone was that of a loyal employee who could never be induced to criticize her boss. "None of them suited his needs. We're desperate, Ms. James. Mr. Bauer's due in North Carolina by the weekend for a conference in the Great Smoky Mountains."

"And you'd like me to drive him down." Eva rolled her eyes at her roommate, Ayn, who was shamelessly eavesdropping on her half of the conversation. Ayn wagged her head broadly in the negative.

"Of course, you'll be generously compensated for your time."

Eva glanced at the two-inch silver cuff encircling her wrist. A large multicolored tourmaline was set into it. Even at bargain prices Mexican-style, it was an ex- pense she had not figured into her holiday—but one she had not been able to resist. "How generously?" The amount named made her eyes widen. "You *must* be desperate."

"We are. We're also aware that you're expected in Albany on Monday. We'll fly you directly there from North Carolina."

"How will Mr. Bauer get home?"

"With a few days' grace, we're certain to find someone who's not afraid of him." Despite her frequent use of the royal "we," Ms. Roberts sounded like an indulgent aunt. "Mr. Bauer's bark is worse than his bite."

Eva chuckled. That was not his opponents' experience. The money was a generous incentive. But there were other considerations. "Does Mr. Bauer know you're contacting me?"

The voice on the other end hesitated. "Actually, no. But each time he's lodged a complaint against a driver, he's mentioned your abilities as a point of comparison."

"Still, it's possible he might not agree to this." Eva heard Ayn exhale a breath in exasperation.

Ms. Roberts said crisply, "He'll be delighted."

"Let me think about it, Ms. Roberts."

Ayn hopped up off the sofa arm. "You're joking?" When Eva shrugged, Ayn began scrambling around the room, swinging her arms ape-fashion and making monkey noises.

Eva purposefully turned her back on the antics. "I must see if it's possible to change my own arrangements, Ms. Roberts. I'd rented a van and planned to move my things to Albany this weekend."

"Consider it done," Ms. Roberts answered promptly. "You make whatever arrangements you need. We'll pay for them."

Sensing she was being outmaneuvered by a pro, Eva hedged. "I'll call you with my answer in an hour."

She hung up the phone with a sigh and glanced down at the pile of luggage at her feet. She had just walked in the door from her vacation. Ten days of sun and water had lifted her spirits considerably. If only she had not yielded to the temptation to read her phone messages the moment she opened her door, she would not be right back in the emotional turmoil she thought she had left behind.

"You aren't seriously considering taking the job?" Ayn asked in amazement as she lifted thick bangs off her forehead with an upsweep of her hand. Her skin was so pale, it seemed translucent, a fact she emphasized by dyeing her short hair a deep garish maroon. "Well, are you?"

Eva shrugged, unwilling to be interrogated.

"What is this? Anytime Mr. Organ Grinder jerks her chain, Little Eva is expected to perform?" Ayn began scratching her armpits and making Cheetah sounds.

"Don't be rude," Eva said indignantly as a blush stung the tender skin of her slightly sunburned face. "I can use the extra cash. Furnishing a new apartment is expensive."

"Then you *are* thinking about it!" With a groan of frustration, Ayn flung all ninety-one pounds of her five-foot body into the hammock that served as seating and extra sleeping space in their tiny fifth-floor, walk-up apartment. At twenty-five, Ayn was an actress who was most often "between gigs." To pay the rent between parts, she waited tables and worked for a children's party organizer as a clown and mime. "I don't get it. Why should Bauer expect you to drop your life to run to his aid? You don't even work for him anymore. You're a lawyer. Or have you forgotten?"

"I don't think returning a phone call from Mr. Bauer's secretary qualifies as a display of senility," Eva said evenly as she picked up her things.

"Before you've even unpacked?" Ayn scoffed. Fluttering her lashes, she simpered in wicked mimicry, "Of course, Mr. Bauer. Anything *you* want, Mr. Bauer."

Eva straightened up gracefully, her natural reserve coming to her rescue. "Who asked for your opinion?"

"Certainly not you. But you're going to get it, anyway," Ayn said irrepressibly. "I've seen your face whenever you mention his name," she continued, watching Eva with absolute attention. "He rocks your world."

"Possibly you're right," Eva murmured. She had long ago given up arguing with Ayn. A didactic personality, Ayn saw the world in big bold print: Black or White, Right or Wrong. "The point is," Ayn went on, as if encouraged, "you're looking for any excuse to see him again. You're in love with the man." Her smile was positively smug. "Admit it."

Realizing that Ayn was not going to give up until she got some sort of answer, Eva said reluctantly, "I'll admit that I haven't decided what I'm going to do."

"I give up!" Ayn scooped up her workout things and headed for the door. Suddenly she did an about-face. "Look, I'm sorry if I was rude. I just don't want you to get hurt." She smiled slyly. "I'm terrible at piecing together a broken heart. Later."

"Bye." Eva gathered up her bags and headed for the bedroom. To be perfectly honest, she had been hoping for a message from Nick. Something wonderfully romantic, something desperate, something that would make her agree to see him again before she left town. The chance to chauffeur him halfway down the Atlantic seaboard was not what she had in mind when she had fantasized a reunion between them. The pitiful thing was, she was considering doing it.

Self-respect probably did demand that she refuse the offer. Common sense went against bending her own hectic schedule out of shape to accommodate the needs of a man who had not even bothered to call her.

Every reasonable objection took its turn at the podium of her mind as Eva unpacked and then showered. But when she came out of the shower, wrapped in two thick terry-cloth towels, all she could think about was her last glimpse of Nick's face as she let him off at his apartment ten nights ago. He had looked as if he were resigned to losing something very important in his life. And that was how she had felt. Yet neither of them had stopped the other from leaving.

What might have been.

That phrase seemed as sad as any line about regret.

She had hoped for a more definite sign, a stadium-clearing home-run declaration of how she should handle her feelings. What she had gotten was one of life's enigmatic little bunts. Another chance, but just barely.

She pulled the towel from her head and shook out her wet hair. For nearly a year she had wanted to melt Nick Bauer's icy exterior, to heat up his smile and ease the frozen lines of sadness from his expression. But it went deeper than desire. Though Ayn had taunted her with words to the contrary, she could face facts. She *was* in love with Nick Bauer. And, she suspected he felt something more than lust for her.

It was just as obvious that she could not leave things as they were, unresolved.

Eva reached for her comb as a secret smile curved up the corners of her mouth. Two days alone with Nick. Two days to make him realize that he loved her and that love was worth a risk. The temptation was simply too good to pass up.

Gazing at the mirror, she studied the provocative image of herself wrapped in a towel. If she accepted the job, it would be on her terms. No uniforms. No cap. No trousers. And no formality. Melting an iceberg required concentrated heat. Nothing less than a blowtorch was going to work with Nick.

Nick boarded the elevator on the top floor and punched Lobby. Slumping against the mahogany-and-brass-paneled wall, he let his bag and briefcase slide to the floor. He had been working all night, tying up loose ends before he left town. His eyes felt gritty. His muscles still trembled slightly from his dawn workout in the company's private gym. If he were lucky, he would be able sleep in the limo. As it was, he was not looking forward to spending two days on the road with a stranger behind the wheel.

Despite what everyone thought, he had not fired his last three drivers out of misdirected anger over the departure of Eva James. He was not that petty. But he did not hesitate when excuses were offered. The first driver thought he was in a demolition derby. The second bellowed profanities out the window at the slightest provocation. He did not need that kind of image. The third man simply did not know Manhattan. Twice he had gotten so lost, even Nick was not certain where they were.

Nick plowed a hand through his silver hair, streaked dark by dampness from his shower. He was resigned to the loss of Eva from his staff, but not his life.

He had told himself repeatedly that he should leave well enough alone, but how could he? Now that Eva was out of his sight, she was never out of his mind. At odd moments throughout the past ten days, he had found himself thinking about her smile, remembering the exact tilt of her head of when she was listening intently to him. The scent of her perfume lingered with mysterious intensity in the limo. The memory of her quiet huskily sexy voice echoed in the silent recesses of the back seat. The absence of her bright smiling eyes sharing confidences with him via the rearview mirror reminded him that he was once more absolutely alone.

It was not like him to brood. It was not like him to daydream, or to look back or acknowledge regret. But he was not thinking or feeling much like himself lately. His thoughts and feelings were inextricably tied up in Eva James. If business commitments had not made it impossible, he would have made a first-class fool of himself by following her to Cancún.

He glanced at his watch. It was 6:47 a.m. He had tried to reach her twice the day before, knowing she was due back from Cancún, but had gotten her answering machine. It was too early to call but he had to talk to her. Maybe she would agree to let him drop by before he left town.

Feeling as anxious as a teenager who had finally screwed up his courage to ask a girl out on a first date, he pulled the cellular phone from his pocket and dialed the number he knew by heart.

The number rang four times before he heard fumbling sounds on the other end. Finally a very groggy female voice said, "Who the hell is this?"

"Nick Bauer. I'd like to speak to Eva James."

He heard what sounded like a snort. "Too late. She's run off to join the circus! *Ooh! Ooh! Ooh!*"

Nick frowned as he punched the off button. Obviously he had awakened Eva's roommate from a deep and disturbing dream. Why else would she have made ape noises just before she slammed down the phone? But damn, he had missed Eva!

The elevator chimed as it reached his destination. A few minutes later he was facing the balmy, cloud-scattered morning of what was expected to be a very hot July day. The heat extracted a mutter from him as two deep lines appeared on his forehead. The reminder of a forecast of thunder showers along the Atlantic coast further soured his mood. He had counted on seeing Eva before he left but he had not known just how much until this moment.

Eva had been waiting nearly twenty minutes when she finally saw Nick emerge from the building. She exited the front seat with a quickening pulse. In the early-morning light he was hardly more than a silhouette. Still, it was enough to set her emotional register pinging with physical excitement.

She noticed he was favoring his left leg and knew without being told that he had pulled another all-nighter. Most times, the injury from the plane crash he had survived was unnoticeable. But, when he was exhausted, the iron grip of control he held on his body relaxed a fraction and the vulnerability was evident to one who looked closely.

She had deliberately not rehearsed the moment in her mind, afraid that whatever she hoped for would be a mistake. She rounded the front of the limo and paused by the bumper. And waited.

Nick blinked when he noticed the female figure standing by the limo. It couldn't—He whipped off his dark glasses. "Eva?"

She smiled as he came to a standstill a few feet away. "Hello, Nick."

She wore a suit, as per regulation. But, unlike the trousered uniforms she had worn all year, the short fitted beige jacket was shaped to reveal her feminine curves. The matching flared skirt was a mere twenty inches long, leaving a good deal of her tanned legs exposed. Her hair hung free, the deep copper waves curving over her shoulders. She watched his eyes darken in admiration as his stern features relaxed into a boyish grin. That look was worth every moment of preparation, she decided.

"It's wonderful to see you." He glanced at the empty front seat of the limo. "But what are you doing here at this hour?"

Nick didn't know about the arrangement.

With a distinct jolt of surprise Eva realized that Ms. Roberts had lied to her. Annoyance flickered through her thoughts but she quickly tamped it down. She had seen Nick's face when he recognized her. It had lit up like a Christmas tree. Not a bad beginning. But she had to be careful.

"I believe we are traveling to North Carolina together," she said in a neutral tone.

Surprise flooded Nick with warmth. "*You're* driving me to North Carolina?"

Eva nodded slightly. "If you have no objections."

"God, no. None at all." His gaze swept her a second time, lingering on legs that seemed to go on forever. The view was spectacular. A pair of tanned legs had never looked silkier or sexier or more tempting to the touch. The day was looking up. Everything was suddenly looking up. He was going to have Eva to himself for two whole days!

When his gaze came back to her face he wondered if she could guess what the sight of her was doing to his nervous system. He noticed the pink flush on her high cheekbones and hoped it was caused by his nearness, not the tropical sun she had been basking under. "Your vacation looks good on you."

"Thank you." Her gaze flickered over his tired features, honing in on his mood. "You, on the other hand, look like the dog's dinner. You shouldn't work all night."

"Had to be done." He flexed aching shoulder muscles. "There's no one to look after me since you left." He grinned suddenly but a shadow of doubt remained in his gaze. "Why didn't you return my calls?"

Eva's eyes widened. "What calls?"

Nick frowned. "I called twice yesterday and each time left a message on your answering machine. I even woke up your roommate this morning. She said something about your having run off to join the circus. By the way, does she make monkey noises for all callers?"

"That's just Ayn," Eva murmured ominously. First Ms. Roberts and now Ayn. It seemed that everyone felt they had a stake in her life and were playing the odds in their favor. She reached for his bag. "Allow me."

Nick shook his head. "I can't believe you agreed to this," he said as he followed her to the trunk, luggage in hand. "Aren't you supposed to begin a job in Albany on Monday?"

Eva turned and looked directly into his tender dark eyes. "Would you rather I hadn't accepted?"

He regarded her with equal frankness. "Why did you?"

Her smile was enigmatic. "Ask me again in forty-eight hours."

He watched her walk away with a renewed sense of wonder. There was definitely something different about Eva this day, and it was not only that he had an uninterrupted view of her gorgeous legs. She seemed more self-assured and yet wary—no, *aware*—of him. That was it. She was making her interest in him more obvious but by such subtle degrees that he did not know whether to go after her and enfold her in a hot passionate embrace or simply wait and watch the show. He decided, rather reluctantly, to follow plan B.

Once he had had a moment to think about it, he knew he had made a mistake the last time they were together. He had led with his libido instead of his head. He knew then he had been dealing too long in a social world of high-powered, high-pressure, independent, but high-maintenance women who spoke their minds and demanded instant gratification of what they wanted. Eva was different. Eva was a class act. Whatever her feelings, she was not about to get swept up in the moment.

A master negotiator, he knew success or failure lay in the details. He wanted Eva and was prepared to find a way to make it impossible for her to simply walk away a second time. He had two days. He would be certain he got the details—the mood, location, actions and words—right this time.

When she had opened the door for him, he paused before getting in, laying his hand over the one she had rested atop the door frame. "I'm glad to see you, Eva." His dark eyes searched her face for a response. "Really glad."

Eva nodded, not willing to give voice to her feelings just yet. "Do you have any special requests or needs for the journey?"

"Yes." His hand tightened over hers. "I want us to travel together as friends not employer/employee. Agreed?"

"Certainly, si—" She smiled again, the beauty of it drawing his attention to her generous mouth. "Nick."

The way she said his name, soft and husky, gave him more reasons to be glad. "Good. I'm going to need a couple of hours sleep and then we'll talk, Eva. Really talk."

Eva returned to the front seat with a sense of relief. He had been happy to see her even though he had not expected her. She knew he did not like surprises or sudden changes of plans that gave him no time to rehearse his reaction or approach. Yet he seemed to trust her. Suddenly she knew how to handle the next few days. She would keep him off balance, gently forcing him to complete spontaneity and emotional honesty. Then when she had him at his most vulnerable and receptive, she would discover what lay at the heart of the Ice Man.

She turned the key in the ignition, feeling as if an adventure was getting underway. For the next two days she had her very own Prince Charming all to herself. She intended to see that he learned all about the uses of enchantment. Only, this was the twentieth century. This time, Cinderella was in the driver's seat.

Nick licked his fingers clean of chicken juice and spices. "I had no idea fast food could taste so good."

Eva smiled at him over the bronzed perfection of her spit-roasted chicken leg. "You should broaden your horizons, Mr. Bauer."

They sat in the shade of a highway rest stop, eating an order of chicken and fixings she had bought at a drive-thru window a few miles back. Nick had awakened from his three-hour nap with a voracious hunger and while Ms. Roberts had scheduled lunch, complete with directions, for noon at an elegant little restaurant just north of Baltimore, he had opted for convenience over elegance.

"I haven't had macaroni-and-cheese since I was a child," Nick said as he scooped up another forkful from the disposable container.

"I thought rich kids ate gourmet lunches made by nannies," Eva responded with a smile.

"Maybe they do," Nick said when he'd swallowed. "I wouldn't know. We were cranberry farmers. During the rough times, macaroni-and-cheese with diced franks was dinner."

Eva glanced doubtfully at him. "You grew up poor? But I've seen your mother's home in Greenwich. That's no farmer's cottage."

He grinned with pride. "I paid for it. And the improvements on the homestead that my brother and his wife run now. Business is better now that they have the equipment necessary to produce like the big boys."

Disbelief lingered in Eva's tone. "So why hasn't any reporter ever picked up on the poor boy/rich boy image?"

"I'm too good at covering my tracks," he answered without encouraging further comment.

"But with all that's been written about you, and your wife," Eva added, plunging boldly into what she knew was an off-limits topic, "I had the impression you were Back Bay Boston bred like her."

Nick put down his fork and regarded her for a moment in silence. Eva held his penetrating gaze though she began to wonder how she had found the nerve to mention his wife when no one else ever did to his face.

"I am a private man, Eva. I come from private people. When I first made my reputation, I had already decided how to handle the publicity that comes with being a prominent figure, in such a way that it would not turn my family's life into a circus. To keep the gossips from digging, I offered background materials I thought were relevant, and invented the rest. Janet, my wife, came from money and breeding. We met in school."

"Harvard," Eva supplied. "Not bad for a cranberry farm boy."

He smiled. "It was Janet's world we offered the press. She didn't mind and my family was grateful for the smoke screen. First it was convenience and then it was reality."

"You mean hobnobbing with East Coast movers and shakers?"

"Hmm." He looked down at the pile of chicken bones on the plate before him. "Sometimes I miss the simple pleasures."

"Like driving a car?"

He looked up, a smile his eyes. "You think I can't drive?"

Eva shrugged. "I've never seen you behind the wheel, Mr. Bauer. Do you even own a car?"

"Three, actually." He looked a little uncomfortable. "I suppose you're right. There's nothing stopping me from driving myself around."

"Nothing but common sense and expediency," Eva answered. "I don't begrudge you the limo. It's practical and time-saving."

He saw the challenge in her eyes. "But you doubt I could drive it."

Eva laughed. "Since you don't have a chauffeur's license, we're not going to find out on my watch."

He reached out and stroked his thumb against the corner of her mouth. "Salad dressing," he said as he stroked at it a second time.

Though little more than a whisper of a caress, it set heat scorching through Eva. Giving in to the urge to touch him, she reached up and encircled his wrist with her fingers. Bringing his hand back to her mouth, she deftly licked the dressing off his thumb with the gentle stroke of her tongue.

She saw his eyes darken as the satiny surface of her tongue stroked his thumb. "Eva, I—"

"Wait." Eva pressed her free hand to his mouth. "It's about three more hours to D.C. and then, according to the itinerary I was given, you have meetings scheduled with a senator and then two representatives on Capitol Hill."

Nick groaned. He had forgotten the appointments. He had forgotten everything but Eva. Even now his body was urging him to throw the whole weekend over, to get behind the wheel and drive them off someplace where no one would find them until they were good and ready to be found. But, of course, he never let his passions rule him. If he started now, it was bound to frighten her away.

"I suppose I'll have to keep the damned appointments," he said in a frustrated voice that sounded more like strangled anger. He saw her stiffen ever so slightly and deliberately took a deep breath to ease his tension. "But promise me you'll have dinner with me tonight."

Eva shook her head, matching him mood for mood better than he knew. "You have an evening engagement. Some investors who would like to persuade you to back their industrial waste reclamation center on the Hudson." She smiled. "They're doomed to disappointment because their specs don't come anywhere close to meeting the ecological requirements you backed last year."

Nick's face was a study of surprise. "How do you know that?"

"The package Ms. Roberts couriered to me last night included the last-minute details of your meetings as well as an itinerary. Out of curiosity, I read the background check on the company." She paused. "I hope you don't mind."

"Not at all. I trust you implicitly, Eva." His gaze intensified. "I'm left with just one question. Why didn't I hire you as an attorney?"

Eva's gaze was equally frank. "I don't know. Why didn't you?" Her tone was light, the question rhetorical, but he could not brush it aside.

Why *hadn't* he hired her once she had passed the bar? Because she had seemed to know what she wanted to do? She wanted to work in domestic law, issues dealing with women and children. She had said repeatedly that her best chance to influence legislation was by working in Albany. But was that the right answer?

Suddenly he knew it was not. He had, unconsciously perhaps, ignored the chance to hire this bright

savvy woman because six months ago he had not
wanted to commit to a permanent professional relationship with a woman who made him feel as unset-
tled as Eva James did. He saw now that by refusing to
even consider her, he must have wounded her in ways
he had never even thought about until this moment.
The realization came at a vastly awkward moment for
she was looking at him as if she could read his mind
thought for thought. He felt foolish and gauche and
ashamed.

Deciding to let him off the hook, Eva glanced skyward. "It's going to rain by nightfall."

Nick knew that tactic well. She was strategically
backing off from the moment. Another person might
have created a scene, made him feel worse than he already did. But Eva, bless her, was extraordinary in
more ways than one.

Grateful for her finesse, he glanced up at the pale
blue sky, crowded with metallic edged cotton-wool
clouds. The heat stung the back of his neck and glis-
tened on his cheeks. "I suppose we'd better go, if I'm
going to have time to check in and dress and still make
those appointments on time."

He rose to his feet as she began clearing the picnic
table. "Leave it. I'll do that." When she looked ques-
tioningly at him, he said, "You put yourself out for
me, Eva, when you don't have to. Don't let me take
advantage again."

Eva regarded him quizzically but she could see
something was going on behind his eyes that was very
important to him. "Okay."

When he had finished throwing away their trash, he approached her as she stood by the car waiting for him. "Eva, let me take you out tonight, somewhere quiet, secluded, nice."

For the first time Eva allowed him to see her joy. "I'd love it, Nick."

She leaned forward and kissed him quickly on the lips and the smile she gave him afterward made him feel as if he had swallowed sunshine, so fierce was his pleasure.

Chapter Three

Nick barely listened to the ersatz political conversation going on at his table and took even less part in it. Behind his glasses, a pale amber shade for evening wear, his full attention was focused on the woman who occupied the table at the far corner of the elegant dining room.

More than an hour earlier, he had seen her enter, admiring the absolute poise with which she crossed the dining room to be seated alone. Every detail of her had drawn his eye. Her cloud of softly waved copper hair, the elegant stride of her long legs encased in sheer silk stockings, the simple body-skimming champagne-colored dress cunningly cut to cling to her high full breasts and drape the slender contours of her body, the subtle swing of her hips that made the flared layers of her sheer skirts swirl flirtatiously about her legs. All of it had mesmerized him. Though her gaze had been straightforward, her expression matter-of-fact, she had turned heads throughout the restaurant. And no wonder. Every man present sensed, as he did, that there were hidden depths in this woman worth exploring, if only she would allow it.

She had seated herself and smilingly ordered a glass of wine before turning casually to survey the room. He had not realized how tensely he had been anticipating the moment until her gaze finally met his. Like a laser beam, Eva James's glance had burned cleanly through his cool veneer to ignite the inner man. He had even felt his cheeks warm. And lower down... Well, that didn't bear thinking about under the circumstances.

Through three courses and sixty-five tedious minutes, he had had to covertly watch her consume alone the meal he had wanted very badly to share with her. He glanced down at his own half-eaten plate, wondering what one of the most expensive meals in Washington, D.C., had tasted like. He could not remember swallowing a single mouthful of it. It was simply a reminder of how far afield his plans had gone. Annoyed, he signaled an unobtrusively hovering waiter to remove it.

"No appetite?" inquired the woman on his left.

"A little rich for my tastes," Nick replied, reluctantly turning his attention to the senate aide who had been making a concerted effort to hold his interest. "You were telling me about the bill coming up for a vote next week. What are the chances it will emerge intact from committee?"

As the woman launched into an overly detailed explanation, designed to keep his attention, Nick retreated behind an enigmatic expression. He knew that one no would guess that behind his glacial reserve he was seething with frustration.

When he had agreed to drinks after his meetings, he had not expected the appointment to turn into this interminable dinner obligation. Unwilling to give up on his hope of having a quiet tête-à-tête with Eva, he had called her hotel room to say he had made a reservation for her at the same restaurant where he was dining. He had planned to slip away from this table once she arrived. Those hopes had been ruined when the incumbent senator from New York, who happened to be dining here, was induced by her dinner partners to join their table. Once that occurred, dinner had become a quasisocial obligation he could not bow out of, since several of his business clients were backing the woman. So, while he tried to remain civil, the one person in the world he really wanted to be with ate alone just yards away.

Finally the aide's attention was drawn away by a question from the other end of the table. With an inaudible sigh of relief Nick removed his glasses and leaned back in his chair, mentally deserting his dinner companions as he let his gaze drift again across the sea of soft-lit gleaming surfaces of china, crystal and silver to where Eva sat. She, too, seemed to shimmer. At least he could enjoy the view.

With every movement of her head, the jewels in her earrings winked provocatively behind the curtain of her bright hair. Candlelight played over the surface of her skin, entrancing him. The elegant movement of her hand as she reached for her coffee cup gave him ridiculous pleasure. Everything about her drew his interest and approval. It was as if he had never really seen her before this day. Perhaps he had not, had not dared allow himself to see the woman who could move him so easily. Though it was probably impossible, he thought he even detected the faint scent of her perfume in the air. He had to find out what it was about her that so tantalized him. And tantalize him she did.

A smile formed on his usually austere mouth. He felt as if he had made a delightful secret discovery. But, of course, he was not the only one watching. Even men entertaining attractive dates of their own were making quick covert glances at the lady. He wished he could tell everybody in the room that she was his.

As he continued to watch, she lifted a chocolate-dipped strawberry from her dessert plate and brought it to her lips, staring off into middle space. It seemed a completely natural, unconsciously sensuous act as she bit into it. He saw the pearly gleam of even white teeth. Then the pink tip of her tongue slipped out and over her lower lip to catch any drops of sweet berry juice. The mercury in his personal thermometer shot up several heated degrees. When she suddenly turned her head toward him and offered him a shining moist-lipped smile, pure desire executed a double twist in his groin.

Oh, Lord!, he thought ruefully. Was she deliberately trying to seduce him? But no, Eva James did not do that sort of thing. Or did she? He did not know how she behaved with a man who attracted her. He had never been just a man in her eyes. Now, more than anything, he wanted to be just that, a man who attracted her.

Yet, Eva came with strings attached.

He thought of the old blues line, "If you don't want my peaches, don't shake my tree." It deepened his smile. That was Eva James. Lush and ripe and sweet, but with a woman's prerogative to expect love and a lasting relationship.

Did he have the right to pursue one without offering the possibility of the other?

"Pretty woman," the man on his right said when another lull formed in the table conversation. When Nick turned to him, the man nodded in the direction in which Nick had been staring. "Want to ask her to join us?"

Nick shook his head. "She wouldn't."

"Why not?" The man smirked. "She's already eaten—alone. No woman dresses like that if she wants to remain alone. I think she came here in the hopes of meeting someone."

"No doubt she did," Nick murmured, regretting that his fixed interest in Eva had drawn his companion's attention.

"Then, if you aren't going speak to her, I will."

"That wouldn't be wise."

The man laughed. "Why not?"

Nick leveled his dark gaze on the man. "Because she's waiting for *me.*"

"Oh. *Oh!* Why didn't you say so?" The man grinned sheepishly. "Some men have all the luck."

Yes, thought Nick. *So what am I waiting for?*

He rose from the table, placing his napkin beside his plate. It took only a few minutes to pay his tab and disengage himself from the obligatory handshakes, but when he looked up again, he was annoyed to discover that Eva was no longer at her table.

He strode over just as a busboy began clearing her place. He demanded, "Where did the young woman go who was sitting here?"

The startled young man said, "How should I know?"

Nick hurried out into the street, only to catch a glimpse of copper curls as a cab pulled away from the curb. After hailing his own cab with an imperious gesture that forestalled the doorman, he gave instructions for the driver to follow her.

Drumming his fingers impatiently on his knee, Nick muttered a deprecation against the sticky heat pouring in through the cab's windows. Finally he leaned forward and said, "Don't you have an air conditioner?"

"No, man. Ee's broke." With his Rastafarian braids swinging as he turned his head, the driver smiled. "But the night, ee's like a good woman. Clinging. Wet. Hot. Yeah, man!"

"Right." Nick slumped back against the seat, which felt greasy and slick from the Potomac's humidity. Nothing about this evening had gone as he had hoped. By now, he and Eva were supposed to be sated with good food and wine, and thinking about other appetites that might be mutually satisfied. Instead he was composing lines of apology.

In the distance, the night sky lit briefly, like a dark hallway with a faulty bulb. He wrenched his tie loose and unbuttoned his top button. Maybe rain would take the edge off his mood, but he doubted it. Nothing short of the cooling touch of Eva James was likely to soothe the fires burning beneath his surface.

The taxi ride seemed to take forever. They were staying in a hotel in Alexandria in order to be south of

D.C. and thereby avoid the morning rush-hour traffic in the Capitol.

When he finally arrived at the hotel and entered the lobby, he saw the elevator doors closing on a flash of champagne chiffon. He rushed over and pushed the up button repeatedly until a second elevator arrived. On the ride upstairs he wondered what he was going to say when he caught up with her.

As he stepped off the elevator, he again thought he caught a whiff of the perfume she was wearing. Wanting her was doing things to his head he had never experienced before.

He went directly to her room and knocked. At first there was no reply. He used his fist to deliver the second knock, startling an elderly couple who were just exiting their room.

They gave him a scared-rabbit look as he muttered, "Sorry," and then the door before him opened a fraction.

The right side of Eva's face appeared in the space. "Yes?"

Nick smiled. "Eva, I need to see you."

Her eye widened. "Now? Is something wrong?"

"No—Yes." He pushed an impatient hand through his hair. "Look. I just want to talk. Can I come in?"

He saw her reach for the chain. "Give me a second before you enter. I was undressing." She closed the door and he heard the chain slip free. Then the door opened a fraction.

Once the possibility of her half-undressed state registered in his mind, he forgot all about the request to wait a moment before entering. He pushed open the door at once.

She was halfway across the room, her back turned as she scurried away. He noticed two slips of pink silk. One formed a narrow band across the middle of her bare back, the other an inverted triangle that left exposed the outer curve of each luscious globe of her derriere so that the slightly wider tan line was exposed. The rest of her was long and leggy and tanned to perfection.

He sucked in a breath as she passed the mirror. It reflected back to him the deep plunge of her lacy bra that left a generous portion of her breasts exposed. She was quite curvaceous, more so than he had imagined—and he had imagined plenty over the last hours! He heard her throaty giggle just before she ducked into the bathroom and closed the door.

By the time she reentered the room a few moments later, his mind was so smoked by the images burned into his retinas that he had to blink to clear his vision. She had put on a floor-length black robe of Oriental design with pagoda sleeves and stenciled with pink camellias. His mind automatically peeled back the black silk in search of the pink lace beneath.

"Do sit down, Nick." She waved him toward a chair while she perched on the end of bed. She crossed her legs so that the robe parted, revealing her slender but well-formed calves. He noticed her shell-pink toenails and wondered if her well-shaped arches were ticklish. When his gaze returned to her face, her smile was warm, her golden brown eyes bright with amusement. "Was there something in particular you wanted?"

Yes. You.

He nearly said the words aloud. His gaze moved from her eyes to her mouth. It was a lovely female mouth, all full softness and a tender deep rose in color. The color was natural. He had long ago discovered that fact. But he had not yet had time to fully explore the taste and texture and response of the woman to whom it belonged. Fissures of desire appeared, radiating heat through his icy reserve.

"I wanted to apologize about dinner."

She smiled. "There was no need. You did, after all, pick up the tab. Besides, I recognized one of your dinner companions. The senator must have been delighted to have been seen in your company this early in her reelection campaign. The publicity will be as good a fund-raiser as having the funds committed by your clients."

He gave her a rueful smile. "I'm glad you understand. Many women wouldn't have."

Eva laughed. "I'm *not* many women, Nick."

"No," he said consideringly. Minute by minute she was becoming the most singular woman of his experience. The whisper of silk as she crossed her legs sent a ripple of response through him. His gaze betrayed his thoughts by sliding toward her legs.

"Was there anything else, Nick?"

He did not move a muscle. His clever wit had suddenly deserted him. His libido was definitely in charge. It said they were alone. She was dressed like an advertisement from one of those sexy lingerie catalogs. The bed dominated the room, inviting use. What was he waiting for?

He saw her attempts to hide a yawn behind compressed lips and remembered with guilt that while he had slept half the way to D.C., she had been behind the wheel.

"You must be tired," he said at last. *Bad move. Never give a date an out.*

"Are you tired?" Eva rose to her feet, drawing his gaze upward past the exotic curvature of her breasts to her slightly flushed face. Was it his imagination or was the pink in her cheeks a deeper shade than only moments before? "I'm not. In fact, I'm very restless." She gave her shoulders a slow, flexing roll that parted her robe, revealing a scant inch of the pink lace that covered her breasts. "It's all those hours sitting behind the wheel. After a long trip I usually need exercise before I can sleep."

"I didn't know that," Nick admitted. "I suppose I've always been too busy to wonder how you spend your free time when we've traveled together."

"I'm an expert at room service," Eva answered. "And I haven't missed a decent movie in the last year. But tonight I thought I'd take a walk to stretch my legs."

An idle lustful thought about those lovely legs of hers and what they might feel like wrapped about his hips, made him smile. Deep down, something like a glacial shift took place. "It's not safe for a woman to walk alone at night."

She smiled and canted her head. "Would you like to go with me?"

He nodded, glad for any excuse to remain in her company. "My pleasure."

"Good. I'll just finish changing."

In less than a minute she was back in a silk tank top, walking shorts and sandals. She looked at his expensive suit and smiled. "You should change. They say it's going to rain."

"No need." Nick shrugged out of his coat and slipped off his tie. When he had opened his collar and rolled his shirtsleeves up to the elbow, he indicated the door.

Eva scooped up her umbrella, looked at it a moment and then tossed it back on the bed. Smiling, she winked at him. "Let's live dangerously."

"Are you certain you want ice cream?" Nick questioned, having hoped to whisk her into an elegant little bar that served imported champagne. They needed dark and seclusion and time alone together.

"Absolutely," Eva maintained. "It's still hot enough out to melt asphalt. Nothing but ice cream, *real* ice cream, will do tonight."

She took him casually by the arm and steered him into the open doorway of the ice cream parlor just across the street from the Potomac riverfront in Old Town Alexandria.

The place was filled with a blend of tourists, teenage couples, young parents with sugar-revved children, a pair of young sophisticates guiltily debating the relative nutritional merits of fresh strawberry mousse versus double dutch fudge.

When she had thoroughly scanned the list of exotic possibilities, Eva turned and smiled devilishly at Nick. "What will it be?"

Unwilling to be enticed by the caloric fare, Nick shook his head. "Lady's choice."

"Well, then—" Eva turned to the young man behind the counter "—we want a cinnamon waffle cone filled with a scoop of this and this and this." She pointed to three flavors of chocolate ice cream. "Topped, of course, with hot fudge, whipped cream and sprinkles."

The young man's eyes widened as he grinned at her. "And a cherry?"

"Oh, yes, a cherry." Eva gave him a provocative look. "Mr. Bauer is *very* fond of cherries."

"I am not," Nick answered indignantly.

Eva swung around to him, her eyes wide with wicked glee. "But you are. You always order two with your Manhattans. Tell me I lie."

He blushed, actually blushed as he became uncomfortably aware of the other customers' knowing smiles.

"Is that how you do it?" he asked as they stepped to the other end of the line to pay for the order.

"Do what?" Eva replied innocently.

"Anticipate my needs by watching and listening when I'm not paying attention?" he whispered.

Eva reached across him to snag a pile of napkins, brushing his arm with hers, but she did not look at him. "Do I do that, anticipate your needs?"

"Constantly," he murmured as he paid the cashier. He turned to her and he stood so close, she could see her reflection in the nearly black depths of his eyes. "It's like you read my mind."

She slanted a sly smile his way. "I do."

"Read my mind?"

"Of course."

They stepped out into the steamy night as distant lightning cast its pale iridescence momentarily over the sky. Pausing at the corner, Eva turned to him. "Here." She dug her spoon into the overflowing cone and offered a spoonful to him.

He recoiled. "I'm not going to eat that. I can feel my arteries hardening just looking at it."

"You will eat it," she said, holding the dripping spoonful before his face. "After all, do you want to live forever?"

He arched a single taupe brow. "Quite possibly."

She looked at him with a suddenly somber expression. "Why, Nick? What do you have to live for?"

She saw the unexpected question hit him like a blow to the solar plexus. As he stared at her in perfect surprise, she decided to go for broke. "What do you have to look forward to? Who would you regret leaving behind?"

She did not wait for him to reply but pressed a spoonful of the gooey chocolate concoction on him. Obediently, he opened his mouth and she scooped it in.

His eyes lit up as the rich flavors melted and blended on his tongue. "Real ice cream," he murmured. "It is, to be honest, quite sinfully good."

Eva beamed at him as if he had successfully accomplished a difficult task. "See? One has to take the plunge once in a while if only to be reminded what one is sacrificing in being righteous."

"You're dangerous," he said when she held out another mouthful.

"Exactly. Tonight I intend to foster your every reckless impulse."

"Really?" His eyes glittered as another flash of lightning registered in their depths. "So what am I thinking right now?"

Eva looked straight into his dark eyes, richer and more seductive than any chocolate bar. The distant rumble of thunder bolstered the more civilized sounds of traffic, laughter and music flowing from the various shops along the avenue. "You're hoping I don't eat all the Rocky Road."

His smile deepened. "Wrong."

"Then stick around. It takes time to read a man who's not accustomed to admitting to his secret desires." Eva turned quickly away and began strolling toward the waterfront.

Nick followed her.

They strolled the river walk, watching the dark water and admiring the Capitol lights on the opposite bank. While Nick talked about his early experiences as a lobbyist in D.C., Eva kept feeding him ice cream and smiling. It seemed like the most natural thing in the world when they paused to sit on a bench and he finally put his arm about her shoulders. The fact that she could not steady her pulse despite the casualness of his action was her own damn fault, she told herself. For all the romantic interest he had shown in her thus far, she could be a sister, or cousin. It was time to up the ante.

She turned toward him within his embrace, bringing her face to within inches of his. "Nick, I want you to—"

The bolt of lightning made no sound yet the air seemed to hiss softly a second before the *crack* of thunder shook the night. An instant later the first drops of rain scattered about them.

Eva rose to her feet and lifted her arms wide. "Oh, good! It's going to rain."

Nick came to his feet beside her as the rain abruptly shifted from random splashes into a hissing downpour. "Let's get out of here!"

Eva shook her head. "Not me. I love warm summer rains." She danced a little away from his outstretched hand. "Come on. Let's see how wet we can get."

"Are you crazy?" Nick took two stalking steps toward her and caught her by the arm. "This is becoming a certifiable downpour."

Eva laughed as she leaned against him, bracing herself with a hand flattened against his chest. "Didn't you ever play in the rain as a child?"

"It's lightning, Eva. That's dangerous."

Eva smiled. "I know. Sometimes a little danger is good."

She saw his expression in the glow of the next, softer flash of light. His features were perfectly composed, despite the rain slicking them. His black eyes looked like smooth wet stones from the bottom of a deep well. He seemed so cool, controlled, untouched by the rain pelting them or the sounds of rolling thunder or the lash of the stormy breeze. But she knew it was all a lie. Beneath her hand his heart was beating a little too fast for a man purported to keep his emotions locked inside a block of ice.

Without hesitation she gave him a gentle push to disengage herself from his grip. "Loosen up, Counselor. There's no one to see if you make a fool of yourself."

She turned and with a laugh of challenge sprinted gracefully across the grass.

Nick was after her in a shot, half amused, half furious that she had chosen this moment to become whimsical. The rain fell in a hard steady slant, drenching everything in its path. Within a few yards, his shirt was plastered to his back and his hair was matted to his brow, releasing dribbles of water into his eyes.

She was not easy to catch. She reached a closed kiosk ahead of him, where several other people had sought shelter. As she ducked in under the narrow overhang he heard her laughter at his expense and it needled him. When he reached her side, she suddenly sprinted away again out into the rain.

For a moment he resisted following her. Even as he debated the dangers of letting her go, she suddenly stopped and began swirling round and round under the canopy of the night. Arms raised, her head thrown back in joyous abandon, she spun slowly, looking like some gorgeous pagan priestess offering homage to benevolent gods.

He watched in vexed admiration as the sky repeatedly lit up, throwing her slender figure into high relief against the darkness.

"Your girlfriend?" asked one of his fellow stranded pedestrians.

"Not exactly," Nick responded. "She's my chauffeur."

The man chuckled. "Is that what they're called nowadays? I suppose 'personal secretaries' have gone out of style."

Nick smiled. There was no use protesting that Eva was far too independent to be any man's mistress.

Finally she stopped spinning and stood simply staring at him. He shook his head. Did she really expect him to go out and get her? He saw her extend her hand and crook her finger at him. Angry at himself for being confused by her actions, and unable to think of an alternative, he stalked out into the rainy night. At that moment she turned her back and began running away again.

Muttering four-letter Anglo-Saxon expletives, he took off after her, absolutely determined that she would not escape this time.

He caught up with her within a few yards and snagged her by the wrist. She spun around to face him, breathless laughter escaped her smiling mouth. A brilliant spear of lightning forked through the sky and she cringed and turned into his shoulder. Even so he heard her laughter continue.

"What the hell kind of game are you playing?" he demanded over the cannonade of the thunder.

Her smile was brilliant even in the darkness. "Having fun, Nick." She sounded happy, excited. "You do know how to have fun, don't you?"

"You want to know what I call fun?" The edge in his voice would have etched glass as he began dragging her toward the nearest protection, an empty bus shelter.

He pulled her in ahead of him but did not release her arm. "This, Eva, is what I call fun." He closed the distance between them and, hauling her against him, bent his head to kiss her.

Chapter Four

Nick was surprised by the chill of her wet lips and then shocked by the warmth that quickly replaced it. He heard her sigh as she leaned deliberately closer against him, her body suddenly all soft curves and womanly warmth. And then her arms were moving up about him, one hand resting on his damp shirtfront while the other gripped his sleeve above the elbow. This is what he had been waiting for for nearly a year—to touch and be touched by Eva James.

Desire zigzagged through him as the kiss went on and on, spinning out the notes of desire with the sexy persuasiveness of a long, slow, jazzy saxophone solo.

One kiss melted into another, feeding on the passion of the moment. Her lips were soft and mobile beneath his, seeking the shape of his, testing the firmness, then finally tugging his lower lip in between hers. There was nothing tentative about her kiss, no hesitancy that sometimes colors a first encounter. She seemed to know just what she wanted, and what she wanted was him. When his tongue made a foray into her mouth, she immediately touched it with her own and a jolt of pure lust shot through him straight to his groin.

He pulled her in even closer and scooped her hips into his. Slanting his mouth across hers, he gave up to the sheer pleasure of kissing her as long and as thoroughly as he had wanted to for nearly a year. She was like incandescent heat in his arms, searing him with her touch. Deep inside him, some hard cold knot began to dissolve.

Eva sighed and snuggled against him, murmuring womanly sighs of pleasure as his hands went exploring. One short hour ago she had given up any hope of being with him tonight. She had watched in resignation while he dined, wishing she could just hear his voice or see his eyes. Now his warm mouth was on hers and she was learning that even without the use of his clever wit and forceful voice, he was a master of persuasion. He was melting her with his desire, robbing her of both breath and any thought of reluctance. It occurred to her fleetingly that she had never been kissed more thoroughly, or more stimulatingly. Her smile formed a silken passage for his tongue. She had been right. Beneath the ice there was the hot passion of a flesh-and-blood man.

When he found the shape of her breast through layers of wet silk she felt the already puckered nipple stiffen in response to his fingers. She had never been this close to him before. Even though he had kissed her twice, she had never dared touch him in return. Now she did not want to waste a single moment.

She pulled his damp shirt from his waistband and ran her hands in a loving massage over the hard contours of his back. Despite the rain his skin was hot and smooth.

Nick no longer heard the rain, nor saw the flashes of lightning, nor felt the deep rumble of thunder. There was only Eva—sweet, sweet Eva—inflaming his body with her erotic play. His heart thundered in his ears. His body shuddered and flushed in response to her touch and taste. He felt so hot and ready that when she feathered her fingers across his distended fly, he thought he might explode through pressure alone.

"Wait. Wait," he said breathlessly and kissed her forehead. He pulled a little away, shaking his head and chuckling in amazement at his own lack of control. "There's got to be a better place to finish what we've started."

Eva looked up at him, her eyes enormous with the heat of her desire. "I wondered when you'd notice."

He grinned at her. "What if I hadn't?"

"Then I guess we would have risked being arrested for lewdness and public display."

Laughing at her boldness, he kissed her again, hard and swift. He looked around quickly and noted to his dismay that it was raining even harder than before.

She sneezed.

He rubbed his hands up and down her bare arms, feeling the goose bumps that had formed there. "You're freezing."

"I didn't think it would cool off so fast," she answered, wrapping her arms about her body to stave off another sneeze. "Do you think you can hail a cab?"

"If there's one to be had in this weather," he replied in exasperation. He enfolded her against his body for a moment to warm her. "I'll be right back."

He ducked out into the rain and headed for the nearest cross street. Miraculously, an empty cab turned the corner just as he reached the intersection. He jumped into the street to flag it down and stepped into an ankle-deep puddle. He jerked open the door even before the taxi had come to a complete halt. Looking back over his shoulder, he shouted to Eva, "Come on!" But she was already dashing toward him through the downpour.

"You folks particularly fond of water?" the cabbie asked with a big grin when his passengers were inside. "If so, you might want to see the Tidal Basin."

"Another time," Nick answered and gave the name of their hotel. He turned to Eva who had begun to shiver in earnest. "Driver, kill the air conditioning. The lady's turning blue."

The cabbie made noises of protest but one glance at Nick's face made him comply.

"Here." Nick stripped off his shirt and wrapped the soggy cotton about Eva shoulders and bare arms. "It won't dry you but it's a barrier of protection," he added with a frown of doubt.

Eva cocked a brow at his bare chest. "What are you going to say when we get back to the hotel?"

Nick stripped the moisture from his face with a hand and laughed. "Who the hell cares what other people think? All that's important is that you get a hot shower and then go to bed before you catch a cold."

Eva chuckled. "I'm very much afraid you're right." She sobered, looking up at him from the snug circle of her arm. "After all, I must work tomorrow."

Nick did not protest her hint that their time together was over. It was his fault their evening together had not begun earlier. "I've enjoyed the evening, Eva—even if it didn't turn out quite as I'd hoped." He lifted a foot and rocked it back and forth so that his shoe made squishy sounds as water dribbled from the leather.

"You've ruined an expensive pair of shoes," Eva observed.

He shrugged and then settled her against him within his arm's embrace. "It was worth it. I haven't had this much fun in years."

Eva caught his hand and squeezed it lightly. "Good. I enjoyed it, too."

Nick knew she meant all of it, not just the steamy kisses they had shared. He leaned his cheek against her damp hair, inhaling the elusive scent that he had been imagining for days. One thing was certain, they were not done with one another. She had kissed him as if she were trying to set his socks on fire.

The dull red numbers of the LED clock glowed like malevolent eyes in the darkness. 3:07 a.m. Muttering, Eva flipped over on her stomach and punched her pillow. But it was no use. Her eyelids seemed to be on springs, snapping open at the least provocation. They flew open as ice tumbled like wooden blocks from the automatic ice-maker just outside her door. They flickered in response to the faint but maddening cheerfulness of the elevator chiming its arrival on the floor. Even the silence was ominous. From deep within the bowels of the hotel, a noise too deep to register as sound seemed to vibrate her bed. Finally the air conditioner kicked in, spewing eddies of refrigerated air across the king-size bed.

· With a groan of resignation, Eva flipped over onto her back. She might as well face it. Sleep was still as elusive as it had been three hours ago when she left Nick in the hallway.

His final kiss at her door, a beautifully controlled demonstration of his power to arouse, had left her with no doubts that there were depths to this man's passion she had barely begun to explore. When he had lifted his head, those dark eyes smoked by passion had begged entrance into her room, and her bed. All it would have taken was a sigh of invitation on her part and she would now know what it was like to make love to him. Sated and sleepy, she could be snuggling spoon-fashion against his warm nakedness, her hips scooped intimately against his groin, his lips brushing her neck, his hands playfully cupping her breasts and stomach.

Eva bolted upright, sending the covers sailing toward the foot. *That* was that! Sleep was gone for at least another hour. She was now as tightly wound as piano wire. Even her skin felt a size too small.

She reached for the light and flipped it on. Maybe a shower, a stinging cold shower, would relieve the tension. But somehow she doubted it. She would probably just end up adding a case of the shivers to her miserable condition.

"Dumb! Dumb! Dumb!" she muttered softly.

Why had she not given in to the moment? She had felt her restraints dissolving under his kiss. He would not have looked back if she had not. Why had she? Because she was playing for keeps. And she knew she just might lose.

Eva propped her elbows on her crossed legs and rested her chin in weary resignation on a palm.

This is what I call fun.

She knew he had said that in response to her silliness but she could not quite erase it from her mind. She should not have been surprised to learn that a man who had cut himself off from emotional entanglements would equate sex with recreation. But she did not want to be a diversion for him, however pleasant.

When she looked at him, she saw her future as it could be. She could picture him in quiet moments, at the end of hard days, needing the small comforts of her smile and privacy. She could envision them sharing the pleasures and frustrations of their professional lives, perhaps ultimately working together.

She could also imagine his features captured in the tiny face of their firstborn. She could visualize him in earnest concentration as he learned to change a diaper or hold the fragile life they had made in love and tenderness and joy. Most of all, she could imagine his all-too-rare smile permanently replacing the sadness that now lurked in his eyes.

She could not picture him as a short-term lover, however intense and romantic the relationship. Nor could she imagine having once loved him, ever getting over him. And that was the source of her conflict. She had not invited him into her room because she did not want to lie to herself or hurt herself. She wanted it all, or nothing.

Eva sighed, sinking further into her dismal thoughts. So here she sat in the middle of the night, neatly caught between the conflicts of her heart and mind. Or maybe the struggle was between her love and pride. No, it was hope and desire. She hoped he would admit that his desire for her was more than lust. Lust was good, definitely good, but in her plan to thaw out Nick, she had simply set herself afire.

She cast a baleful look at the clock: 3:13.

Nick punched the remote reflexively, channel-surfing without paying much attention to the late-night fare flicking past on the screen. Beside him on the nightstand were two empty minibottles of Scotch and a half-eaten can of nuts. Not that he needed the calories after Eva's ice-cream sundae but he did not like what alcohol did to his empty stomach these days. Yet the alcohol had not made him drowsy nor lessened by a single degree the urgent need pumping like adrenaline through his body.

He glanced at his clock. 3:13. He could not sleep. Could not read. Could not work. Could not settle long enough to watch a movie.

He tossed the remote aside and sprang to his feet and began stalking the room. He had tried a hot shower and then a cold one. He had done enough sit-ups to make any personal trainer proud. He had attempted to work on a crossword puzzle, had nearly dressed and gone out in search of a club or a late movie, anything to get his mind off Eva James.

"This is ridiculous," he muttered. "Insane!" Her kisses had left him restless, rigid and amazed that he was not too old or sophisticated to be left in a condition of permanent rut. Horny did not even begin to explain the condition of his body.

His gaze lit on his door. Eva lay in the room just across the hall. He imagined her sprawled in delectable abandon across turned-back sheets, arms lifted in invitation. Then he heard the echo of her voice inside his head.

What do you have to live for?

She had challenged him with that question. Why did he want to live? Well, because everyone did. The will to survive superseded rational explanation. But sometimes the price of survival was brutal. Only by shutting down his emotions had he been able to function that first year after the deaths of his wife and son. Gradually, it had become a habit. Yet there was a price. The isolation had become so complete, at times he felt his soul had freezer burn.

Why had he not told Eva that? And why had he not admitted that he was afraid to feel again, to open himself up to the possibility of loss? Because, in admitting that much, he would have had to admit how he felt about her, how she made him feel.

Nick flexed his hands, as if something he wanted very badly was within reach—if only he would grab for it. For six long lonely years he had backed away from anything and anyone that looked like commitment. But no woman until Eva had ever made him feel this slow, deep thaw inside.

She had been all heat and warmth and womanly curves in his arms. Her desire had been freely and fearlessly given. Yet, she, too, had backed away. Why? Was there something of which she was afraid?

Three long strides brought him to his door. He slid back the chain and bolt and opened it.

The hall was softly lit so that the glow of light under Eva's door was unmistakable. A smug smile curved up his mouth. So, she could not sleep, either! He stepped out into the hall before he remembered he wore only his underwear, and that it did not begin to hide his state of tumescence.

He hastily backtracked into the privacy of his room. As he grabbed his robe he debated the merits of knocking on her door. He did not want to do anything that she might misinterpret, or interpret too clearly. They were still in a quasiprofessional relationship. He turned toward the phone and dialed quickly.

She picked up on the first ring. "Hello?"

"Eva?"

"Yes? Nick?" she added in surprise.

"Yes. I saw the light on under your door. I wondered if you were all right."

"I'm fine. I just can't sleep."

Nick smiled. "Me, either. I wonder why?"

"Maybe it's the chocolate ice cream. All that caffeine."

"Perhaps." He paused for the space of two heartbeats. "Eva, you asked me tonight why I want to live. That's a hell of a question."

"I know." She sounded mildly amused. "Right up there with 'Why was I born?' and 'What's the meaning of life?' That sort of thing."

"Exactly. So, I'm curious. Why should you care about the answer?"

"We're friends, aren't we?"

"Yes. Still, I've known people my whole life I would never think of asking that particular question."

He could almost hear the wheels turning in her head.

"Maybe I asked, Nick, because you seem to need to think about the answer more than most people do."

"Why would you think that?"

"You're alone. Absolutely alone. If you were happy about that condition, it wouldn't have entered my mind to question it."

"So, you think I'm unhappy."

"Aren't you?"

He tensed. "What possible interest could that be to you?"

"You're right. Maybe it's none of my business."

"No. I didn't mean that." He paused, his voice huskier when he continued. "There's something between us. You know it. I know it. It's three-thirty in the morning and we're talking on the phone when one of us could just as easily cross the hall. Then neither of us would be alone."

"Are you certain that's true?" She suddenly sounded as leery as he felt. "Would you really be less alone in my bed, or just distracted from your solitude?"

"It's a little late for metaphysical debates, Eva." His voice dropped in register, deep and rousing as a caress. "What if we just try it and find out?"

"I'd like to, Nick, but..."

"You're afraid you won't like yourself in the morning," he finished dryly.

"Oh, I'd like myself just fine," she answered in perfect honesty. "And I'd like you better, more than you'd be comfortable with. That's the trouble. You wouldn't want me to begin to fashion silly daydreams of our future because you don't believe in happily ever after, do you? Only, I'm afraid I wouldn't be able to stop."

Eva held her breath as the silence on the line lengthened. It was as close as she had ever come to admitting her feelings for him. As the seconds added up, she suspected with a terrible sick wash of feeling that she had made a mistake.

"Sorry," she said a little harshly. "I thought we were being honest. It must be the time. Lord, it's nearly four. I'd better get some sleep. See you later."

Her receiver had nearly reached its cradle when she heard him shout a little desperately, "Eva!"

She brought it slowly back to her ear. "Yes, Nick?"

"Don't give up on me." He sounded distracted, his perfect tones for once roughened by unmanageable emotion. "I may not be worth it but I don't want you to give up. Understand?"

"I understand."

"You're important to me, Eva. Sorry if I rushed you."

She chuckled. "It wasn't too much of a rush or I wouldn't be lying awake, would I?"

She could almost feel his smile of relief but his tone was a little tight for genuine amusement. "If you only knew what you do to me!"

"Oh, no, you don't!" she said, managing to keep her tone light. "I need at least three hours of good sleep. Remember, you'll be putting your life in my hands come daylight."

"I'll trust you with any and every part of me, Eva, whenever you say."

"Good night, Nick."

Eva set the receiver down with a wide smile of triumph on her mouth. Suddenly, sleep seemed a very real possibility. The sooner she fell asleep the sooner it would be morning, and she would see him again.

The third cup of coffee was as strong and bitter as the first. As she added more one-percent milk to her cup Eva spied Nick's unique silver hair amid the crowd stepping off the elevator.

Something that went deeper than attraction came alive inside her whenever he was within sight. As he crossed the lobby dressed in natural linen trousers and ivory tab-collar shirt, his signature dark glasses shutting out the world, he was the picture of leisurely sophistication. Yet, she knew things about Nick a casual observer wouldn't suspect. He hadn't slept. That fact was betrayed, as yesterday, by the barest hint of a drag in his left leg.

I love him. That natural, necessary emotion burst upon her thoughts and remained. So there it was.

Last night, she had dared tease and taunt him, just enough to break through his aloof veneer, and been rewarded with a rare glimpse of the passionate man he kept hidden. A slow kitten-in-the-cream smile curved her mouth. The man packed more potency in a single kiss than any other man she had ever known. But that was only half her goal. They were more than just physically compatible. She had one day left to prove it to him.

She lifted her cup, her nails tapping a little nervously against the cup. As she watched over the rim, he scanned the lobby in search of her. Usually she left a message for him at the desk, telling him when to expect the limo out front. Today she had not. She decided to keep him off balance.

She saw him speak to the concierge. The man responded by pointing in the general direction of the hotel's coffee shop. When Nick noticed her sitting just inside the entrance, his face lit up in greeting.

Eva stood up as he neared her and watched his happy expression alter as he realized that she was in uniform. He snatched off his glasses, revealing two deep lines on his brow as his espresso-dark gaze swept her navy blue, brass-buttoned blazer and trousers. "What's this, Eva?"

She smiled just a degree or two, ignoring his request for an explanation of her change in dress. "Coffee, Mr. Bauer?"

He shook his head. "I ordered room service." His frown deepened as he continued to stare at her uniform but he did not say anything else about it. "I phoned your room at six-thirty, hoping you'd join me." His lifted an accusatory stare to her smiling face. "You didn't answer."

"I must have been out jogging down by the river. I needed the exercise to wake up. Then, too, I had to service the car."

The lines between his brows eased a fraction but his tone remained disapproving. "You might at least had left me a message. I've had the hotel staff looking for you for more than an hour.''

''Sorry, sir.'' Eva lowered her gaze, a slight frown pleating her own brow. So, despite the fact that she had kissed him the night before as if he held the last breath of air in the world, he had expected her to revert back to an eager-to-please Bauer employee this morning. Disappointment dragged at her. He had never before seemed petty, or arrogant.

She picked up several sheets of paper that lay on the table by her saucer and offered them to him, willing herself to sound efficient, calm, yet impersonal. ''I picked up your faxes. Ms. Roberts's note said you may expect the final estimates on the Jansen project before noon.''

He accepted the papers but his tone was laconic. ''Thank you.''

''It's what you pay me for,'' she answered with just enough edge to her voice to draw a sharp look from him.

''I suppose I do.'' He looked sheepish and disgruntled at the same time. ''Did you sleep well?''

''Well enough. Kind of you to ask, Mr. Bauer.''

He stared at her, not bothering to disguise the injured affront in his eyes at her renewed formality. ''I didn't sleep well, Eva.''

Despite his harsh expression, Eva wondered if she was being too judgmental. Perhaps he had been genuinely concerned for her safety and was disappointed they had not been able to share a private leisurely breakfast together.

She ignored the female urge to reach out and lace her fingers through his and lead him back to the elevator, and her room. She did not doubt that he would make love to her. It was exactly what he wanted, what she wanted. But common sense warned her against such tactics. She was gambling on something bigger than getting into his bed. She wanted entry into his life.

He caught her hand as she reached for the check. "About last night..."

Eva shook her head and slowly slid her hand out from under his. "Not here, Nick."

For an instant she saw naked longing smoldering in the pith of his dark eyes, then he slipped his glasses back into place. "Whatever you say, Eva. Whatever you want."

Eva turned away with new resolve. At three in the morning, he had asked her not to give up on him. He had no idea how single-minded she was going to be about keeping that promise.

A few minutes later they were both blinking into the glare of another muggy morning. The Potomac wore a metallic sheen. A smoggy pall hung grayish-brown in the smothering summer air. Last night's rain, brief and scattered, had evaporated as a steamy omen of another sweltering day.

"God! What a day!" Nick muttered.

"Inversion on the East Coast," Eva answered as she swung the rear door open for him. "Could be in the triple digits by midday."

To her surprise, he lifted her hand from the frame and pushed the rear door shut. "I'll sit up front, thank you."

Eva met his obstinate expression with a sly smile. "Front-seat passengers are against policy."

"I made the policy," he answered shortly. "I can break it."

She gave him a snappy salute. "Yes, sir, Mr. Bauer!"

Chapter Five

"I couldn't...save them."

Nick bit out the words, as though forced by torture to admit them. "Couldn't do...anything...for them." He took a long slow breath that ended on a funny little catch of sound. "A man should be able to protect his wife and child. I failed them."

Eva kept her eyes fixed on the highway. This unexpected confession had come out of nowhere. She could not even remember the inconsequential remark that had led him into it. Or maybe there had not been one. They had been on the road two hours, were deep in the Virginia horse country of white fences, pristine stables and manicured paddocks. That was it. He had mentioned his wife's love of horses. The next moment he was talking about his marriage, and then the end of it.

Eva swallowed back her own feelings. This was the very first time he had ever mentioned the crash to her. It did not take a genius to figure out how much the effort was costing this very private man, or that he was making the effort for her. It was crucial that she say something comforting.

Eva glanced at him. He sat rigidly, staring ahead as if he, not she, were driving. His profile might have cut glass. His tone had been impersonal, seeking to retreat even from his words. Only the barest tremor at the corner of his mouth betrayed how much control he was exerting over himself. This was the crux of his loneliness, the source of the glacial barrier that kept him emotionally separated from every other person in his life. It had never before occurred to her that he might blame himself for the deaths. She knew that it would be useless to mouth the usual comforting things that every other person who dared must have said to him at the time. He respected frankness, not platitudes.

"You say it's your fault. Did you cause the geese to be sucked into the engines?" she asked quietly.

His head whipped toward her, surprise registering in his face.

"Didn't you think I would be curious about the crash? I went to the library and read newspaper accounts," she baldly admitted. "So I ask, how did you fail?" She glanced at the highway between each question. "Did you single-handedly bring the plane down? Did you pick and choose who lived and who died? Did you turn away in fear? Where did you fail?"

Nick shook his head, his mouth flattening out under the pressure of his titanic grip on his self-possession. "It's not that simple."

"I read how you saved three other passengers' lives though your leg was injured." Despite his daunting frown, Eva went on in a stronger voice. "Ms. Roberts told me you were so badly concussed that you didn't even remember where you were for the first three days you lay in the hospital."

"I didn't want to know." His voice was a bare husk of its usual vibrant tone. He turned to stare out the front window again but she knew he was really looking inward.

She took a deep breath, feeling an empathy for him as strong as any she had ever known. He did not need her tears or sympathy. "You'll never reason it out, Nick. What happened won't ever conform to logic or measurable accounting. It wasn't an act of checks and balances, a measure of good and bad. It was a horrifying random accident. You loved your wife and child. Your grief has been so long and so deep. But, Nick..." She waited until he turned his head toward her. "They are gone and you are here. Would you have wanted your wife to live the last six years as you have done—alone and unloved?"

"Of course not." Some memory, softened for a moment, the pain in his expression. "Janet loved life." He shrugged a little. "She would have wanted me to go on living mine."

"Then do it," Eva said softly.

He turned to her, his gaze gradually retreating from the past and reentering the present. A rare smile of indulgence lifted the pain and eased the pressure on his fine mouth. "I don't know what I did to bring you into my life, Eva."

She smiled. "As I recall, you tried to block my employment. I had to storm the citadel and demand to be recognized."

"So you did. And you've been whittling away at my barriers ever since." He lifted his hand and touched her cheek with the back of his fingers. "Don't stop." His touch drifted down her cheek to her neck where his fingers encircled her nape in a feather-light touch. "I need you to keep after me."

With a shrugging gesture, Eva hugged his finger-tips between her cheek and shoulder, feeling the elation of a dangerous barrier safely crossed. "Perhaps you should be careful what you ask for. You just might get it."

"I'm counting on it—and on you, Eva." He leaned his silver head back against the cream leather headrest and closed his eyes. Yet his hand remained curved about her nape, a gently weighted reminder of a new bond between them. "I'm counting on it," he repeated wearily.

He fell asleep so quickly, Eva did not bother to respond. She knew some infinitely difficult but necessary moment had been passed. Whatever happened now would be about the present and, just maybe, the future.

"He never loved me. I was part of his 'bigger plan,' the most expendable part, as it turned out."

"And you never suspected the truth until it was too late?" Nick watched as Eva chewed a forkful of salad.

They sat in the cozy little nook of a country store a few miles outside the Cherokee reservation in the Great Smoky Mountains of western North Carolina. The building had once been a country feed-and-grain store. Now it was an arts-and-crafts mall filled with stalls selling local Indian and country crafts, farm collectibles and antiques. The small lunch corner was decorated in gingham and eyelet. They had stopped on impulse, Eva having allowed Nick to sleep through most of the day. Somewhere between debating buying a handmade war bonnet and consuming ice tea and salads, the topic of Eva's marriage had come up.

Eva pondered her answer. "I was just twenty years old. I grew up on a tight budget in a small town. Bill Rawlston seemed every woman's dream mate—handsome, brilliant, the boy wonder at an electronics firm in Hartford and from money. We met at a party given by mutual friends. He was several years older. Who was I to question his arrogance and self-assuredness, especially when he was directing his considerable charm my way?"

Her lips twisted ruefully. "I thought he was perfect, and so mature. He listened patiently to whatever I had to say, solicited my feelings every time we were together. Of course I fell for him. Big mistake."

She saw the hand Nick had rested on the tabletop move in her direction. She forestalled his gesture of sympathy with a little movement of her head. But he did not retreat. He looked her dead in the eye and said, "Tell me about it."

She studied the symmetrical beauty of bone and muscle of the man sitting across from her. It suddenly struck her that, in many ways, Bill and Nick were alike: handsome, smart, wealthy. But that was where the similarities ended. Bill had had no capacity for real emotion, certainly lacked the ability for self-examination, or regret. The subtle but defining marks of character that had been missing from Bill's pleasant face were there in spades in Nick's. No self-absorbed man could have eyes that embodied such strength, such sadness, such tenderness. She had seen firsthand that fierce protective look come alive when he thought some worthwhile cause might go wanting for "political expediency's sake," or when he saw someone being taken advantage of. At this moment the tenderness was for her.

She felt a rush of emotion in the region of her heart. He was as focused as if he were awaiting critical last-minute details of a business transaction instead of the trivial facts of her very brief and unhappy marriage.

Eva pushed a leaf of dandelion green around her plate, trying to recall the young unhappy bride she had once been. But the memories were so distant that it seemed as if someone else had lived that life.

The dispassion translated to her voice as she continued. "I'll make this fast. He asked me to marry him after only two months. I felt like Cinderella when Prince Charming brought the glass slipper to her door. So I kissed my senior year at college goodbye and married him.

"It wasn't until after we married that I realized that, for Bill, asking wasn't the same as caring and that listening wasn't the same as hearing. He had perfected the manners of a sensitive modern man but they were only a tool. The fact that I was miserable from day one didn't signify. He had what he wanted—a dutiful, subservient, pliable wife."

"I can't imagine you as either dutiful or subservient," Nick interjected. A new intimacy entered his dark gaze. "Pliant, I have been imagining all day."

Eva avoided looking at him but was grateful for the smile in his voice. "He was selfish even in bed but I was inexperienced, assumed it was my fault and that it would get better. But after six months he came home from work one day and said he wasn't certain *I* had made the right decision in marrying him after all. That if *I* had really listened to my heart, *I* would have realized that I didn't love him, not with the absolute devotion with which he needed to be loved."

"Bastard," Nick murmured.

Eva nodded, finally lifting her gaze to meet his. "About a week later I heard the rumor that he had resumed an affair with the senior executive officer in his department which he'd broken off shortly before we married. She was eight years older than he, and in a position to do his budding career some good. I walked out."

Eva speared the cherry tomato trying to escape over the rim of her plate. "I was only mildly surprised and frankly relieved that he didn't even attempt a reconciliation." She lifted her fork to inspect the tomato. "No trial separation. No marriage counselor. Just a quick divorce." She popped it into her mouth.

"No settlement?"

Eva shook her head emphatically. "I refused to pursue the settlement my lawyer told me I was entitled to. Bill was right. I'd made a mistake. Money wouldn't have changed that."

Twin fault lines of anger etched Nick's brow. "A decent man would have offered."

Eva gazed fondly at him, loving him for the fact that he could care so passionately about things that had occurred long before they met. "Think of the experiences I'd have missed if I hadn't had to work for a living! At least now I know my worth and I won't ever sell myself short again.''

Nick held her shining gaze with the intensity of his own. "You don't ever need to. From where I sit you seem to be calling all the shots. So, why is there no man in your life now?"

Eva shrugged. "I've had other priorities."

Nick expected that answer but it gave him a kind of perverse pleasure to have her confirm that no man shared her life in any important way. "And now?"

Eva gave him an enigmatic little smile and looked away.

They sat by a window sporting a window box brimming with bright summer flowers. Eva had shed her uniform jacket as a concession to the heat but her once-starched shirt was quickly wilting. Three glasses of ice tea were barely keeping her hydrated. Beyond the window, the limo seemed to dance in the midafternoon heat that bounced off the sidewalks and street. Several kids had surrounded it, trying to peek into the smoke-tinted windows. Usually she kept all gawkers at a distance but she did not have the heart to chase them off. Besides, it was too hot to go out into that heat again until she absolutely had to.

She glanced up and spoke to the waitress as she approached. "I was hoping it would be cooler near the mountains."

"Ninety-seven in the shade," replied the apple-cheeked blonde in a red-and-white gingham Colonial-style dress with white frilly apron. "It's a day for skinny-dipping, sure enough."

Eva's eyes lit up. "Is skinny-dipping on the menu?"

The young woman laughed as she tore their check off her pad and laid it on the table. "It could be."

"Really?" Eva ignored Nick's surprised expression.

"Oh, there's a gorge not far from here where one of the creeks forms a natural swimming hole." She winked. "All the local folks know it. Been there myself."

"How hard it is to find?" Eva asked, her gaze kindling with mischief.

The young woman grinned as her speculative gaze swung from Eva's smile to Nick's incredulous expression. "Maybe five miles, up in the Smokies." Her gaze shifted toward the window and beyond to the black limousine baking in the sun. "Of course, the road's narrow and twisting, just a ribbon of blacktop, really. Drops off steeply in places."

Eva had followed her train of thought. "You'd be surprised at the spaces I've threaded that monster through. If there's a road, I'll manage."

The waitress smiled. "Tell you what, I'll draw a map for you." She took a paper napkin and sketched roads and directions on it. "Perfect day for it," she said as she handed her handiwork to Eva.

Eva scanned then pocketed the map. "Thanks."

"Sure thing," the waitress answered. "Folks around here go up there all the time. Of course, it *is* against the law. But most times the sheriff's got better things to do than chase people away from the swimming hole."

She reached for the bills Nick handed her, her eyes widening in appreciation when Nick said, "Keep the change."

"Thanks. You folks come back anytime." She paused in backing away, her gaze lingering appreciatively on Nick. "You want to be sure and get back down that road before too long. Radio says to expect rain later. You ain't never seen weather until you've experienced a Smoky Mountain thunderstorm. Enjoy your swim."

Nick chuckled when she was gone. "She thinks we're crazy enough to try it."

Eva stood and reached for her uniform jacket that hung on the back of her chair. "I am."

Nick's taupe brows lifted ironically as he came to his feet. "Are you serious?" His dark eyes took on a definite gleam. "I didn't pack swim trunks."

Eva smiled wickedly at him. "Neither did I."

The world changed the moment they turned off the main highway through the Great Smoky Mountains National Park onto a blacktop road so narrow there was no stripe to divide it. Suddenly, eerily, they were gliding through a sheltering, cooler, quiet world where cathedral-high trees formed the forest closing in about them.

With a conspiratorial glance at one another, Eva and Nick simultaneously reached for their window controls, pushing the down button. Immediately, mountain air swept in to replace the need for the air conditioner, bringing the scents of the wilderness on its cooling breeze.

High hedgerows of rhododendron whispered past the road on either side. After a few moments they began the climb in a tight curvy zigzag. On one side of the car, the mountain loomed as a dark verdant presence. On the other, the land fell steeply away in places until they were looking out over the tops of trees whose branches they had been beneath only minutes before. The breathtaking climb took every ounce of Eva's concentration as the limo's engine occasionally strained in hauling its weight up the incline. In places in the valley below, where the mountains shouldered away the afternoon sunlight, the land had begun to grow misty. Yet, overhead, the sky was a bright hard blue shell.

When the road finally leveled off a bit, Eva turned a smug smile upon her passenger. "Told you I could do it."

Nick cocked a doubtful brow at her. "Getting back down is going to be another challenge."

Eva shot him a confident smile, her gaze lingering a fraction longer on him than was absolutely wise. Despite the dark interior, he seemed to shine. She supposed it was his hair, the pure silver white that attracted every photon of the meager light into it and served it back with enhanced brilliance. She could have sat watching him forever, or until she got up the courage to touch him. She could never look long at him without wanting to touch.

Suddenly he looked over at her and snared her gaze. She knew he could read the longing in her expression, in her eyes. To distract herself, and him, she said, "People claim moonshiners still lurk in these moun-

tains. Although, a few years ago marijuana became
the leading illegal cash crop.''

"How would you know that?" Nick questioned
though he was more interested in other things. He had
seen the slight but betraying tightening of her hands on
the wheel when he looked at her. He felt it, too, the
slow but inexorable rise in the tension between them.

Eva offered him a superior smile. "I read."

Nick reached out to touch a lock of silky hair curving over her shoulder. He folded the ends of the curl
over his forefinger with his thumb and used it like a
feather to tickle her jawline. A warm wash of color
rose under her skin and spilled into her cheek. Heat
spread into his groin. ''What else do you know about
the area?''

Eva recognized his tone of voice as skeptical. He
used it when he wanted to rattle an opponent's confi-
dence. "A great deal, actually. The Great Smoky
Mountains National Park is the largest publicly owned
wilderness area east of the Mississippi. More than
three hundred thousand visitors come through here
each year. There's bass fishing in summer and, amaz-
ingly enough, skiing in winter months. Despite the in-
flux of all those visitors, the older people in this area
of Appalachia still speak in a dialect that has its roots
in sixteenth-century Elizabethan English.''

"I'm impressed with your knowledge."

Eva could not turn her gaze from the road this time
for they were beginning the descent into the gorge
marked on the paper napkin map. "I always take time
to learn about the things that interest me."

"So I've noticed." Nick watched as she expertly maneuvered the limo through a steep downward turn. She often went the extra mile to check on the clients with whom he did business. It was not just idle curiosity with her. She had a good sharp mind that she enjoyed exercising. He knew now that at least part of her interest stemmed from the fact that these were things that concerned *him*. In so many ways she had made herself a part of his life without being intrusive. It was yet another of the rare qualities she possessed. He could not—must not—lose her.

He slid a hand under her hair and began to gently massage the tendons of her neck. "You're tight as piano wire. Is it fatigue?" His thumb branched out to stroke under her jaw. "Or is it me, Eva?"

Eva glanced at him, absorbing the heat from the smoky surface of his nearly black eyes, and wondered how he could ask. "I'll never knowingly lie to you, Nick."

Nick chuckled. "That's a classic Eva answer—subtle, evasive and with enough mystery to keep me intrigued. Very well. Keep your secrets, for the moment."

A moment later the car swept into a turn that flattened out into a sunny spot formed by a natural break in the mountain range. The grass just off the road was matted by regular use but the only vehicle there now was a pickup truck full of teenagers who had piled into the back. They whistled and waved as Eva pulled the limo to a halt beside them.

"Who's the celebrity?" cried one of the girls as Eva swung open her door.

"Sorry, just a CEO," Eva called out as Nick emerged from the other side.

Their groans were classic examples of disappointment.

"What brings you all here?" called another of the group.

"Looking for a little fresh air," Eva answered.

"You all don't want to stay late," called the driver and pointed at the sky. "Weather's coming on. On the other side of the mountain now but it'll come on fast."

Eva glanced up at the clear blue sky and shrugged. A moment later, as the truck pulled away to accompanying hoots and waves, she thought she heard faint rumblings, but decided it must have been the truck's muffler.

"What do you think?" Nick asked.

She met his doubting gaze across the roof of the car. "I think I'm ready to go skinny-dipping." She shed her jacket and tossed it into the car before closing the door and turning to cross the grass toward the water.

The gorge was a small flat-bottomed canyon cut long ago between the mountains by the action of the narrow stream that ran swiftly in the distance. At one end of the narrow valley a steep cliff rose abruptly, forming a protective barrier from winds and heat. It was here that the stream bowed out into a pool. Cool lacy ferns grew at the base of the larger trees surrounding it. In the deep shadow of the cliff itself, thick moss covered the ground cast in permanent twilight.

"It's perfect," Eva said enthusiastically when she reached the mossy-strewn bank. "It must be ten degrees cooler here."

"Exactly," Nick answered as he came up behind her. His gaze lingered in admiration on the feminine contours of her back and hips. "So why don't we just sit and enjoy the view? There's no need to get wet."

Eva spun around on him with a mischievous glance. "Isn't there?"

Nick met her challenging gaze with its touch of feminine reserve. He had anticipated that the morning drive would be one long-heated encounter punctuated by double entendres and scintillating sidelong glances until neither of them could stand it any longer and sought a way and place to end this slow dance of desire. Yet he had slept away a good part of the day and what conversation they did have had been about past hurts and old mistakes. Still, the tension had been there.

Now, as their gaze locked, he recalled with absolute clarity of detail what had nearly occurred the night before. He felt his muscles tense. He wanted— no, needed—to kiss her again. He could almost feel her sharp little teeth sink into his lower lip, recall the taste of her on his tongue. The perfume that had been teasing his nostrils all day as he sat beside her suddenly seemed more potent in the open air.

Yet something he could not even give words to made him very reluctant to start what he so badly wanted to finish. "I'm not certain we have time for this, Eva."

She smiled. "It's only four o'clock. You're not expected at the conference site until at least 6:00 p.m. But, if you'd like, I can call to reconfirm."

He put up a hand to stop her, yet his next words were no more encouraging. "What if someone should come along and see us?"

Her expression changed to one of mild surprise. "Since when have you cared what strangers think?"

He did not give a good damn, but he did care about her. "What if it's the sheriff?"

Her smile reappeared and he wondered if it would taste like sunshine, for it certainly heated his blood. "You'll explain, using that Bauer charm of yours, that you didn't know it was against the law. We're from out of state, and we won't ever do it again."

He watched her as she kicked off her shoes and crunched her bare toes in the grass, wondering why that simple gesture seemed like calculated erotic playfulness. He took a step toward her, a slow smile forming on his face. "You're making light of a potentially damaging situation."

"Damaging to what?" she responded as she reached up and unbuttoned the first button on her shirt.

"My image," he said doggedly, lowering his gaze to keep her from guessing his thoughts. "Think what would happen if the press got wind of me swimming in the nude with my chauffeur."

"The publicity would certainly alter your public image," she answered with a chuckle. "I can see the TV news headlines now. 'Ice Man Bauer Thaws With Nude Companion.' Or better yet, 'Bauer Bares Butt— Photos At Six.'"

Eva laughed again but the look on his face said that he did not share her amusement. She placed a fist on each hip and gave him a thorough glance from the top of his head, gleaming like a polar ice cap in the sunlight, right down to his shoetips. "Just what is it you're afraid of revealing, Mr. Bauer?"

Of my reaction to seeing you nude, dear Eva.

Nick considered his options. He could simply drop his trousers and show her. Or he could tell her. Or he could . . .

Eva turned away from his stubborn expression and began unbuttoning her shirt. She had never done anything like this in her life, not if she didn't count skinny-dipping as a preteen with her cousins on her grandmother's property. But to brazenly reveal herself to a man she had never made love with—what could she be thinking of? No, she was not going to think. The time had come for action. Put up or shut up. Fish or cut bait. Sink or swim. Winner take all. The clichés ricocheted off the walls of her mind like Ping-Pong balls. Ultimately it came down to this. For eleven months, fourteen days and somewhere in the neighborhood of eight hours, every glance, thought and smile between them had been steering them toward this moment. Whatever happened, she would not be sorry unless she did not take this chance.

When the last button came free, she quickly stripped off her shirt to reveal a bra of rose satin and lace. At least she had worn her sexy underwear, she consoled herself. Though, at the time she put it on, she thought it would come off in a different setting, for a different reason. But, as swimwear, her bra and panties were as modest as a bikini. Back still turned, she slid open her zipper, eased her trousers down over the fullness of her hips and gave them a shove toward her feet before she could change her mind. She thought she heard a sound behind her but she was not about to turn around to discover what had caused it. It would be too humiliating if Nick had gone back to the limo.

Nick, standing dry-mouthed and staring, had not gone anywhere. The only direction his mind was thinking of taking him was full-steam straight ahead.

He took several slow soundless steps toward her as she reached back with both hands to unhook her bra. His next breath halted somewhere in middle passage as he came to a stop directly behind her. He watched in rapt fascination as the satin straps of her bra slid down her lightly tanned arms. As she moved her arms forward they sailed off the ends of her fingertips as the bra sank to the soft thick grass.

He was so close to her, all he had to do was reach forward beneath her extended arms to cup each breast from behind. He had glimpsed her nakedness in her hotel mirror the night before and knew her breasts were full and naturally weighted with large easily aroused nipples. The muscles in his stomach contracted—hard. Yet he did not touch her. He was no boy, grabbing at what he wanted, but he wanted her so badly he hurt.

Eva heard the small expulsion of breath close behind her but she did not have the nerve to turn around. Instead, she sprinted off in the direction of the water, calling over her shoulder, "Last one in is a rotten egg!"

Nick stopped thinking about the sheriff or the consequences or anything else but the sight of Eva James running across the grass in her panties, her breasts swinging provocatively as she challenged him to follow her. He stripped off his clothes in record time, leaving a trail toward the water.

When he realized what she was about to do, he shouted a warning. But it was too late. She leapt into the placid pool in a graceful diving arch.

As water fountained up in iridescent drops, he ran toward the bank where she had jumped in. He swore under his breath in anger and relief as she surfaced with a whoop of delight.

"It's cold! Bracing! Wonderful!" she cried in breathless exclamation.

Nick did not share her enthusiasm. "Dammit, Eva! No one with half a brain leaps into an unfamiliar body of water. It's not safe." He knew he sounded like a parent, but his heart was beating a ragged tattoo of fright. She might have struck her head on a submerged object and been severely injured, or killed.

"You're right!" she called to him as she swam toward the shore. When she reached chest-high water she looked up at him with a contrite expression. "I'm sorry if I scared you." Her sudden warm smile seemed to brighten the day. "It *is* wonderful."

Nick's lips twitched. Cold and bracing did not sound exactly wonderful to him. But at least she was okay.

He stood on the bank in his boxer shorts, watching her head bob in and out of the crystal water dappled with green and gold shadows. He could see her breasts clearly, bobbing in the water. Her nipples were hard rosy pebbles just below the surface. She was complex and complicated, a strange blend of practical reason and whimsy. Yet no other woman had ever made him feel so completely in tune with her, and with himself. When he'd married, he had been too young, too eager to make it, too focused on his career to fully appreciate the emotional joys of loving a woman. And then he had lost the chance to grow into that knowledge.

He wondered now, watching Eva, if it were possible to feel as he felt about her and not call it love. He very much doubted it.

Eva dog-paddled in place, water streaming from the ends of her hair. "Well? Are you or aren't you going to drop the veil, Mr. Bauer?"

Nick glanced back over his shoulder to the trail of garments they had left. When he looked down at her again, he said with a slow grin, "You seem to have forgotten the rules of skinny-dipping."

"Right." She splashed about for a moment and then triumphantly held up a soggy bit of pink silk and lace. After twirling it twice about her head, she flung it toward the shore. The panties landed with a wet smack on top of his bare right foot.

"There!" she cried smugly. "That's the price of admission. Are you up for it, or not?"

The gibe narrowed his eyes and widened his smile. "With you, Eva, I'm always *up* for it." Grinning, he shoved his boxers down and stepped out of them.

Eva had a glimpse of his quite impressive arousal before he cannonballed into the water with a splash that created a wave, momentarily submerging her head.

Chapter Six

When he surfaced, Nick gasped in astonishment. "Jeez! It's freezing!" He shook his head like a wet dog, sending droplets flying in all directions. Eva squealed as the shower struck her but she did not mind.

After a moment he slicked his hair back with both hands and smiled at her. "You are a madwoman."

Eva shrugged, finding her footing in the chest-high water. "And yet you are quite willing to follow my lead. Amazing, isn't it?"

His smile broadened, every feature in his face relaxing to accommodate it. She had never seen him smile so freely before. Gone were the tight-pinched edges at the corners of his mouth, which betrayed his need to control even his pleasure. Her gaze drifted over him as he stood closer to the shore in waist-high water. The fine trace of hair on his chest was surprisingly dark and lay smoothly against his skin. Only at the base of his belly, which she had caught the barest glimpse of before he dove in, did it flare into crisp tight curls with reddish highlights. She smiled at the memory. How like nature to adorn this supremely self-contained man with an "ice cap" of hair while hinting at hidden fires lower down.

She began to swim parallel to him, moving her arms in lazy arcs to slice the water. "It just takes a moment to get used to," she promised as she flipped over on her back. "This is just what we needed to cool off."

Forgetting the shivers creeping across his skin, Nick watched her floating toward him, her rose-crowned breasts bobbing above the surface. Though the rest of her body was submerged, he caught provocative glimpses of it through the clear spring water. She looked like a sea nymph: lithe, seductive and oh-so-desirable. He suddenly felt the futility of what she had described as "cooling off." His internal temperature was rising by the second.

When she came within reach, he stretched out a hand and snagged her by the arm, pulling her to him until their skins were sliding wetly along one another's. The feel of her was cool and slick and unbearably seductive. His inner thermometer spiked toward the boiling point.

"Come here," he commanded softly as he drew her to her feet beside him. His hand slid warmly under her chin, turning her face up to his. He bent his head slowly, giving her time to realize what was happening, and how it would happen, and why.

Sensing that he was about to kiss her, Eva did not wait. She surged up on tiptoe to meet his mouth with her own, her arms coming up to encircle his neck. There was no need to pretend that this was anything other than what she wanted. She loved him, had waited so long to know what it would be like to love him with her body.

His mouth was hot despite the water surrounding them. She felt that heat curl and settle in her stomach, and then his tongue was stroking the warmth in her to a higher intensity. Her knees seemed to lose their strength. She had to clutch his shoulders to stay upright in the water. His hands moved. One plowed into her hair to hold her head for his kiss. The other formed a firm barrier at her back to hold her up and against him. She leaned into him, grateful for his masculine warmth and strength and hunger.

He took his time, kissing and tasting and loving her with just his mouth until she thought she would weep. He did it sweetly and powerfully, offering an astonishing variety of erotic pleasure in the deceptively simple act of a kiss.

Nick savored her mouth, feeding the feeling that he was aflame in sensations of her. At first her skin had been cool to the touch, her lips trembling from the brisk mountain breeze. His own body had responded to the chilly water by contracting to less than impressive proportions. Yet, the moment their lips met, the cold and wet and chill disappeared. Suddenly her skin radiated warmth, her lips heating to the pressure of his mouth and breath. He could feel the thrill of desire vibrating just under the surface of her skin. He reached up to cup a breast. She moaned softly into his mouth and he tasted her desire.

He reveled in how easily she came to life under his touch. And how swiftly he responded in need. The subtle mystery that was Eva James melded into a woman who was all forthright seductiveness. How he wanted her! No other woman had ever been so eagerly and unapologetically excited by him.

He had known it would take no more than this, to kiss her, to touch her, to taste the invitation on her lips, and he would be aflame, unable to wait or even think of anything but being—at last—inside her. He pulled her closer so that she would know what she did to him, and the magnitude of his need for her.

Sensing the change in his anatomy, Eva slid a hand down his back then around the curve of his waist to the front. She marveled at the differences in texture of his skin, from the denser thickness of his back and waist to the finer, thinner skin of his belly, as her fingers glided down his stomach. His muscles contracted involuntarily as her hand met the barrier of their hips and her hand slipped lower. He moaned as if in pain when she encompassed him but he only drew her in, trapping her hand between their lower bodies as he cupped her bottom with his hands.

So much for the Ice Man image, she thought with a secret satisfaction that curled her toes. Nick Bauer had his own personal volcano and he seemed ready to erupt.

When she finally released him, the hard ridge of his sex boldly prodded the womanly place at the apex of her thighs. Spreading her legs slightly, she straddled him and then tightened her thighs to hold him there. He groaned softly into her mouth, his fingers pressing into the soft flesh of her bottom as he lifted her on tiptoe to bring their bodies even closer together. Her breasts flattened out on his chest, the nipples aching as they grazed the hair on his chest. Then he began moving his hips. The easy thrust and retreat of his hips was matched by the frankly sexual forays of his tongue between her lips.

Eva could not catch her breath. Everywhere they touched, she seemed to be on fire. Inside she was melting, liquefying with the pleasure of what he was doing. The pressure building between her legs was a sizable hint of what he would do next. Yet he never actually touched the place that ached so unbearably.

"Nick—" she said on a ragged breath. "Nick—please!"

"I hear you, Eva." Nick searched his mind frantically for a plan of physical geometry that would allow him to make love to her where they were.

He gripped her low down and lifted, saying urgently, "Wrap your legs about my waist!" But the pond bottom was too slippery. When she tried to climb him, he nearly lost his footing and she began slithering down his front. There was no wall to press her up against and no water float to hold her up. As design after carnal design failed, the realization that this could not be done came as such a disappointment that he snatched his mouth away from hers with a snarl of despair.

Breathing hard, he felt himself slide free of her thighs as her body floated away from his. The release was wrenching as if he had withdrawn from inside her.

He swung his head desperately toward the bank and saw the firm soft blanket of grass. Did he dare risk taking her in the open where anyone might come along and see or, worse yet, interrupt them?

"What's wrong, Nick?"

When he looked back at her, her expression was almost dazed. She leaned in toward him until her breasts, floating in the water, just grazed his chest. "Don't you want me, Nick?" The question was a subtle command. She wanted him, here and now, whatever the risk.

Heat surged through him as his body shuddered with renewed urgency for release. "Hell, yes!"

But he was a man accustomed to planning things. He was no Lothario but he had an idea of how he had wanted it to be the first time between them. Coupling quickly in a mountain gorge was not it. Yet, when he looked at her seductive gaze, at the passion-blurred curve of her generous mouth, it suddenly seemed important only that they satisfy the raging hunger burning out of control.

He drew her with him toward the bank with a chuckle of self-awareness. "This isn't exactly the place I would have chosen, Eva, but I don't think I can wait."

When they reached the shore and waded out, he stopped and turned to her. "Will you let me make love to you now? Here? In the grass?"

Her body trembling as much from desire as from the breeze on her wet skin, Eva searched his face for any sign of reluctance but all she saw in his expression was the absolute intensity with which he awaited her next words. She smiled at him with the secret knowledge of the passion they had aroused and not yet assuaged. But the moment was too important for flippancy. Her need to share her love for him—with him—was too intense to trivialize with only a lustful smile.

She said in a perfectly serious voice, "If you feel what I feel, this is the right place."

The smile he gave her was perfect in its tenderness and joy. *He loves me,* she thought. And then he drew her in and embraced her.

For a long moment they stood still within one another's arms, as if the agreement had not just been made. But then his hands lifted to frame her face and he turned her mouth up to meet his and Eva felt the world drop away, leaving only them in this wild natural Eden.

One moment they were on their feet. The next she felt herself being laid back in the grass. She did not know who moved first or if they had kissed a long time or just once but suddenly, the frantic fever of passion overcame them once more.

His hands and mouth were everywhere. His lips devoured hers, then touched her brow, her eyes, then skimmed down to her breast, tugging and sucking her so that she whimpered with pleasure. His hands stroked her, calming and rousing, as her own did him. And then his fingers moved low down to stroke inside her so sweetly that her body found the rhythm irresistible.

The first wash of pleasure surprised her in its intensity. The tiny internal convulsions of her body that caressed his fingers were just short of painful. Even as her hips rose instinctively against his fingers, she stiffened, embarrassed by her body's uninhibited hunger. But then she heard him crooning approval in her ear.

"Yes, Eva. Yes! You're so responsive, so good."

Even before the sensations began to ebb he was kneeling between her parted thighs.

For a moment she stared up at him. His breath was choppy, his silver hair stained dark by water, his teeth clenched with the effort of self-control. His concentration was so intense, he looked almost angry, yet in his nearly black eyes she saw a needy vulnerability more appealing than his strong attractive body. The complex play of emotions he had always been so adept at keeping hidden softened and humanized his classically handsome face. The sight shattered her with love. He was saying something to her but she did not understand the words. It did not matter. She felt his hands on her thighs and then the hard press of his sex nestling between them.

His thrust was not gentle. She realized that he had spent the last of his reserve of control to bring her to pleasure. Now as he slid snugly within her, it was he who cried out in momentary surprise. There was no pain in his action, only the intense sensations of this deep invasion by a force large and powerful and demanding. Her hips arched naturally to meet and accept the seminal invasion, her body easing with each movement to expand in accommodation. But the effort forced deep moans from her. Pleasure more staggering than any she had ever experienced quaked through her.

Nick tried to stop the runaway locomotive force his body had become. They were both wet from the pool, but deep inside, she was even wetter, and impossibly hot. Driven by the wondrous sensations, he was all rough greedy hunger. His thrusts were deep and hard and impossible to contain. He had never felt more randy, more governed by his emotions, more out of control.

He bent over her, searching like a blind man for her mouth as though her kiss alone could keep him from exploding into a million pieces. He found it, the soothing warmth of her lips invading his senses. This was Eva under him, the one woman in the world who, after so long an isolation, made him feel that he might again find peace, and a homecoming. He moaned in gratitude as her sweet mouth anchored him and his erratic rhythm steadied into deep satisfying surges that carried them both toward the final short distance to completion.

Eva felt him tensing, the short hard thrusts pushing her over the edge of pleasure as his deep grunts signaled his own fulfillment. She held on to him as if the grass beneath them had suddenly taken flight like a magic carpet.

"*Oh*...oh, yes!" Nick's voice carried in it the swift urgent hunger of his body as it found release with hers.

He buried his face in the junction between her neck and shoulder with a small sigh and after a few seconds stilled. But every muscle of his body remained taut with the need still pulsing at the apex of their joining. It was as if he had climaxed without his body knowing it. He felt ready to begin again, immediately.

"I thought—I don't think—" he murmured into her hair and then began to chuckle.

Eva gently stroked his back as his laughter shook them both. She had known it would be like this, all skyrockets and Catherine Wheels, consuming every previous memory of lovemaking before it. Now there would only be this overwhelming memory of Nick's body, and his complete and total possession of hers.

The sharp *crack* of lightning startled them both and then a cannonade of thunder seemed to shake the ground beneath them.

Eva tilted her head back as Nick lifted his skyward. To the west, pewter clouds were boiling over the rim of the mountain peak. Even as they watched, another flash of lightning stretched outward from the roiling thunderhead into the clear blue beyond. At that moment they heard the whistle of the wind as it swept suddenly down through the gorge followed by the feel of rain-cooled gusts along their naked bodies. A moment later thick fat drops of summer rain pelted them.

Nick rose quickly to his feet and reached down for Eva. "Come on!" he cried, pulling her to her feet. As he put an arm around her to shield her body with his, the sky opened upon them.

Scampering across the grass like two naughty children, they headed for the limo. Nick punched the combination into the automatic lock then grabbed the handle of the rear door and swung it open, moving back so that she could climb in first. He leapt in beside her and slammed the door.

With hair plastered to their foreheads and rain running down their faces to dribble off their chins, they simultaneously broke into laughter. At that moment lightning breached the semidarkness within the tinted windows. They instinctively reached for each other as thunder jarred the limo.

"God, you're beautiful!" Nick said as he cradled her face in his hands. "Beautiful! And wonderful! And more than a little mad!" He punctuated every phrase with a kiss dropped lightly on her lashes, nose and finally her mouth.

For a moment Eva gave up to the delicious sensation of his kisses. All the feelings that she had been so uncertain of expressing rose up from deep within her, nearly choking her with their intensity. She pushed against his chest and came out of his slackened embrace with a shaky laugh that ended in a sob as two unexpected tears slid from her eyes.

"You're crying." Frowning he pulled her to him. "Did I hurt you before? You were so tight."

Eva shook her head, as surprised as he by the sudden overflow of emotion. "No, no. I just—" She looked at him, eyes gleaming with love. "I've just wanted this for so long."

He gave her a long strange look that eased into a wicked grin. "Then why didn't this happen before?"

"Because," Eva said in her most reasonable tone, "I *knew* it would be like this." She lay her head on his shoulder. "Just hold me."

"This is better," Nick said in satisfaction as he sprawled unselfconsciously on the leather seat and drew her down beside him. "Why didn't I think of the limo in the first place?"

Eva's gaze slipped over the boldly displayed contours of his chest and belly down to his groin, her eyes widening at what she discovered at the end of the journey. "You had—or should I say *have*—other things on your mind."

Nick looked down at himself and smiled. "I don't usually recover so quickly." He cocked his head at an angle to look at her and grinned in pure male smugness. "Now you know. You do this to me every time I'm near you."

Eva drew a deep shuddering breath. Yes, now she knew, and it was still a wonder and unbearably exciting.

She licked her lips, an unconsciously voluptuous reaction, as she placed her hand deliberately on the expanse of silky hair just below his navel. "We have nothing to put on. Our clothes are out in the rain."

"Yes, I know," he said with a sigh. "You're hell on a man's wardrobe. I'm going to have to invest in rubber suits if we keep this up."

Eva smiled as she lazily swirled a finger through his groin hair. "I, for one, rather like the results."

"Eva," he said low in his throat, "you're asking...for trouble."

Eva leaned over him and, cupping his face in her hands, kissed every inch of it she could reach: his brows, his eyes, the hollows beneath his cheekbones and most of all, his slightly swollen, passion-blurred mouth. When she was done, she released him with a big sassy smile. "I love you, Nick Bauer."

To her dismay she saw the shadow of doubt enter his eyes before he quelled it. "Eva," he began, his voice sounding a warm note that did not match his wary gaze, "I'm more flattered than you know. Surely you've guessed how I feel about you."

"Of course I haven't," she answered forthrightly, but her gaze shied away from his as she moved to trace the tip of his arousal with a fingertip. "You've never said two direct words about your feelings for me."

He thrust his pelvis suggestively under her hand. "Would you like another demonstration of what you do to me?"

Eva stilled, her gaze as frank as his was cautious when they met. She wondered inconsequentially if he felt as awkward as she did. Nothing in his expression answered the question. He had won his reputation by knowing how to deal with difficult and delicate situations. Yet this was something she had not counted on. Even stark naked Nick Bauer possessed hard-to-penetrate layers of reserve.

"I suspect I know how you feel, Nick," she said slowly, choosing her words as carefully as if the wrong one would bite her. "The question is, do *you* know how you feel?"

She saw the flash in his eyes as his razor-sharp mind kicked in before he replied. "Why don't we find out?"

He lowered his head to kiss the tip of one of her breasts. He took his time, massaging it to puckered fullness with his tongue before drawing it strongly into his mouth. She arched instinctively to the pressure, sighing deep in her throat. Within seconds her sated body was once more aching with the need to again be possessed by him. Though she knew it was a delaying tactic on his part, she could not fault him for choosing so delightful a method.

When he moved away from her, his face was slightly flushed and his mouth was curved with satisfaction. "I know how you make me feel. Wonderful. Content. Alive. I haven't felt any of those things in six years.

Maybe never like this.'' His hot-coffee eyes seemed to drink her in. ''Isn't that enough for the moment?''

She did not try to hold him off as he bent over her. Instead, her arms tightened about his shoulders, drawing him against her. There were so many other things she wanted to say to him. Things like ''I love you, I want to marry you, be your family for a while, and then add to it. I want to give you children so that you will know that you never need to be alone in the world again.'' But, for now, she accepted what he was offering: this moment.

She kissed him, a deep soul-searing kiss that offered in equal parts tenderness and passion for this man whom she loved more than she had thought was possible. That love had made her daring, reckless, sparing neither pride or dignity. No wonder the Romans had depicted Cupid as a cheeky trickster with a broad sense of humor. She had it bad. And now, she knew, she would never ever get over him.

He parted her thighs so that she straddled him and then entered her with a thrust that forced a groan of contentment from him. As he began moving strongly against her, swelling to life in that secret place where she held and caressed him, Eva closed her eyes and gave a sigh of pure desire. Hopeless to resist. Impossible, really. Then she even stopped thinking and welcomed the sweet wonderful feelings he alone aroused.

Afterward, he pulled her down on the wide leather seat beside him and tucked her into the curve of his arm. They lay a long time in the semidarkness listening to the tail end of the storm that had whirled unnoticed around them while they'd made love. The thunder was muted now, the lightning less frequent and softer.

Yet it was Nick Bauer's storm of conscience to which Eva was attuned. She could hear the rapid beat of his heartbeat and knew that he was thinking hard about what he should do and say next. As much as she would have liked to make it easier for him she knew she must not. She had risked everything emotionally on this afternoon. It was now his moment of truth to meet, or reject.

Nick held on to Eva as though she might suddenly bolt. Yet he knew the truth was just the opposite. It was he who had to keep from fleeing. He lay beside her with thundering heart and sweaty palms, every nerve shockingly alive. Her love had split him open, exposing his false sense of self-sufficiency for what it was—a cloak for his fear.

I love you. She had said the words bravely, fearlessly. He knew her too well to suspect that she had said it to wring a similar confession from him. She had said the words because she meant them. The declaration made him proud, and humble—and scared him to death. Her companionship this past year had been the greatest gift of his life. But he was not ready—was not prepared—

Nick flinched from the excuses forming in his thoughts. God! Was he really that much of a coward? He had wanted to be with Eva this weekend more than he had wanted anything in six years. He had emerged from her embrace feeling as if he had just begun to breathe again. Yet he had been prepared to accept so much less from her than a declaration of love. No, that did not quite explain this fear ripping his gut. The truth was he did not want the responsibility of her love because he was very much afraid he might fail her, and break her heart. Yet, if he did not offer her something, he would lose her.

"Stay the weekend with me."

Eva lifted her head from his shoulder to look at him. "You mean at the conference? How would you explain my presence to the others?"

His expression was pure Nick Bauer: cool aloof, superior. "I never explain."

Eva tried not to react to his cocksure attitude—but she could not dismiss the implication. He was not uncomfortable with the idea of bringing a woman with him to a business conference because it would not be the first time. Only she felt the shrinking inside her as she imagined the smirks and sly glances that would come her way. His business partners would assume she was his mistress. Yet, even that would might not have mattered if he had spoken of his feelings for her. He had not. Perhaps she had made a terrible mistake after all. Perhaps he did not feel as she did. The ache inside her redoubled.

"I won't simply have an affair with you, Nick."

Exasperation colored his expression as he angled his head to look at her. "I'm not talking about an affair." He hugged her tighter. "We've only just really found each other, Eva. I don't want to let you go yet."

Yet. Eva shook her head, feeling colder and lonelier by the second. "If I stayed with you now, Nick, we would have an affair. I know what I want. That's not it. I can't pretend otherwise."

His arm slackened. "All right, Eva. We'll do this on your terms. Go on to Albany, if you must. Just promise me that we can be together next weekend."

He glanced at the opposite seat where his day planner lay open but then changed his mind about reaching for it. He shrugged. "It doesn't matter if I have appointments. I'll break them. I'll even book a regular flight on Fridays for you so that we don't have to waste the precious time it would take for me to drive up to Albany." He smiled encouragingly, "See, I'm willing to change my priorities around for you. Doesn't that count for something with you?"

"Yes," Eva said miserably. "It means you like sex with me well enough to inconvenience other people in order to have it."

His face went blank. "That's a distortion of my intentions, Eva, and unfair."

Eva bit her lip, wishing she could forget everything but the fact that he wanted to be with her, was here now lying skin to skin with her, but she could not. He was erecting barriers, retreating behind the reasonable sensible tone of the Ice Man. "You're right. I'm sorry. And I'll admit I'm tempted." She touched his cheek. "But remember when, two weeks ago, I told you half the women in New York were in love with you while the other half just wanted to sleep with you?" He nodded slowly. "Well, I'm the one who wants to marry you, Nick."

Her words hung in the air as an appalling silence grew between them.

Eva felt her cheeks warming as he continued to look at her with eyes that flashed warning signals. For the very first time she wished those tell-all eyes were hidden by reflective lenses. It was as if the past two days, the last hour, had never been. She had gone too far too fast, and ruined everything.

She sat up and moved out of his embrace. "I suppose I shouldn't have said that, either."

"No. No." He sat up and touched her face to turn it back toward him. It wounded him to see the pain on her face and he wondered a little desperately how all the beauty they had just shared could turn to ashes so quickly. "I admire your honesty. It's all just...so sudden, Eva."

Eva laughed in spite of herself. "Oh, Nick, you sound like the heroine in a Victorian novel."

To her astonishment, he blushed! "God, Eva!" he muttered savagely. "You're making this so hard!"

He visibly pulled himself together, then exhaled a long breath before continuing. "Things are simple for you. They aren't for me. They haven't been in a long time."

Because he could not bear not to touch her in some way, he took her hand and held it between his, willing her to feel his sincerity. "I know that I want to be with you, that you make me happier than I've been since I can remember. But I don't know if that's love." An indefinable sadness entered his expression. "I don't want to cheat you of the chance to have something I can't give you."

Eva reached out to stroke his hair gently. "Nick, your emotions are in full working order. I think you've just forgotten how to listen to them. But if you don't feel as I do, you can't fake it."

"I don't know what I feel," he said bitterly. He turned to her, his face contorted by pain. "But, damn it, Eva, I won't let you walk out on me!"

Eva searched his face. What she saw was a man more afraid of being hurt than she was. She touched his mouth, hardened and thinned by anguish, and felt the tension in his lips ease under the gentle motion of her fingers. She had wanted to bring him joy, not sorrow. She now knew what it was like to lie in his arms, sated and happy and deliriously fulfilled. She knew she could make him laugh and feel carefree, and hot with desire. How could she walk away from him, even if staying might break her heart?

For the first time since stripping out of them, Eva wished she had her clothes on. Suddenly she saw herself as a stranger might: naked, wet, still flushed from the madness of making passionate love with her boss. Her boss. She had a job to do.

"All right, Nick. You win. We'll take this one step at a time. But I can't—I won't—stay with you. I've got to start my life in Albany. We'll talk when you get back to Manhattan."

"You promise?"

"I promise."

Eva looked around as if she expected her clothes to magically appear and saw the time on the clock in the console. "You're going to be late," she said absently and mostly to herself. "I'll open the trunk. We're going to need dry clothes."

Eva opened the door and stepped out. Rain still hissed down as a slower but steady gray drizzle. It took only a few steps to reach the front door and open it. That done, she punched the trunk release. Nick was there waiting and quickly drew out two suitcases before slamming the trunk shut with more force than was required.

Eva moved toward him as he moved toward her, hardly aware that she was standing in front of him in the rain with nothing more than her expression of resolve to shield her. She saw his eyes travel down her, pausing to watch as crystal raindrops dripped off the tips of her breasts. She followed the raindrops' path down his broad chest to the base of his belly. Even now he was half-ready to love her again. She knew it would take only a careless gesture, or sigh of approval, and they would be back where they had been minutes before, draped one over the other on the wide leather seat of the limo.

She reached out and took her overnight case from him. "I'll change up front," she said briskly and started to turn away.

Nick caught her by the elbow. "I know you're angry."

"I'm not angry, Nick." She leaned forward to place a kiss beside his mouth. "I don't regret the afternoon. It's been a dream of mine for a long time. But even dreams end, don't they?''

"Why do we ask so much of life?" she heard him whisper to himself as she turned away. "Why can't we be satisfied with less?''

His voice sounded plaintive, despairing. Was it still so very difficult for him to consider loving again? For her it was the most natural, necessary wish of her life.

Chapter Seven

It was slow going back up the mountain. The black-top was damp and littered with debris from the squall that had ripped through the gorge. On the drive in, Eva had seen signs warning of the possibility of rock slides but had not thought much about it. Now the warnings took on new significance. There was not much room between the sheer cliff on one side and the sudden drop-off on the other. The sharp turns, often hidden by overhanging branches until she was upon them, made her edgy. A blockage in the road might mean a major delay. It occurred to her that she had not asked if there was another way out of here and that they were not passing other vehicles on the road.

Though it was only late afternoon, the sun had disappeared behind the mountains and the road lay in deep shadows of twilight. Even without the air conditioner on, the chill of rain-cooled air made goose bumps form on her skin. In her haste to dress, she had pulled on what was easiest—jeans and a T-shirt. The rain had ruined her uniform, not that she would need it after today. Her days as Nick Bauer's chauffeur were over.

With misgiving, she flicked her gaze to the rear-view mirror. Nick, dressed equally casually, sat staring straight ahead. Was he watching her? Her gaze went back to the road. She had not been able to gauge by his expression what he was thinking. His sunglasses, which he had not worn all afternoon, were back in place. She had not suggested that he ride up front with her, as before, and he had not made any attempt to join her. A wriggle of disquiet slipped through her. The man behind the mirrored lenses seemed a remote stranger.

A few moments passed before she was able to again risk moving her gaze from the road. What she saw in the mirror surprised her. Her gaze automatically skipped away from the sight. She blinked, then concentrated on the slick black pavement snaking out ahead. She must be wrong. She glanced again. She saw a single tear slide out from below the edge of his dark glasses and streak silently down his right cheek.

The sight both appalled and exhilarated her. If he could feel so much anguish, then there must be equal room in his heart for other emotions like joy, and hope and love.

She breathed a sigh of relief when the limo crested the top of the mountain pass. Here the sun still shone brightly and the road widened out with a clearing where there was a scenic-view parking area. She slowed and took a long panoramic view of the valley below, looking smoky blue and draped in rain from the retreating storm clouds. Then she turned her attention to the road, slipping the limo into second gear as they started down the other side, which led to the main highway.

The limo took the first curve smoothly, hugging the road beautifully. The drop-off on this side of the mountain was more gradual and trees grew thickly by the side of the road. As she headed into the next curve Eva had the feeling that she could relax a little. The worst was over.

The tractor-trailer cab appeared out of nowhere, swinging out from behind a blind curve straight into her path.

Eva hit on the brakes with a cry of warning and wrenched the wheel to the right, for the alternative would have meant plowing into the side of the mountain. She heard Nick yell her name as she fought for control. The tires slid on the wet surface and slipped off the edge of the blacktop. The limo fishtailed and then she felt the impact as the cab's front bumper caught hers. Metal scraped metal and something exploded in front of her. The air bag, she thought after a force like a fist had slammed into her face and chest.

Nick swallowed blood and cursed viciously as he fought semiconsciousness. He could smell burned rubber and gasoline fumes. For a moment it seemed he was reliving a nightmare.

This couldn't be happening. My God! Not again!

He forced his eyes open and saw the padded ceiling of the limo directly above him. He was lying at an awkward angle, his chest and neck hurting from the restraint of the seat belts on impact.

"Eva!" He said her name before his thoughts could fully organize. "Eva? Are you okay?"

Instead of her reply, a shadow appeared at the window nearest him. It was a man's head.

"You folks all right! God as my witness I didn't see you!"

"There's a woman up front!" Nick shouted to his rescuer. "Can you see her?"

The man moved to look in the front window. "She's still there," he called back "Oh, Lord! She's lying mighty still."

Nick ignored the implication of those words. He did not have time for panic, or fear. He had to act. He released the restraints and wrenched himself upright so that he could look into the man's face. "You've got to get us help. Fast!"

"Sure! Sure thing!" The trucker was younger than he first appeared, probably no more than twenty-five. "I got a CB in my cab. I'll call the sheriff."

Nick thrust his head out the window. "Don't you leave, damn you! I've seen your face. If you leave us, I won't call the authorities. I swear I'll hunt you down myself!"

Nick was surprised by the man's reaction to his threat. After all, what in reality could he do? But the man paled and his face screwed up. "Look, I'm only going to make that call. There was a rock slide on the other side. Came down so quick, I couldn't stop. I swear I wasn't driving reckless. The sheriff will be able to tell you that. I'll be back, I swear!"

A moan from the front seat caught Nick's attention. Scrambling across the shambles of the back seat he moved to reach Eva.

"I'm here, Eva," he said as he tried to squeeze through the mangled metal to reach the back of the front seat.

"Nick?" Her voice was faint.

"Thank God, you're alive." Nick tried to see her through the broken panel of glass that separated the seats but the roof had caved in, blocking his view. "We've got to get out of here."

"I can't. I'm caught. My leg." Eva gasped out the words, too shook up to really evaluate how badly hurt she was.

Fear splashed through Nick. "Are you bleeding? Can you tell? Eva! Answer me!"

"No. I don't think so. I hit my head but—" Eva reached up with her free hand and touched her face. Her skin felt tender and abraded but no blood stained her fingers when she took her hand away. Still, she knew she would soon be black and blue from the impact of the air bag. Despite the throbbing in her head she made herself concentrate on each of her arms and legs, trying to determine her situation. She was wedged in between the front seat and the console, the roof forming a new abruptly slanted angle just above her head. She could move her arms but her legs would not move. "I think the steering column collapsed. My legs are trapped."

His heart was racing but Nick did not allow the panic to enter his voice. "Don't worry. I'm going to get help. Okay?"

"Nick?"

"Yes, Eva?"

"Don't leave me."

"Not on my life!"

"Nick? I didn't mean that. You need to get out. The car could go over the edge at any minute."

"Don't worry. You plowed into a tree. The limo's not going anywhere." He hoped he sounded convincing for he could feel the slight rock of the car body in the wind. That could mean the car was pitched at an unstable angle despite the tree trunk he could see through the cracked front window.

"Lucky thing you have insurance," she quipped, followed by weak laughter.

"Damn lucky," he muttered, but he did not share her laughter. He looked out of the window to see if he could see the truck driver returning but the man seemed to have disappeared. "Hang on, Eva. I'm going to see if the car phone is working."

"Just dial 911."

"Right."

Eva heard him curse at length as he felt about in the dark interior. He is frightened, she thought. Scared for me. I did not want to hurt or frighten him. It must be bad.

Nick located the phone under his left shoe and punched in the number. "Operator, this is an emergency. There's been an automobile accident. I need the North Carolina State Police emergency line. How the hell should I know? You're the operator. Right. Hurry."

The connection came through with surprising ease. "I've been in an auto accident on—" Nick lifted his head toward the front seat. "Where the hell are we, Eva?"

"I didn't get the name," she answered softly. "Tell them it's the road into the Gorge Road off the Blue Ridge Parkway."

Nick repeated her instructions and after a short pause to listen, he exploded with uncharacteristic emotion. "I don't give a damn about the difficulties created by the storm. We've got bigger difficulties. There's a woman trapped in a car. Get somebody up here! Now! Look for a rock slide across the road. We're on the other side. Bring whatever it takes to get the woman out. We mustn't be left up here after dark or they'll never find us."

Eva listened as Nick calmly explained their situation to the police, urging them to send help. She wondered if the storm had flooded or blocked the roads. How long would it take for help to arrive?

At that moment gravel rattled and ran as the car settled a fraction lower on the incline.

Nick bit back a curse as metal cried and creaked. After a moment the movement stopped. He shoved away a tremor of fear. "Eva," he said levelly as he edged toward the front seat again. "You've got to see if you can free yourself."

Eva shook her head. "It's no use. I've tried. I don't think anything's broken but I'm going nowhere until somebody comes with heavy-duty equipment. But you must get out, Nick, while you can. Okay?"

"Okay. I'll come around your side and see if I can open your door."

Eva shut her eyes as she heard the back door being forced open. The luxurious limo sounded more like a tin can being pried apart. At least he would be safe. Now she could concentrate on worrying about herself. She felt something warm trickle down the side of her face and realized she was sweating despite the fact she felt cold in every other part of her body. Nerves, she told herself. Just nerves. Really, she had nothing to worry about. Nick was nearby. He would, somehow, protect and save her.

She heard his footsteps crunching gravel as he walked round the car. She knew he was assessing the damage, and probably calculating the odds of how much trouble she might be in if there was another rockfall.

When she heard another man's voice, she tried to twist her head around to see who it was. Perhaps rescuers had arrived. But she could not see a thing. "Nick? Nick!"

A few heart-pounding seconds later the front door on the passenger side was wrenched open and Nick's face appeared in the sunlight streaming in. "It's all right, Eva. I was talking with the trucker who hit us. He's called for help, too, but it's going to be a while." His smile took on a reckless slant. "I'm going to keep you company while we wait."

"No. Don't!" she said a little desperately but he was already climbing in, angling his body to avoid the jagged steel where the impact had bent the frame and narrowed the space between seat and console.

"You shouldn't be in here," she tried again. "Something could happen."

He smiled at her, the sight of it increasing her pulse, and slid in as close to her as he could. "Do you remember what you asked me last night? God! Was it only last night? You asked me why I wanted to live, Eva. I didn't have an answer then. Now I do. I want to live so that I can be with you."

Eva bit her lip. "Nick, don't. Please."

"Please don't what?" He reached out to gently touch her shoulder. "You think I'm just babbling to keep you occupied? I could talk about the weather if that were the case." His brows contracted over his thoughtful expression. "I'm not a stupid man, Eva. Stubborn, and shortsighted, yes. I'm not accustomed to making errors in judgment so I didn't understand where I'd gone wrong. I thought that as long as I didn't allow anything to become too important to me, nothing could hurt me again. That was wrong thinking. A man can plan his life, figure all the odds, play all the angles to his advantage and still not see the whole picture." He smiled again. "What I missed in all that calculating, Eva, was you. I hadn't planned on you coming into my life."

"I know." She stared at him helplessly for it suddenly seemed that he was more in need of comfort than she. "I'm sorry."

"You should be," he said philosophically. "You messed up my perfect little plan, Eva, and I don't think I'm ever going to recover."

The car shuddered as a new rockfall slipped and slid down the cliff behind them. Nick heard her moan in fright as rocks settled and shimmied past the wheels. "Hold on, Eva. Help is coming." He held his breath for she had turned her face away from him. "Do you hear me, Eva? Eva?" He pushed himself farther across the seat but he could not quite reach her. "Eva, I need you. You mustn't leave me."

Eva turned her head slowly toward him. "I'm not going to leave you, Nick." He saw a smile flicker on her too-pale face. "I'm going to stay right here…and fight for you…and marry you…and give you children…and make you smile."

Nick felt emotion squeeze his heart. "You always make me smile."

"And then," she continued as if he hadn't spoken, "I'm going to see that you live long enough to become a grandfather." She was still smiling but it had become more of a grimace. "But you'll never look any older. You'll always be a silver-haired heartbreaker."

"Only yours, Eva. Yes, I'd like that. If you still want me."

How humble he sounded. "I want you." She slowly moved her hand from her side and stretched it out toward him. "Hold me, Nick."

He took her hand and squeezed it tight as he held it to his cheek. "You're so cold, Eva. I wish I could warm you." He ran his hand strongly up her slender arm and across her chest as far as he could reach. "As soon as I can, I'm going to hold your body close to mine and make love to you until you can't walk."

Eva chuckled weakly. "Hush, Nick. You're not supposed to make an injured person's pulse race."

He smiled but his eyes were full of worry. "Does it hurt much, Eva?"

"No, it doesn't hurt at all. That's what's so strange. I don't feel a thing, except for this damned itch under my right arch. I can't scratch it."

"The itching is good, Eva. It means you've still got feeling in your legs."

She squeezed his hand. "I'm so glad you're here, Nick."

"I'll always want to be wherever you are, Eva." He touched her face gently, stroking her cheek. "Eva? Just for the record. I love you."

Eva nodded. "I know. And it's okay to be scared of loving me. But you won't be disappointed. I'm a tough lady. You should have known that the day you let me in the door of Bauer Associates."

"I plan to install you permanently at Bauer Associates, if you'd like that, Eva, and permanently in my bed."

"*Yours* and *mine*."

He choked on his laughter. "You're pushing, Eva."

"It's just my biological clock ticking," she said on an answering gust of dry laughter.

For the twenty minutes they talked about anything and everything that came to mind. As if by mutual agreement they both seemed to realize that their more powerful thoughts and feelings would have to wait for another place and time.

The sound of the rescue team did not make a clear impression on either of their minds until the police sirens penetrated the canopy of trees. "Help's here, Eva," Nick said excitedly. "They're here."

Unfortunately, neither the ambulance nor the heavy-duty equipment could make it past what turned out to be a series of small mud-and rock slides down the mountain road. The police arrived on foot and the medics were dispatched from the scenic-view parking area several hundred yards up the mountain where a helicopter had been able to land.

Eva lost track of the time it took for them to winch and pull the car to safety. She ignored the slow progress of separating metal from metal in order to free her without hurting her. She answered the medics' questions calmly and avoided looking at the needle they stuck in her arm. Instead, she let her mind drift back over the earlier hours of the day, visualized floating naked in the pond, the taste of Nick's mouth, the feel of his body surging hot and hard upon hers.

When the medic who was monitoring her through the ordeal commented that her pulse was a little faster than he would like, she merely smiled at him Sphinxlike and then lifted a knowing glance to Nick, who hovered close by. As their eyes met, his brows lifted knowingly and she knew he had guessed, perhaps shared, her thoughts.

Finally she was lifted out after being fitted with a neck brace and backboard, as a safety precaution. As carefully as if she were made of spun sugar, she was placed on a stretcher.

"How is she?" Nick demanded of the medical team for the fortieth time.

"She appears to be doing just fine," the medic answered. "No apparent major injuries. But we can't say for certain until she's been thoroughly examined at the hospital."

"I'm going to fine," Eva assured Nick. Her gaze moved from Nick to the medic. "Just how will you get me down from here?"

"First class, as a matter of fact," the medic answered with a cheerful smile. "Hope you like to fly. We came in by helicopter."

"I'm going with her."

Eva's stunned gaze met Nick's determined stare. Of all the things he had eliminated from his life, flying was number one. "You don't need to do that, Nick."

He looked down at her with a steady brilliant gaze full of love and determination. "Yes, I do."

He said the words with such conviction that she knew he was testing himself as much as any bond between them. She had encouraged him to take tiny risks these last two days. But as for everyone, some had to be made solo. Yet, she was going with him, and he knew it.

They made the trek up to the parking lot in near silence, Nick supporting the stretcher on her right side near her head so that he could hold her hand.

He flinched only once, when the blades of the helicopter came to life. But he climbed in and sat down beside her, his expression set, but not afraid.

Nick squeezed her hand rhythmically as the copter shuddered, as if by doing so he was pumping blood though her. "Now you just hold on. It's almost over, baby. I promise."

"Yes, darling," Eva answered calmly, loving him for loving her this much. "There's just one other thing I need."

Nick bent lower over her. "What? Name it and you've got it."

Eva smiled up into his concerned expression. "Kiss me, Nick, for luck."

He grinned at her. "Anything to please my lady."

He covered her mouth with a gentle sweet kiss that brought tears to her eyes. But it was not nearly enough for her. She reached up and caught a handful of silver to deepen and lengthen the kiss.

When he lifted his head his eyes were dark with the passion she had only begun to explore. "You're one reckless woman," he said in admiration.

"Only with you," she answered with a wicked chuckle.

"Get well quick, Eva. I have a few thousand things I want to do with you." He laughed, free and easy. "Some of them are even done out of bed."

Eva smiled back, certain of herself and him, and the future.

Finally the medic gave the high sign and said, "Take her up!"

To Eva, the whirling sound of helicopter blades seemed like the music of the most beautiful love song in the world because Nick was there beside her, in spite of his fear, his memories and his emotional scars. If he could do this, in spite of it all, then the meltdown was complete, and both of them would bask in the resulting loving heat for the rest of their lives.

* * * * *

A Note from Laura Parker

Many of you like to know where a writer gets his or her story ideas. I've often found that envy can stimulate the imagination. My husband usually takes a limousine when he's on a business trip and imagining that luxury made me think what a pleasure it would be to have someone at your beck and call, yet still be in the driver's seat, so to speak. Wrapped in that isolating silence, away from the cares of the world, what sort of relationship might develop between a cool self-contained attorney and his very discreet personal limo driver? Especially if that driver were an attractive, smart young woman who could teach her boss a thing or two about going along for the ride? And what if that intimate world of the limo became their only refuge during a violent thunderstorm?

Ever since I was a child, I've loved thunderstorms. On a hot summer afternoon, after a day of shimmering heat that has made the asphalt sticky and my neck prickly with heat, salvation would show up in the form of a rolling boomer packing a sound-and-light show that I've always found a thrill. The sudden stillness in the air beforehand like the breathless anticipation before the moment of passion. The first flickering of light, beautiful and otherworldly. Then the sudden fury and passion of the storm fueled by the accumulated heat and overcharged elements. Finally the cooling calming rains in the aftermath of the power spent. Well, I've always found it very satisfying and very sexy. Hey, I'm a romantic!